EVENSONG

Also by Stewart O'Nan

FICTION

Ocean State

Henry, Himself

City of Secrets

West of Sunset

The Odds

Emily, Alone

Songs for the Missing

Last Night at the Lobster

The Good Wife

The Night Country

Wish You Were Here

Everyday People

A Prayer for the Dying

A World Away

The Speed Queen

The Names of the Dead

Snow Angels

In the Walled City

NONFICTION

Faithful (with Stephen King)

The Circus Fire

The Vietnam Reader (editor)

On Writers and Writing by John Gardner (editor)

SCREENPLAY

Poe

EVENSONG

A Novel

STEWART O'NAN

Atlantic Monthly Press
New York

FIRST EDITION

Printed in the United States of America

First Grove Atlantic hardcover edition: November 2025

Library of Congress Cataloging-in-Publication data is available for this title.

ISBN 978-0-8021-6643-2
eISBN 978-0-8021-6644-9

Atlantic Monthly Press
an imprint of Grove Atlantic
154 West 14th Street
New York, NY 10011

Distributed by Publishers Group West

groveatlantic.com

25 26 27 28 10 9 8 7 6 5 4 3 2 1

For the real HDs of Pittsburgh,
and everywhere

Oh the mystery of it all—life,
death and the passing of time.

Barbara Pym

Time passes.

Virginia Woolf

EVENSONG

The Humpty Dumpty Club

It was their nightmare, right there in the name, a shattering fall not from the battlements of a castle but headlong down a flight of stairs, Joan Hargrove, their wise, organized leader, queen of the highlighter and color-coded file folder, bringing her accounting skills to bear on the club's every move. They'd never had another president.

Thursday she hadn't shown up for bridge at Emily's—no surprise. They all knew she'd been battling a stubborn summer cold she'd brought back from Chautauqua. Susie had just run her over some butternut squash bisque from the Co-op, and Joan had seemed fine, a little tired, still in her bathrobe and slippers, carrying around a box of tissues. Why she decided to take her trash down to the garage that night was a mystery none of them could fathom, though both Kitzi and Emily were just as fastidious. City of Pittsburgh pickup wasn't until Monday, and if the kitchen can was full, she could have asked Susie. She'd lain there through the morning, her tabby Oscar mewling, confused.

"That's why you should always have your phone on you," Kitzi said, breaking trump.

"You can't always," said Emily, who thought them a bother.

"That's why I have my Star Alert," Arlene said, fishing the plastic pendant with its red panic button out of her blouse. She had low blood pressure, a condition she brought up constantly, though it had been years since she'd had an episode. It was one reason she'd joined the club: so she wouldn't have to rely on her sister-in-law Emily as much. Having spent the entirety of her adult life happily free of attachments, the idea of women banding together to support one another appealed to her. She and Kitzi had been charter members, along with a dozen others from their church choir, most gone now; she'd recruited Emily after Henry died, using bridge as a sweetener. The two of them couldn't stand each other yet were inseparable. Here come the Maxwell sisters, friends joked, and it was true, over the years they'd come to resemble each other, an observation Emily, once a beauty, resented.

"Plus, slippers on stairs?" Kitzi said. "That's a dangerous combination."

"I called her that morning to see if she needed anything," Susie said. "I thought she was sleeping."

They imagined the phone ringing upstairs in the spotless condo, Joan broken and helpless at the bottom, the cat sniffing at the garbage strewn everywhere.

"I should have gone over."

"No," the rest of them protested.

At sixty-three, Susie was the baby of the group, an active member of the choir they'd long aged out of, freshly adopted after a late divorce. A fledgling pescatarian and tireless recycler, she worried about the ozone and the oceans and the Ukrainian refugees, nurturing a perpetual state of angst the other three, being of a more sanguine generation, blamed on her youth. Her ex-husband had been a lawyer for US Steel, stonewalling the unions and the EPA. Now that she was single, she was trying to undo the damage one noble cause at a time.

"How were you supposed to know?" Emily said.

"Accidents happen," Kitzi said, leading with the ace. They were going to make their four hearts easily; if Arlene had signaled that she had the king, they could have bid five, but Arlene's game, like her hearing, wasn't as sharp as it used to be. She miscounted and dropped easy tricks, bid timidly and then let Kitzi play the hand, content to be the dummy.

To their collective shame, a male neighbor on his morning constitutional had discovered Joan, investigating the open garage door, a harbinger of chaos in her gated community. She'd broken an arm and a leg yet survived.

"It's amazing how things happen, isn't it?" Susie said. "It's kind of a miracle, really."

"I wouldn't go that far," Emily said. The leg was a bad compound fracture, a contraption of stainless steel rods jutting from her cast. Joan was Pitt, class of '55, two years behind her. Her orthopedist at Shadyside said she was looking at seven months of physical therapy, which Emily—shocked by Joan's scabbed and swollen face—took to mean she'd never walk again. She'd have to move to assisted living, Emily's deepest fear, though scores of former members swore by Longwood. When Emily visited, which wasn't often, it was clean and pleasant enough, if not the Valhalla her friends from Calvary and the University Club claimed. Half of the East End was there, burning through their children's inheritance. When her son Kenny mentioned the possibility, she scoffed, saying she could never afford it, a deflection even he didn't fully believe.

"I'm going to go see her after practice," Susie said.

"Weren't you just there last night?" asked Kitzi, who'd only been once so far, busy with Martin and her election board duties. "Plus you're taking care of Oscar."

"Oscar's a sweetie," Susie said.

"I can go tomorrow during the day," Arlene volunteered.

"Oh, we have so many people going tomorrow," Kitzi said. Under Joan, the club had flourished, and there was a steady stream of current and former HDs paying tribute, their cards and flowers crowding the windowsill.

Kitzi flushed out the ten, then laid down her hand. The last tricks were all hers.

"You could have made the baby slam," Emily said.

"I wasn't sure about the king."

"When is Darcy leaving?" Arlene asked, meaning Joan's daughter, an econ professor who'd flown in from Austin and needed to be back for the start of fall semester. They all thought she should stay longer, though, as Joan herself pointed out through a haze of painkillers, while she was in the hospital there was nothing anyone could really do for her.

"Not till Sunday," Susie said.

"I can do Monday," Arlene said. "I've got nothing going on."

"That's fine," Kitzi said, making a note.

"Tomorrow I'm taking Francine to the podiatrist," Emily said. "What else is on the docket?"

Kitzi had sent them all the September wish list as soon as she could get into Joan's email, yet they still looked to her as if she were in charge. She didn't expect Arlene or Susie to take the reins, but she'd thought Emily, with her definite opinions about everything, might share the burden of connecting the needful and the willing, if only out of pride. Now it seemed she'd inherited the job by default.

"Someone needs to pick up Peggy Follansbee's prescriptions at Giant Eagle."

"When does she need them by?" Arlene asked.

"It just says pickup tomorrow."

"Is that the Squirrel Hill Jyggle," Emily asked unhelpfully, "or the one in Edgewood?"

"I'm guessing Squirrel Hill."

"It could be the Market District in Oakland," Susie said. "Peggy just moved into Webster Hall."

"Do you have her number?" Kitzi asked.

"Roberta would. I can call her."

"It's fine," Kitzi said. "I'm sure Joan has it somewhere."

"It might be new."

"I can do it if I know where," Arlene said.

"I'll figure it out," Kitzi said.

It was three, they were finished. Emily told them to leave the dishes, but they dutifully marched their cups and saucers into the kitchen, where she tried to push the leftover sugar-free sugar cookies no one liked on them. It was a ritual, Kitzi finally relenting, saying she'd take a couple for Martin, and Emily stuffing a Ziploc bag.

As they gathered in the front hall, from her bedroom upstairs came a single warning bark from Angus. Outside the day was balmy, the Oldhams' honey locust rippling in the breeze. Susie had somehow convinced them to carpool in her tiny hybrid, since they were coming from the same direction, which Emily thought was smart, especially given how Arlene drove. She checked the mailbox—not yet—then waved them away before heading back inside.

Alone again, with the house quiet around her, she thought not of Joan in her hospital gown but of Henry, the IVs taped to the bruised crook of his arm, how he'd asked her to take care of Arlene and not give up on their daughter Margaret, demands that even now seemed unfair, if not impossible. What would she ask, and of whom—God? There was no one else left.

Angus barked, and she frowned, trying to hold on to the thought, unhappy as it was. She needed to do the dishes and figure out dinner.

"All right, Mr. Doofus," she said, climbing the stairs. "I'm coming to save you."

Oscar the Grouch

Sunday afternoon Susie waited until Darcy was gone to go over to Joan's. She'd offered to drive her to the airport, but Darcy said she'd just Uber and thanked her for everything she'd done—sincerely, Susie thought, yet beneath her gratitude she could sense the same apprehension she'd felt radiating from her all week. Who are you, and what are you doing in my mother's house?

A daughter herself, Susie understood that kind of primal jealousy but thought Darcy's radar was off. Susie and Joan had never been close. She wasn't some usurper brazenly insinuating herself into the will, she just happened to live a few blocks away, within walking distance of Calvary. By rights, looking after the apartment should have fallen to Kitzi, Joan's oldest friend and second, but Kitzi was in Squirrel Hill and had her hands full, between her husband and running the club. It was more convenient for Susie to check on things, and did Darcy really want to clean up her mother's blood?

Joan lived behind the church in Shadyside Village, an enclave of luxury town houses segregated from East Liberty by a high brick wall, while Susie was directly across Walnut Street in the Kenmawr, a once exclusive prewar building that Emily and Arlene lampooned, pronouncing the name with a haughty Brahmin accent as if it were still full of cosmopolitan couples of their generation and not aging shut-ins and sullen Chinese CMU students who vanished at the end of the semester, leaving behind piles of Ikea furniture by the dumpsters. She and Joan were both transplants, finally downsizing from much larger digs after their children had scattered and, in her case, for the most part happily, her husband.

Before she'd gotten to know Joan, she visited Shadyside Village once a year, at Christmas, caroling with the children's choir. Now she made the walk every day, the sagging brick foursquares chopped into apartments and cars with out-of-state plates parked bumper to bumper and cracked recycling bins and spray-painted garbage cans giving way, once she'd checked in at the security booth, to a cloistered island of calm. Inside, the roads were all soothing circles, white concrete rather than blacktop, mailboxes standing between the sidewalk and the curb like the suburbs. The condos were unadorned, sided an identical dark chocolate brown, each with its own brass coach light, stubby driveway and garage. There was no parking. The grass, the bushes, even the trees were uniform, evenly spaced, the only concession to the chaos of city life the bright red fire hydrants.

Today, as always, the place was strangely depopulated, though she could hear the rumble of traffic on Penn Avenue beyond the wall. She'd sung at both services that morning and her back was hurting her. Knowing that she had to drive over to see Joan later, she'd taken a gummy rather than a Vicodin, which made the make-believe world even more unreal. Who would want to live in a place like this? The question was moot—even with the generous settlement from Richard she could never afford it—yet she still imagined coming home and the garage door opening, welcoming her the way it had all those years in their rambling Colonial out in Fox Chapel. This was the placid life she'd left behind for the Kenmawr; it was too late to ask for it back. As she followed the curve of the road, a Porsche SUV with tinted windows approached, slowing for a speed hump. She waved, defiant, feeling like a trespasser, sure that somewhere someone was watching her on camera.

Joan's punch code was her birthday, which Susie thought she ought to change. She'd have to work on her. The door rolled up to reveal her old Forester gathering dust, the wheeled garbage bin against the far wall reminding her that tonight was garbage night. She lifted the lid: empty. It wasn't a competition—it was silly, really—and yet she was pleased that Darcy had forgotten, if she'd ever known.

It had been a week and the stairwell still smelled of blood and Renuzit. She'd scrubbed the carpet until only the faintest outline remained. She wasn't superstitious but kept to the wall, sidestepping where Joan had lain, marveling, as she pulled herself up by the handrail, at how far she'd fallen. In a month Joan was going to be eighty-nine. It really was a miracle, despite what Emily might say.

At the top she cracked the door an inch and peeked through in case Oscar tried to make a break. Joan painted him as an escape artist, though so far he'd been skittery, holing up under the bed in the guest room until she put his food down. The hall was empty and gray, the kitchen, the living room.

"Hey, buddy," she said. "It's just me."

She was too polite to ever say it out loud, but Oscar was actually kind of a jerk. Her first day in the house, he'd arched his back and hissed at her, baring his fangs, then left a black nubbin of a turd in the middle of Joan's bed as a protest. "I know," she told him, "you want Mommy, but Mommy isn't here. You've got me." She understood he was traumatized and that she was a stranger, but did he have to spill his water and scatter his kibble all over the kitchen floor? Most of the time he hid. When he did break cover he kept his distance, sitting and staring at her from the hallway like a demon out of a Stephen King movie. She tried to sweet talk him and he wheeled and stalked away with his tail in the air. He reminded her of Richard, expecting her to do everything for him, then ignoring her.

When he didn't come, she picked up his empty bowl and knocked it on the counter a few times before filling it and setting it back on the mat.

"Oscar!" She shook the box like a maraca. "Come on, bud, come get your kibbles."

Sometimes it took him a while, and she stood at the sink, filling the watering can, trying to lure him with kissing noises.

As she suspected, Darcy hadn't watered the plants. Susie did them clockwise, starting with the African violets on the windowsill, droplets beading like mercury on the parched dirt. She tended to drown her own and tried to be sparing.

In the guest room she set the can on the floor and knelt down to look under the bed, prepared to find Oscar glaring back at her, but there was just dust.

"You are tricksy," she said, and pushed herself upright. "Come out, come out, wherever you are!"

He'd show himself when he was ready—maybe slip in behind her when she was doing the ivy in the guest bathroom—but when she went to refill the can, he wasn't there.

She shook the box. "Let's go, Oscar Mayer, dinnertime."

She waited, listened. The windows were double-paned, insulating them, like the heavy drapes and wall-to-wall carpet, from the greater world. At her place, day and night, she could hear buses, sirens, church bells. Here there was nothing but an unbroken whine of quiet like a ringing in her ears. She closed her eyes and might have been drifting in space.

"You're going to make me look for you, aren't you?"

Her back hurt, and, feeling absurd, she set the can in the sink, went into the living room and got down on all fours, lifting the dust ruffle to peek under the sofa. She clambered to her feet again, grimacing and rubbing her hip. Later she'd take a Vicodin to sleep, a habit she knew was bad for her, if not outright dangerous, but otherwise she'd be up all night listening to the bells count the hours.

"I give up," she said. "Olly olly in come free."

In Joan's room she closed the door behind her so he couldn't escape.

"Where are you?"

Maybe the balcony. It adjoined the neighbors'. Darcy could have locked him out by mistake, but he wasn't there either.

He wasn't under the desk in Joan's office or in her little laundry closet. She was running out of possibilities and imagined how she'd tell her. It was Darcy's fault, but she'd be the one who'd have to break the news. Or not. She could find him. She could at least try. When she first started watching Oscar, she'd text Joan pictures of him eating or just being cute. She'd find a good one and put it on a flyer and go around posting them on phone poles—except Shadyside Village didn't have phone poles. They probably had a bylaw against flyers anyway. She'd have to go door-to-door, admitting her guilt. How late was Staples open?

She was checking the linen closet at the end of the hall when the doorbell rang, a single long trill. She stopped, caught, as if she shouldn't be there. She debated not answering it. Maybe they'd go away.

The bell rang.

It might be a delivery, more flowers or something she had to sign for, but she hadn't heard a truck. It was Sunday. The silence made her acutely aware—as she was in the laundry room of the Kenmawr or the elevators at night—that she was alone.

The bell rang again.

"All right, all right, hold your horses."

She used the garage door because it was more public, in case she needed witnesses. As it rolled up, before she could even see who'd rung the bell, Oscar sauntered in, twitching his hips as he passed, totally ignoring her.

The man the door ultimately revealed was older than Joan. Hunched over a cane, he wore a dove-gray fedora and baggy navy suit, his hand a mottled mass of veins and age spots sporting a gold Masonic ring. At first glance she thought he was blind because his glasses were black and oversized, enclosed on the sides like welders' goggles to keep out the light. His cheeks and mouth were sunken, his lips wet and trembling.

"Lose something?" he asked.

"Yes, thank you. Where did you find him?"

"He's always catting around here, like me. He sounded hungry. How is your mother doing? We're all thinking about her, she's such a dear soul."

He thought she was Darcy, and while they looked nothing alike, in a way she was flattered. It seemed easier not to explain. What mattered was that Oscar was back.

"She's resting," she said.

"I hope she feels better soon."

"Thank you, I'll let her know."

"You tell her Gloria and Bill say hello."

"I will," she said, and thanked him again, making sure Oscar was in before closing the door. Gloria and Bill say hello. What a character, she thought, out wandering the neighborhood in his Sunday best.

"Okay," she said, "let's get you fed already."

Oscar stopped to sniff the carpet at the foot of the stairs.

"Git!" she said, chasing him up.

She took a picture of him at his bowl for Joan—proof of life. He ate contentedly, as if nothing had happened, like Richard after one of their couples therapy sessions, his appetite a goad. Why did she let him upset her? Joan had warned her—it was just his nature, it had nothing to do with her, the same as Richard. Finishing the watering, she thought there were people who cared and people who didn't, and that she was glad she was the first kind, even if it sometimes meant losing sleep.

Oscar was done and licking his paws.

"Was that good? Yeah, I bet."

Without a glance, he slunk down the hall to the guest room.

"Okay. See ya."

The light outside was fading. She raked his litter box and did the garbage, rinsed the plastic Chinese takeout containers Darcy had left in the fridge and filled his water bowl before closing everything up and rolling the bin to the curb.

Bill must have finished his walk and gone home to Gloria, because the Village was empty again, only the security guard glued to his cell phone. On Walnut a group of students was throwing a backyard barbecue, the smell of charcoal sharpening her appetite. The day was over, and though Oscar had given her a scare, in the end it had been a success. She'd sung twice and gotten outside and taken care of Joan's place and met a new and interesting person, and there was still tonight's visit to look forward to, and the promise of a Vicodin at bedtime, the merciful release of sleep. Walking home with the bells of Calvary and Sacred Heart mingling above the trees, she was pleased with all she'd gotten done for a Sunday, but back in the Kenmawr, eating her leftover baba ghanoush alone, she fell into a dispiriting gloom that lingered as she gathered her things into her bag and drove to the hospital, thinking, once again, as she passed the fancy new high-rise condos on Centre, how excited she'd been to rearrange her life and how mysterious it was that it had taken this shape.

She had to wait in the hall, and then when the nurse opened the door for her, Joan had a tube attached to her nose.

It was oxygen. They were afraid she might have a collapsed lung. She shrugged as if it were just one more thing. "Did Darcy get off all right?"

Susie thought she could have called. "I guess so. She was gone by the time I got there."

"How's my baby doing?"

"Good," she said, but, looking at her, drawn and pale on her pillow with a tube clipped to her nose, she couldn't lie. "He got out. I don't know what happened."

Joan laughed and choked on a cough. "I told you, he's like Houdini."

"One of your neighbors brought him back. Bill."

"How is he?"

"He seemed fine. He and Gloria say hi."

"You know he was the one who found me. Probably saved my life."

"No," Susie said, trying to picture it.

"Did I get a package from Zappos?"

"I didn't see one."

She'd ordered some new sneakers to help with her PT. "It could be behind the hose thingy on the side of the garage," she said, and Susie marveled at how easily she'd absolved her—no matter that it was Darcy's fault. Susie told her how Bill had mistaken her for Darcy, and they shared another laugh. They talked about how Kitzi was holding up and what next week looked like for the club. Even drugged, Joan knew every detail of the schedule, as if, like God, she were planning all of their lives from a distance. How did you become so strong? Susie wanted ask, but just listened, following along, and even after Joan said she was tired and closed her eyes, she sat there watching her breathe, staying well past the end of visiting hours, until one of the nurses poked her head in and said she looked like she could use some rest too.

The Little Red Hen

"Who wants Jean and Gene?" Kitzi asked the room. "Hands."

No one volunteered. It was their big September bridge club, with over twenty members, longtime HDs driving in from Churchill and Mt. Lebanon to show support for Joan. Kitzi had brought up their old card tables from the basement, gently declining Martin's offer to fetch them. He was just trying to be helpful. Even on his best days the stairs were too much for him, robbing him of breath, making his heart monitor go off. He was safely holed up in the den with the door closed, watching one of his survival shows.

She scanned the room like an auctioneer. It would almost be a joke if it weren't so sad. "Someone, anyone."

They avoided her eyes, only partly out of shame. Emily stirred her coffee. Arlene wound her wristwatch. Susie tapped her phone.

Jean and Gene were hoarders. They were a lovely couple otherwise—both of them accomplished pianists and former professors of music at Chatham—but venturing into their home wasn't for the squeamish. Buried somewhere beneath the strata of magazines, grocery bags and junk mail, supposedly, were twin Steinway baby grands, their harps warped and unplayable now. They also had cats, no one knew how many, since none of them was spayed. Gene had lost a leg to diabetes, and due to her eyesight Jean no longer drove. Normally, Joan acted as their go-between—as Kitzi acted as Martin's—delivering their monthly prescriptions and news of the world, since no one else would.

Standing there, stonewalled by the entire club, Kitzi was very aware that she wasn't Joan. She'd made a mistake leaving Jean and Gene for last, and with a twinge of frustration, as if time had run out, she snapped Joan's notebook closed, thanked them all for coming and adjourned the meeting.

"I can go," Susie offered in the basement as they were putting away the tables, but it was too late.

"It's fine," Kitzi said. "I mean, they're right nearby."

While she and Martin had lived in Squirrel Hill for decades, she'd never met Jean and Gene, though she recalled seeing them play once at Chatham, maybe in the '80s, when Emily and Henry and a number of their friends subscribed to the music department's concert series. Gene wore a tuxedo and Jean a black lace mantilla over a flowing floor-length gown, a gardenia behind one ear. She was English, close to six feet and willowy, her body an object of open envy among the women. He was Russian and short—a little person, they'd call him now. His real name was Yevgeny, and he had a great black mane of hair and muttonchops, like a rock star. Their pianos faced each other, their curves perfectly fitted together, yin and yang. At the keyboards they emanated calm, solemnly nodding as they traded phrases, interlacing melodies as the tempo and volume gradually built and clashed and spilled, chords crashing bombastically—and still they maintained a formal reserve, at most swaying, their faces betraying little as they bashed away. It may have been Liszt, she couldn't remember, but she'd thought then how romantic it must be to be connected by their passion for music. She and Martin shared so little, total opposites from the beginning. Even when he was healthy she had to drag him to anything other than a ball game. To have a second, infinitely rich language to speak to each other seemed fantastically thrilling.

She chose midafternoon to go over because that was when Martin had his nap. She made sure he had everything he needed and then called to let them know she was coming. As the phone rang and rang, she imagined Jean sidling her way through the piles, the phone, like the pianos, buried under mounds of sodden garbage. She expected the answering machine to kick in, but it never did. After a few minutes she tried again. When no one answered, she told herself it wasn't unusual. Jean could be hard of hearing or on the john, a predicament she knew too well.

To pick up their prescriptions, she needed their dates of birth, and located them in the rear of Joan's notebook, as well as their Medicare plans, both regular and supplemental. The facing pages were set up like spreadsheets. Primary care physicians, allergies, loyalty cards for Giant Eagle and CVS and Walgreens—the amount of information Joan had was staggering. Out of curiosity, Kitzi looked up herself and Martin, listed along with everyone they knew, like the church directory. Martin's entry was similar to Jean and Gene's, but after hers, in the righthand margin, like a prisoner marking the days, some in black ink and some in blue, Joan had logged a tally of fourteen.

Frowning, she scanned down the page and found another cluster next to Emily's entry: ten.

Susie had two, Arlene three. No one else had more than five.

What did they mean, and why was she flattered that she had the most, as if helping others were a competition?

She took the notebook with her to the CVS on Wilkins, where she waited while the girl behind the counter gave a masked Asian woman a Covid booster, something she'd been meaning to do herself. They were so slow. For years the corner had been home to Merge Motors. When the CVS had first been built, Kitzi thought she'd like having one so close, but the lot was too small. Parking was awful, the aisles were narrow, and there were black gum spots on the carpet. No one seemed to be in charge, or care, and today she was glad to escape with Jean and Gene's pills.

Between the two of them they had eleven prescriptions. Both had one for oxycodone, making Kitzi wonder how Jean managed. It was hard enough taking care of someone when you were dead sober.

She was sitting at the light at Negley when Martin messaged her: Low sodium soy sauce.

"No," she said, and swiped him away.

She slowed for the turn into Chatham, waiting for the line of traffic to pass. On her right, farther up, inescapable, rose Tree of Life, still cordoned off four years after the massacre, the chain-link fence decorated with inspirational posters drawn by local schoolchildren. *Love Conquers All. Together We Stand.* Squirrel Hill was probably the safest neighborhood in Pittsburgh. All it took was one gun nut to take that away from them, and each time she drove by she hated him for making her reconsider—if only briefly—the death penalty.

The line broke and she left Tree of Life behind, following Woodland Road as it wound through a leafy glen worthy of Fox Chapel down to the hidden green bowl of Chatham's campus. The semester was young, and students basked on the long hill where children sledded in winter. The steel barons had sent their daughters to Chatham, and while the new coed university unironically embraced the legacy of its most famous alumna, Rachel Carson, it retained a bucolic nineteenth-century air, with its white-steepled chapel and red brick Federalist halls and Ionic-columned mansions converted into department offices. Like Chautauqua, it was a world Kitzi loved for its timelessness, as if, at least here, the past was not completely gone.

Jean and Gene's house sat halfway up the slope of the bowl opposite the college, a moody carpenter's Gothic tucked into the shadows beneath a stand of old chestnuts. Buckeyes crunched under her tires as she climbed the drive. The garage, a carriage house with a rooster weathervane topping a louvered cupola, was closed. She grabbed the bag from the passenger seat, not bothering to lock the car. On the porch steps rested several folded newspapers sheathed in plastic. As she came closer, she could see they were waterlogged, though it hadn't rained in weeks. On the front door hung a tortuous twig wreath in the shape of a heart. Lace curtains prevented her from peering inside, though she could hear, faintly, turning her head and leaning in, a slow progression of notes like a child practicing scales.

She rang the bell and the music stopped.

She waited, expecting footsteps. The music started again, faltered, stopped.

She rang again and stepped back, ready to show Jean the bag, her reason for interrupting her lesson.

Again, the phrase like a question, ending on a wrong note.

"Hello?" she called. "Jean?" She tried the knob but it was locked.

The music started.

She was sure Jean had heard her, and pressed the bell again, holding it down so that it trilled. When she relented, the music had stopped.

She thought she could hear papers rustling and the knock of something wooden. Then nothing. Behind her, down the hill, a motorbike razzed by. When it had passed, she could hear someone coming. Through the curtain she could see a gaunt shadow approach and then stop, its head bent as if to listen.

"Who is it?" The woman's voice was high and fey, a plummy British soprano that made her picture Glenda the Good Witch.

"It's Kitzi—from the Humpty Dumpty Club? Sorry to interrupt. I have your prescriptions."

"Who are you again?"

"Kitzi, from the Humpty Dumpties."

Still she wouldn't open the door. "Joan typically brings us our things."

"I know. She couldn't make it."

Again, silence, though the shadow never moved. "Thank you, Kitzi. Just leave them, please."

"Is everything all right?"

"Everything's fine. That's kind of you to ask."

"You have some newspapers here too."

"Thank you, I'm aware."

She sounded reasonable enough, understandably leery of someone she didn't know. Kitzi didn't think she should leave without seeing her and Gene. At the same time, being new, she couldn't invoke anything close to Joan's authority.

"Joan's in the hospital," she tried. "She had a bad fall but she's doing better now."

"I'm so sorry. Please give her our best."

"I will," Kitzi said. "Are you sure you're all right?"

"We're fine, thank you."

"If there's anything you need, I'll give you my number. I'll write it on the bag."

"That won't be necessary."

She wrote it anyway. "I'll just set it here."

Inside, a cat meowed as if asking to be let out. The shadow stooped to pick it up and, before Kitzi could say anything, vanished back into the house, leaving the blank white curtain.

"Nice to meet you," Kitzi called after her, but there was no answer. Too late, she realized she shouldn't leave the oxycodone out there where anyone could take it, but the time to make that point to Jean had passed. The music started again, the same tentative phrase ending in failure, and rather than ring the bell, Kitzi retreated.

Was Jean ashamed of someone she didn't know seeing the condition of the house? Besides the papers, there was no hint of the disorder within, the exterior a kind of mask. There was no reason Kitzi should feel insulted, yet, leaving pastoral Chatham behind for Tree of Life and the present, the rejection nagged at her like a job half done. It was only when she got back home and looked in on Martin sleeping peacefully in his defibrillator vest and boxers that she understood she did the same thing, holding the greater world at bay.

She called Joan and got Arlene.

"How's it going with Jean and Gene?" Arlene asked.

"Strange. Is Joan awake?"

She was.

"Does she let you inside?" Kitzi asked Joan.

"She does. It took some time. I try to visit with Gene and see what's in their fridge. I worry that they don't eat."

"Can you call them? They didn't pick up for me."

"I'm pretty sure they don't use the phone anymore. I can write you a note."

"Will that work?"

Joan was afraid they'd gotten too used to her during Covid. It was an important lesson going forward, making sure to rotate personnel—and again Kitzi felt the weight of expectation on her. Today, especially, she wanted to protest. Instead, she thanked her.

The phone gave a muffled clunk as Joan handed it to Arlene.

"Do you want me to try?" Arlene asked.

While Kitzi had managed her visit poorly, she gave Arlene even less chance of success. It wasn't just pride. As much as she struggled with the idea—and the prospect of all the extra work—she had to accept that Joan had made the right choice.

"No," she said. "I'll do it."

Studies from Life

At Allegheny, back in the early '50s, as a requirement for her bachelor's in education, Arlene had had to take an art class. Her Sigma sisters warned her off of pottery (too dull) and sculpture (too hard), recommending instead an easy A called Studies from Life offered by an actual French artist who was rumored to throw beatnik parties out at their old farmhouse during which other art department faculty drank absinthe and smoked reefer and writhed to voodoo-like jazz. To Arlene, Professor Aragon merely seemed French—remote and stoic, almost disinterested, as if their work was unworthy of him, wandering the studio from easel to easel, mumbling cryptic off-the-cuff critiques ("Blue, blue, blue, blue, blue!") and then retreating to an open window to nurse a Gitane he'd left burning on the ledge.

"Everything is too nice," he once said of a landscape of hers, which, being an absolute beginner, she cherished as a compliment.

Studies from Life became her favorite class; she didn't care about the A. They worked on musculature, using live models, which she found strange and exciting. Often she stayed afterward, trying to get the tiniest element right. Professor Aragon noticed.

"You like to paint," he said, seeming concerned.

"Yes, very much."

"You think painting is fun."

"I do."

"Painting is not fun. You paint, you find out."

She seized on this imperative not simply as encouragement but a method of understanding the world. Painting was a way of slowing down and seeing, a way of contemplating the essence of things—a flower, a thumb, a pear, a bowl—and though she'd never sold any of her work, only given select pieces to friends, the time she spent composing was one of the great rewards of her life.

This morning she was working not from life but one of Kenny's photographs of the family cottage at Chautauqua the last summer before Emily had sold it, an act of treason for which Arlene believed she'd forgiven her after twenty years. Rather than a painful reminder of their shared loss, her picture, like Kenny's, was supposed to be a fount of happy memories. The original was going to be Emily's Christmas present; everyone else would get a print.

She was roughing in the panels of the screen porch when the phone rang, and, as was her habit, she let the answering machine pick up.

"Don't forget," Kitzi said, "you're taking Barbara Parrish to the eye doctor at eleven."

The shock of it stopped her in mid-stroke. Was that today? It was impossible, and she hurried into the kitchen, palette and brush still in hand, to check her calendar.

"Oh, poop," she said.

It was ten after ten already. She had just enough time to clean up, sign Barbara out of the Holmes Residence and make it over there, and then one lane of the Highland Park Bridge was closed and they ended up being late. Barbara was having cataract surgery next month. She wore black glasses and needed to be guided up the front steps and into the foyer like a blind person.

"Thank you," she kept saying, holding Arlene's elbow.

"Taking a right here," Arlene said. "Your other right. There we are."

Because they were late, they had to wait extra, giving Arlene a chance to wonder how many of the other patients enduring the nonstop babble of cable news couldn't see the TV. Going blind was one of her oldest fears; she'd imagined it happening to her since she'd first read about Helen Keller. Once, years ago, when her class had gone on a field trip to Penn's Cave, the guide had led them down to a secluded tomb of a chamber and had the children blow out their candles one by one until only his remained.

"You've probably never seen total darkness before," he said, "so get ready." He pursed his lips, his breath bending the flame, and then everything disappeared.

A student whimpered and fingers gripped her arm.

"Now close your eyes," the guide said. "What do you see?"

"Like a red light," one of the boys said.

"Now open them."

She couldn't—and waited till the guide finally flicked his lighter, the flame so bright she had to raise a hand to block it.

She imagined death was like that, an endless, suffocating night. Even now, sitting in the well-lighted office, just the possibility set off a flutter of panic, yet Barbara never complained. She sat upright and alert, listening to the news, every so often cocking her head to catch a stray conversation. When the nurse called her name and asked if she wanted Arlene to come back with her, she waved dismissively and said she'd be fine.

The news repeated on the hour, more of the war in Ukraine, more attack ads calling John Fetterman a socialist. Arlene took out her phone only to find a half dozen text messages—one from Obama—asking for donations to the DNC. As she sat cleaning up her email, she remembered that she needed something from the grocery store but couldn't recall what. It was a common enough occurrence, yet it bothered her, like her painting being interrupted, her whole day knocked off-kilter because she'd forgotten about Barbara. And she'd put it on the calendar, that was the awful thing. If Kitzi hadn't called, Barbara could have missed her appointment.

Arlene shook her head. Emily was right, she thought. I'm losing it.

How had Kitzi known, or was Kitzi just being paranoid? Joan had never called her like that. While Arlene had spent most of her life alone, she wasn't above accepting help, especially from fellow HDs. She and Emily had discussed this more than once and agreed. She didn't want people worrying about her.

She was still fretting over her phone when the nurse led Barbara out. Her black glasses were gone; now she had a gauze patch taped over her right eye. Her left was blood-red, her lashes wet with tears.

"She's feeling a little discomfort," the nurse said. "We gave her some Tylenol-C, so she's going to want to go straight home and rest."

Arlene gave her her elbow and helped her to the door. She was slower than when they came in, and tentative on the steps.

"I can't see anything," she said.

"You're doing fine," Arlene said. "Here's the railing."

Barbara groped for it, her hand closing on air. As Arlene reached behind to help, steadying her elbow with her other hand, Barbara missed the last step and fell forward. Arlene lunged and caught her by the waist, but she was too heavy and Arlene too weak to hold her upright, though she tried. If Barbara had thrown her arms out to save herself, she would have been fine, but she never did. She toppled face-first, slowly folding down with Arlene still hopelessly tugging at her hips until her forehead met the sidewalk.

All Arlene could see, bent over her, was the back of her head. Barbara lay there, not moving.

"Are you okay?"

"I don't know."

"Did you hit your face?"

"Yes."

From out of nowhere a crowd had materialized, spouting advice. Arlene wanted to turn her over but wasn't sure it was the right thing.

"My wrist hurts," Barbara said.

"Don't move," the nurse said, and Arlene was both ashamed and relieved to let her take charge. She dug in her purse for a pack of tissues, keeping them at the ready as the nurse rolled Barbara onto her side.

She had a brush burn on her chin but nothing else. The nurse made her flex her hand while she felt her wrist and forearm. Together, she and Arlene helped her to her feet. The crowd had already vanished.

"I guess I should have eaten something," Barbara said back inside.

"I can get you some juice," the nurse said.

"I feel fine now."

"When was the last time you ate?"

"This morning," she said, but she was unsure of herself, and, like a child taking medicine, dutifully drank the juice while they watched.

Arlene promised the nurse they'd stop somewhere. The only place on the way was a dirty Wendy's on Penn Avenue. Barbara could barely see out of her one eye and kept missing her mouth with her French fries. Arlene fetched extra napkins, all the while scourging herself. What was wrong with her, letting Barbara get ahead of her on the stairs?

It was past two when she checked her back into the Holmes Residence. When Arlene explained to the receptionist what had happened, they called for a wheelchair. With her eye patch and chin, Barbara looked like she'd been in a car accident.

"Thank you," she said. "I'm sorry it turned into such an adventure."

"I'm sorry I didn't do a better job taking care of you."

"Stop saying that. There was nothing you could do."

It was not true, Arlene thought, and continued to brood on it at home, the unfinished canvas reproaching her further, the squandered cottage Henry's legacy. Her memory, his gentle strength and high spirits. In the end they would lose everything—total darkness, despite all of Heaven's promises. It was too late in the day to start again, and rather than hurry and do more bad work, she put the kettle on, hoping to calm herself with a cup of tea, only to discover there was none.

She'd already written it on the list.

"Poop and double poop," she said.

Evensong

Sunday, while the rest of the city was worshipping the Steelers, they came to give voice to their faith. The date had been on their calendars ever since Donald Wilkins released the fall schedule. That morning he'd teased them with a Bach chorale prelude after the recessional, whetting their palates. Now, after months of fasting, they were ready to feast.

Susie walked over early to change. They were premiering a grand motet of Charpentier with Chatham Baroque, and Viv Hapgood, their choirmaster, was nervous, importuning the vestry like a coach, exhorting them as they robed to "Listen, listen, listen!" Everyone knew they were being recorded yet no one mentioned it, as if they were doing *Macbeth*. On a table by the door sat a ravaged flat of bottled water and a bowl of throat lozenges Viv had thoughtfully unwrapped.

The other three drove separately, parking next to one another as if their cars were old friends as well. They had all sung at one point, and though they no longer needed to prepare, they still felt the pull of the new season.

Technically summer was over, but it was still bright out at six thirty, and hot.

"Not exactly the right weather," Emily said, and they agreed. The effect was nicer at dusk as fall deepened into winter, their joined voices a comfort against the gathering night. They were connoisseurs; even this quibble was a ritual, as was their delight at finding the stone interior of the church so cool. Knowing Arlene would forget, Emily had reminded her to bring a sweater, which she now pulled on.

"I'm glad I brought this," she said.

"Me too," Emily said, casting a doubtful glance at Kitzi.

Like the other regulars, they had their own pew, close enough to watch Donald Wilkins work the stops on the organ. It was a small but dedicated group, most of them choir alumni and older donors who kept the music series going. Today they were joined by a middle-aged gay couple in matching blazers and a clutch of nattering undergrads, probably performance majors studying under one of Chatham Baroque's string players.

"I don't see Penny and Helen," Kitzi said.

"They might still be in Maine," Emily said.

"Penny's having a bunion removed Tuesday."

"Maybe that's why she's not here."

"Maybe."

It was the first Emily had heard of Penny's surgery, and she felt hurt. Ever since Kitzi had taken over for Joan, she seemed closed off. Between the club and Martin she had to be stretched thin, yet not once had she come to Emily—maybe out of pride. Having been her friend forever, Emily knew not to ask about Martin, but this was different. Was she wrong? Was she being selfish, wanting to help? She thought the club was all of them, not just one person.

Beside her, Kitzi scanned the chancel windows ranked with disciples, looking for guidance. She'd wanted Evensong to be a respite and now all she could think of was Lillian Cochran going into hospice and how she needed to send flowers.

As always at Calvary, bestilled, Arlene was transported far back into the past. The tousle-headed altar boy racing to the rear of the nave with his taper might have been Henry, wearing PF Flyers under his surplice. Their grandmother Maxwell had left a healthy bequest to the church; supposedly they'd used her face for one of the saints carved into the rood screen, though right at this moment, no matter how hard she tried, frowning with the effort, the name escaped her. Emily would know, but she didn't want to ask her, and so she sat, trying to recall all the female saints she could, certain the majority of them were Catholic.

Soles scuffing on marble, a looseleaf binder tucked under one arm, a hunched Donald Wilkins emerged from the Lady chapel in dark slacks and a turtleneck and crossed the altar rail, his glasses swinging on a chain. He took his seat at the keyboard and propped the binder on the music stand, donned his glasses to find the right page and checked the stops like a pilot preparing for takeoff, then sat back, slumped, his long hands folded in his lap.

"Chop-chop," Emily said, tapping the face of Henry's Hamilton.

Unseen, high above the vault, the bells chimed the hour, and with a thunderous rumble the organ roared to life, rousing them to attention. Emily didn't need to open the program to know the voluntary was Blow's. It was a chestnut, like the introit after it, Purcell's "O Sing unto the Lord," the first hornpiped figure of which brought them creakily to their feet, holding on to the pew in front for support, nodding to the cross as it passed and then to Susie, who looked up from her score, smiling, and while the three of them knew what a stickler Viv could be, and would never again sacrifice their Saturday afternoons to practice, they also knew the glorifying power of processing before a full house at Easter or during Advent, and were jealous. What a thrill it was to be overwhelmed by the sound, the organ's low end reverberating inside them, filling them like a vessel. As the choir filed into the stalls, the three of them sang as if they still belonged to it, all other thoughts forgotten.

Susie, in the middle of the altos, concentrated on the notes. She hadn't slept well last night and then had sung both morning services. After lying on the couch all afternoon with a heating pad, she'd almost taken a Vicodin before walking over to feed Oscar, but needed to be sober for the Charpentier, which she'd struggled with in practice. The pain was distracting. All she wanted to do was sit down, but there were two more verses, and then the Byrd and the Palestrina before the lesson, and as she sang unto the Lord, like an idle notion hijacking one's train of thought, she left herself and floated out over Kitzi and Emily and Arlene and the empty pews beyond to the dim recesses of the organ loft, where she could barely see what was happening in the tiny circle of light up front.

"I've always liked this one," Arlene whispered, and, when Emily didn't respond, added, "And not just because it's by Henry," making her shake her head.

Kitzi glanced at the two of them, left out, as always, of their little in-jokes. Lillian had been a major donor, and Kitzi would be expected to represent the club at the funeral, whenever that would be. Who knew how close she was? The uncertainty was paralyzing. Next week was already a mess, and again she marveled at how easy Joan had made the job look. Fay Dudley and Marion Gill weren't far behind Lillian. She'd need to wear a different outfit for each, a problem so confounding she couldn't begin to think of it, and sang with the others: *And HE shall JUDGE the PEO-ple RIGHT-eous-LYYYYY.*

Now that the choir was in place, they could relax and enjoy the concert. The trio of Chatham Baroque took center stage with their instruments, and, with an exaggerated nod, launched into Byrd's "Have Mercy upon Me, O God."

"It really is like a greatest hits," Emily whispered to Kitzi, who, not wanting to be rude, could only shrug. Normally she was a snob about music too, but today, especially, she could appreciate the dependable pleasures of the familiar.

They were almost through the second verse when someone's phone rang—across the aisle, among a pew of older patrons including Harold and Mimi Cunningham—a cheesy Mozart ringtone, the opening bars of Eine kleine Nachtmusik, strident enough that the bass violist looked over, more surprised than irritated. From her spot in the front stall, Viv Hapgood glared.

It went on, the glib phrase taunting.

Harold and Mimi sat rapt, absorbing the Byrd through their hearing aids via Calvary's wireless feed. A neighbor behind them finally slid across and tapped Mimi, who had to help a confused Harold first find and then silence his phone.

"I'm glad it wasn't me," Arlene said afterward in the refectory, where there was coffee and a disappointing assortment of store-bought cookies.

"I am too," Emily agreed.

"They're professionals," Susie said. "They played right through it."

"Viv was not amused," Kitzi said, making sure she was out of earshot.

"Not so much," Susie said.

"I don't know why they don't say something beforehand," Arlene said.

"We did!" Susie said. "We always make an announcement. At least it wasn't during the Charpentier."

"I guess," Emily said.

"What did you think?" Susie asked, because she was proud of how it had turned out, yet none of them had offered an opinion.

Arlene looked to Emily. Emily looked to Kitzi, and Kitzi looked back to Arlene, as if the three of them were deciding how to vote.

"It was good," Emily said. "I'm not a huge fan of the French." Which everyone knew.

"It sounded good," Kitzi said. "That three-part section in the bridge couldn't have been easy."

"It wasn't."

"I liked it," Arlene said. "It was very soothing."

"I think it turned out well," Susie said lightly, trying not to sound defensive. "Viv seemed happy. It sounded like they were going to use it."

"That's what counts," Emily said.

"Any idea when it will be available?" Kitzi asked, turning the conversation to the future.

"It was written in 1758," Emily said later in the parking lot, as the three of them were standing by their cars, keys in hand. "I think there was a reason it didn't premiere until tonight."

"I didn't mind it," Arlene said.

"It was fine," Kitzi said.

Dusk had fallen and a sharp half-moon was rising behind the steeple, the evening star winking high and bright. It was only October; the whole season stretched ahead of them like a promise, and, satisfied, they bade their good nights, waving across the tops of their cars.

With a finger, Emily signaled Kitzi to wait a second, giving Arlene time to get in.

"Let me know if I can help with Penny," Emily said.

"I will."

"I'm serious. I'm not doing anything this week. I know there's a lot going on. You don't have to do it all yourself."

"I won't."

Emily wasn't sure she believed her, but then, rather than duck into her car and take off, Kitzi nodded. "I'll call you."

For now, it was enough.

At home, Angus was waiting in the front hall as if he hadn't moved since she left.

"And what have you been doing all night?" she asked.

A Bumbler

At this point Susie's interest in men was academic. Statistically, they couldn't all be as bad as Richard. At her age, in her less-than-ideal shape, was it too much to hope for one who was open, one who might be nice? A year ago, when she'd moved to the city, she pictured having dates over for romantic dinners on her balcony, like something out of a Doris Day movie. Wine, candlelight, the perfect dress. She waited to meet her Rock Hudson in line at the dry cleaners or dialing her combination at the Kenmawr's venerable wall of mailboxes, but the only holdovers in the building were women, and the college students ignored her. The only man she met was Bill, but he was Joan's savior, not hers.

Her daughter Alyssa had found her second husband on a dating app—they were both climbers and mountain bikers who worked remotely—and thought Susie might have better luck going that route. Being of a decidedly more private generation, Susie was leery of the internet. The idea of purposely baring herself to the world felt wrong, and foolish. She and Richard used to joke about the "Craigslist Killer."

"How would I even advertise myself?" she protested. "I don't do anything cool."

"You sing. You like to cook. You take care of people. Men like that."

"That's not the kind of man I'm looking for. That was your father. I don't even know what I'm looking for."

"Say that. 'I like surprises.'"

"I don't though. I like things to be calm."

"You like yoga."

"Men don't do yoga. Not here."

"Mom, that is not true."

"I don't want some hippie-dippy guy with a ponytail—ew."

"What *do* you want?"

"I want someone who'll cook for *me*. I want someone who knows who Alice Waters is."

"You should do Bumble. You get to pick who you go out with. The men don't have a say. Dwayne's mom uses it and loves it."

"What does Dwayne think of it?"

"He thinks it's great. He wants her to be happy. I want *you* to be happy."

"I *am* happy."

"I think you could be happier," Alyssa said.

She had no reason to be lonely. After the divorce, she'd kept their friends. It was Richard who left, tearfully confessing to an affair with a partner at another firm downtown. Had she stayed in the house on Mayflower Drive, her life would have gone along as always: her morning walk, coffee, pickleball and then lunch at the club, a few hours in the garden before getting dinner together and listening to *All Things Considered*, at night a well-reviewed novel by the fire. She lasted three months before she called her friend Mandy at Howard Hanna to list it. All that remained were her grandmother's quilts on the top shelf of the closet and the Prius parked out back by the dumpsters, at the mercy of the elements. Bumble was nothing. She'd already made her leap of faith.

"I think it's genius," Arlene said, as if it were a modern marvel. "You choose." Susie had invited her to Point Brugge to mine her experience as a single woman, using it as an excuse to have their mussels—really the broth, a garlicky ambrosia of lemon and white wine.

"I already chose wrong once. You've never used it, have you?"

Arlene laughed, covering her mouth as she chewed her bread. "I did one of those video things once, a long time ago."

"Really? How was that?" Though what she was dying to ask was: Why? Arlene was the most self-sufficient person she knew.

"Strange. It was very new at the time. I did meet some interesting people."

"No one . . . suitable."

"Let's just say there was a range. I don't think any of them were really looking for companionship. One was married, which I guess shouldn't have surprised me. It's interesting, how different people are."

"It is," Susie agreed, though, as she parsed their conversation later, she was more intrigued by Arlene's ideal of companionship. Was that what she wanted? Because she didn't need a man for that. Maybe she was too old for romance, for that kind of happiness, but how would she know if she didn't try?

She signed up with her maiden name as if she were a different person. They needed three photos. Was it cheating that not all of them had been taken in the past year? Her activity level was wishful, lifted from her power-walking era. Likewise, she hedged on the questionnaire, describing herself not as religious but spiritual, politically moderate, in good overall health with no dietary restrictions. She wasn't exaggerating her strengths, as she suspected most people did, just smoothing off her edges. It was like camouflage, a kind of disguise so the matches they came up with wouldn't directly reflect her true self, a prospect that could be hurtful, but this improvised impostor. On principle, she believed that anyone who really wanted to know her should be willing to do some work.

She did confess that she enjoyed walking, dogs, pickleball, literature, fine food and wine, opera and classical music, and she listed her real age. Still, she was surprised when the app suggested two profiles of men in their eighties.

"Send me their screenshots," Alyssa said. "They could be hot."

"They're not. They're old. *I'm* old but I can still see just fine."

"Do any of them have ponytails?"

"Thank God, no. One of them looks like he has false teeth."

"Are there any that could be maybes?"

"Two aren't terrible. One's only fifty-five and plays the violin." She didn't say his name was Peter, preempting any jokes.

"See?"

"He's also been divorced three times."

"What about the other?"

"The other's my age and had his own restaurant."

"Wow. These are gold."

"They're strangers. They could be murderers and rapists for all I know."

"That is true," Alyssa said. "That's why you have your first meetup in a public place—and not a date, just coffee or something.

If you feel something's not right for whatever reason, you say you have to go to the bathroom and take off and never see them again."

"Is that what you did with Dwayne?"

"That's what I did with a number of guys before I met Dwayne. It's just part of meeting people."

Susie couldn't imagine getting naked with one stranger, let alone a number. She didn't even like Richard looking at her. She hated her stomach, and her butt, and her feet. Already she was devising what combination of sleepwear she would have to use to cover herself.

"I don't know if I want to meet people," she said.

"Of course you do. You can't just sit in your apartment the rest of your life. That's not healthy. Go with the chef. Maybe you can get him to cook for you."

"The violinist's better looking. And younger."

"Then go with him. At least you'll get out of the house."

"What if he doesn't drink coffee?"

"Oh my God, Mom, everyone drinks coffee."

She would do it—tonight, before she lost her courage—but how did you choose? She'd only met Richard because he was a groomsman at her roommate Stacey's wedding, the two of them paired for the ceremony because of their height. The reception was at a yacht club on the Cape. They danced to Van Morrison beneath colored lanterns, and when the band stopped, the wedding party moved to the beach, passing a bottle of champagne and some Thai stick around a fire. She and Richard strolled barefoot through the surf toward the point, watching the lights of the summer houses shimmer on the water. In the morning, when they woke in the dunes, she was wearing the jacket of his tuxedo. So much of life was chance. She was afraid she would ruin it by choosing, and in the end, to honor the mystery of the universe, she flipped a coin.

DNR/DNI

Since Kitzi had taken over for Joan, she'd turned her office into a command post, complete with a dry-erase board listing the club's ongoing cases and a map of the city with a green pin for each member's location, and still she was struggling to keep up. To placate Emily, she'd given her Penny and her bunion, as well as running Sukie Beach over to the dentist (no longer trusting Arlene to handle time-critical assignments), and while it was a help, she now had Marion Gill to worry about, along with Lillian Cochran, the two of them sedated and fading in Shadyside's ICU. She assumed they were both DNR/DNI but couldn't ask the nurses' desk how they were doing without sounding like a ghoul. She thought it more politic to call the chaplain, whose number she'd specifically written on a blue Post-it note and pinned to the corkboard but which right now was eluding her.

"You know what I'd like?" Martin said from the doorway, interrupting her search.

Assuming from his tone that it was just more of his normal shtick, she threw him a Medusa stare.

He held his hands apart in front of his face as if gripping an imaginary basketball. "A big BLT with double bacon and extra mayo."

"Great," she said, deadpan. "Go for it. I have to be at the hospital later anyway."

"Do we have any turkey bacon?"

"Stop. I'll be done here in five minutes and I'll get you your lunch."

"I can get it."

"Go away," she said, and he did, moping, and then she felt guilty for being short with him when he'd known all along that she was busy. He could get his own lunch, he wasn't a complete invalid, but his skills ended at assembling hoagies and microwaving leftovers. In frustration she sometimes asked him what he would do if she died first, to which he smugly replied, "You won't," as if it were a joke instead of her worst fear. He slept in his vest in case it needed to shock him to life, and, lying beside him in the middle of the night she jerked awake at the slightest sound—once, out of a deep sleep, her phone buzzing from a spam text message—afraid she was feeling his body seizing, already dead.

What would she do when he died? There was no reason to ask that, because it wasn't hypothetical. Eventually she would find out.

Inexplicably, the chaplain's number was on a red Post-it. When she called, he didn't pick up, and rather than ad-lib something, she pressed End and went to get Martin his lunch.

During Covid, with both of them stuck at home and Trump running the country, they'd fallen into the habit of eating in front of the TV in their sweats, watching the previous night's *Seth Meyers* or *Colbert* to raise their spirits. Now that the world was open again, she'd gone back to wearing actual clothes, while he, housebound, saw no reason. She wasn't sure what day the gray sweatpants he was wearing were on, but they were favorites.

In accordance with their unspoken division of labor, he'd already set out the tray tables and had Seth's monologue cued up, and she felt rushed.

"It's going to take me a little while to make your BLT, if that's what you want."

"I can help."

"It's faster if I just do it," she said, which, while bitchy, was the truth.

Turkey bacon, soy mayo, keto bread—nothing he was allowed to eat was real, and still he was heavy. The doctor had cautioned against sex—needlessly, though both of them let the warning pass without comment, only confirming his suspicions, Kitzi thought.

She was in the middle of flipping the bacon when the hospital called, the ID scrolling the familiar number of the UPMC switchboard, a firewall built to prevent patients from talking directly to their doctors. Lillian, Marion—she stopped herself from guessing which one had passed—so she was happily surprised to hear Joan.

She turned down the burner and covered the skillet with a lid. "This is a surprise."

"Jean just called me. She said someone broke a window last night and tried to steal Gene's car. I don't know, I couldn't quite make sense of what she was saying. Can you go over and see what's going on?"

"I don't think she'll let me in."

"I told her you were coming."

"I doubt that will make a difference."

"Maybe not, but I'd appreciate it if you could take a look around. She was pretty upset."

Kitzi looked at Seth Meyers behind his desk, frozen in mid-sentence, and Martin sitting on the couch with the remote, and thought of everything she still needed to do today.

"Okay," she said.

"Thank you. Let me know what you find out. I worry about them."

"I know you do," Kitzi said, because although she'd only been to their house once, and been denied entry, she understood that feeling of holding sole responsibility for another. It was the guiding principle of the HDs. No one else was going to help them.

First she needed to feed Martin.

"Go ahead and start that," she said, patting the grease off the fake bacon. "I'm watching."

"Something going on with Jean and Gene?"

"That's what I need to find out, I guess, because nobody else can do it."

"You can go if you want. You don't have to babysit me."

"I don't really want to go," she said, handing him his plate and sitting down beside him, but then, as they ate, she couldn't concentrate on the monologue, imagining a burglar breaking into their place and Martin lying there helpless.

"I've gotta run."

"I'll clean up," he said. "Do you care about these guests?"

"No." Honestly, she hadn't even noticed who was on.

Again it seemed she had to pass Tree of Life every day, as if she might forget the terrible state of the world. The midterms were less than a month away, and she worried about the fate of the Senate, and by extension the Supreme Court—the country, really—if Fetterman lost.

The sky was overcast, making the sylvan interlude of Woodland Road feel gloomy, her lights automatically popping on. Chatham was in session, the sledding hill empty, and as she wound up the long drive cloaked in shadow, crushing buckeyes, she realized how secluded the house was. They might have been in the country. There were deer back here, people were always posting them on Instagram.

Getting out of her car, she was surprised how cold it was beneath the trees. As it had the first time, the place looked abandoned, a relic from another era with its lace curtains and filigreed eaves and glass globe lightning rods, the outmoded carriage house like a barn. Nothing stirred, the only sound her footsteps as she crossed the pea gravel. She didn't recall the waist-high yellow grass or the spiked iron fence hemming in the yard like a private cemetery. The CVS bag with the oxys was gone, but another collection of newspapers had amassed on the porch steps. She ignored them and went straight to the door, listening with her head turned for a minute before knocking.

She waited, gazing up at the stilled weathervane, and soon she could hear Jean coming, sidling through the piles, knowing every step might be the one to trigger the avalanche that would finally bury her.

The porch light came on and then the light inside, throwing Jean's stooped shadow on the curtain. "Is that you, Kitzi?"

It was a shock to hear her name. "Yes. Hello, Jean. Joan said you had a problem."

"Yes, well, we're not certain it is a problem, but Gene thought someone ought to check. That car's his baby, you know."

"What happened?"

"That's what we'd like to know. I don't see well enough to be any help, and Gene can't walk, so we're hoping you might take a peek."

With a click, the door opened an inch and a long pale hand reached out a fat set of keys.

Kitzi accepted them, stepping to the side to try to see Jean's face, but the hand withdrew and the door clicked shut again.

"Which key is it?"

"I'm not sure. You'll have to try them."

"'You'll have to try them'" Kitzi mimicked, picking through the ring as she crunched across the gravel. Some were shiny silver copies from Wal-Mart or True Value, some dirty brass. Several were long antiques the color of old pennies like the ones rattled by Jacob Marley.

The lock on the carriage house door was modern and intact: a Yale with a blue bottom. There was a lone Yale key. She turned it and the lock popped open.

"That was easy," she said, and as she pulled apart the massive weathered wooden doors, a tiger cat shot past her into the high grass. While she was looking after it, another scampered out, sat down in the gravel and began cleaning itself.

Inside, the carriage house was chilly as a crypt and reeked of cat pee and something earthier. She could immediately see that one window in the back was broken, a fang of glass still clinging to the frame. In the dim light, Gene's car sat under a heavy canvas tarp splotched with chalky bird shit. Kitzi detoured around it to investigate the window and, in her effort not to brush against the wall, stepped on something soft and squishy that she knew, even before she glanced down, was dead—another cat, shriveled and eyeless—and she ran, pleading, "*No, no, no, no, no*," one hand on the tarp for balance, until she was safely away from it.

"Gross," she said, wiping her shoe on the dirt and scanning around, sure there were more underfoot.

The window had four panes. Only the top right one was broken. The shards on the sill weren't covered in dust, meaning they were new. She peered out into a jungle of weed trees and vines. The window was locked. There was no blood on the glass, no fingerprints. She checked the floor, expecting a brick, a rock or a BB implicating a neighbor's kid, maybe a bird trying to escape the cats, but there was nothing. Obviously, Jean and Gene had heard it break sometime in the night and worried, just as she and Martin would, so she was glad she could give them good news.

When Jean had handed her the keys, she didn't let Kitzi get a look at her. Now, to satisfy her curiosity, Kitzi lifted the hem of the tarp, steeling herself for another cat to fly out.

The car was black as a London cab and perfectly clean, which, after everything, was unexpected. Even the bumper shone as if it had just been polished. It wasn't that old, the taillights squarish, sectioned into red, amber and white like her Honda's. She wasn't a car person. From the back she wouldn't have recognized the make, except for the silver logo that hid the trunk lock, two intertwined *R*'s, and, beneath them, to make it clear even to beings not from this planet: Rolls-Royce.

"That is a big baby," she said.

Where did a professor get the money for a Rolls? Its presence felt illicit, as if they'd bought the car with drug money and were hiding it from the IRS. How old was the Rolls, and what did it cost then? Did they buy it new, walk into the dealership and just write a check? Never in their lives had she and Martin splurged like that—she'd never even ridden in a Rolls—and now they never would.

It was crazy. Neither of them even drove.

She pulled the tarp back over the bumper and picked her way through the cat shit, closed the doors and locked them, yanking hard on the lock to make sure. Now that she knew what was inside, she didn't want anything to happen to it on her account. She wondered if in some way that was how they felt, the car a precious object like a work of art they kept separate from the disaster of the house.

When she knocked this time, Jean took even longer to answer. She apologized; she was cleaning up from lunch.

Kitzi had positioned herself so that when Jean reached her hand out, she caught a sliver of her face—pale as her hands, with wide green eyes, her hair long and white as salt—before Jean shut the door.

"What did you have?" Kitzi asked, trying to picture their fridge, knowing Joan would interrogate her later.

"Just some soup and crackers. What all did you discover?"

She told her about the window.

Behind the curtain, Jean chuckled. "He said he heard it. I didn't believe him. I'll never hear the end of it now. But it's fine, yes?"

"You'll need to get the window fixed."

"Right."

"Do you have someone who can do that?"

"Not at hand, no."

"I can find someone if you like." As she offered, she realized she was making more work for herself, but it was only right.

"Please, that would be a kindness. Thank you, Kitzi."

They spoke through the door as if it were normal. It was only back in the car, navigating the curves of Woodland Road, that Kitzi realized she hadn't told Jean about the dead cat. Was she trying to spare her? With so many, would she miss one?

At home, Martin was watching *Colbert*. He didn't bother to pause it.

"That was fast."

"It was nothing," she said. "Just a broken window."

"Did she let you in?"

"No. I'm still a stranger."

"Weird."

"Not really."

Here was her chance to tell him about the key ring and the Rolls, her glimpse of Jean with her witchy white hair, their whole weird private world.

"Cheesesteak with onions," Martin said, because Stephen Colbert had asked Keanu Reeves what the best sandwich was, and she took her purse into the front hall and tucked it into its spot at the bottom of the closet.

"Did you want to watch this?" Martin asked.

"No, I've got stuff to do," she said.

After reporting back to Joan, she spent the afternoon in her office, trying to track down someone reputable who could repair their window this week, expecting the chaplain to call any minute with news of Lillian or Marion or both. He never did, despite her obsessively checking her phone. She kept it on the counter while she prepared dinner, and on the end table beside the couch as they watched one of Martin's Alaska homesteading shows. Death didn't follow a regular schedule, yet, in bed, when she replaced her bookmark and turned out the light, and still no one had called, she thought that overall it had been a good day.

A Losing Proposition

Parking at Freyvogel's was a nightmare, so it only made sense to go to Lillian's visitation together. There was no question Emily would drive. As much trouble as she had seeing at dusk, even in daylight she didn't trust Arlene behind the wheel. The plan was to get there early, pay their respects and excuse themselves so she could drop Arlene off and be home before dark. The problem with this was that the Fern Hollow Bridge was still out, forcing her to detour around Frick Park, adding a good twenty minutes to the drive. Emily was afraid they were cutting it close and fretted about it on the way over.

"We'll be in and out," Arlene said. "Whoosh-whoosh."

"It's going to be packed."

The Cochran family owned a dozen car dealerships around Pittsburgh and were major donors not just to Calvary but the city's universities and museums. When Henry had been on the vestry, they paid for the church's new furnace. All it had taken was a phone call. Lillian had been the matriarch, and Emily expected

Freyvogel's to be like a board meeting, a parade of fundraisers come to pay homage.

"No one's on time for these things," Arlene said. "It doesn't start until five thirty." It was ten after, and they were maybe three minutes away.

"People will be coming straight from work."

"We're going to be the first ones there. I'll bet you."

"How much?" Emily asked.

"A dollar."

"That's a bet."

They made the light at Aiken, and then the one at Walnut.

"What am I going to spend my dollar on?" Arlene mused, rubbing her palms together.

"You're going to spend it on me," Emily said. "I hope you have one on you."

"I think I do. It doesn't matter: I won't need one."

"Ha, you were going to look."

Freyvogel's was right around the corner. When they turned onto Montfort, there was a line of stopped cars a block long. At the entrance of the lot, a team of valets in black vests was running back and forth.

"There goes your dollar," Emily said. "Looks like we're going to spend it on parking."

"The sign says it's free."

"You still have to tip."

"Oh," Arlene said. "I hate that."

"They get you one way or the other."

"At least you won."

"Whoop-de-doo," Emily said.

Lillian Chandler Cochran

Freyvogel's, like most of the funeral homes they frequented, was a fusty faux-Victorian warren of alcoves and viewing rooms decorated as plainly as an old hotel lobby, with brass lamps, thick pile carpeting and heavy velvet drapes that absorbed all sound, a reverent silence being the preferred response to death. To accommodate the turnout, Lillian's visitation took place in their grand salon, one end of which was dedicated to flower arrangements set on pedestals, the other management's sole concession to the present, a flat-screen TV that ran an endless loop of photos curated by her daughter-in-law Holly, whose name Arlene had forgotten seconds after they'd met.

While Arlene and Lillian had both attended Calvary their entire lives, they'd rarely spoken. During the Depression, when they were girls, they'd been assigned to the same cabin at Calvary Camp up on Lake Erie, sleeping in creaky wooden bunks and washing every morning with cold water, and as she watched the slideshow, a picture of their cabin appeared with all of them gathered on the front steps, their counselor Binny standing like a giant to one side in her Viking maiden braids. She remembered Lillian doing handstands and cartwheels in the grass, and how envious she'd been. Her name had been Lillian Chandler then, as the prayer card Arlene had taken reminded her, filling in the blank. It had been so long ago. She could see her in pigtails, tanned and eating canned peaches at their table in the dining hall, but couldn't recall anything else about her, only a benign feeling that even then she'd been a decent person.

She didn't know the ponytailed coed in the later photos, or the beaming bride, or the young mother in loud prints. Over the years her hair changed color from blond to red to black and back, each fashionable perm and wild blowout making the crowd watching along with Arlene laugh. Here was proof that life went by too fast—Lillian Chandler Cochran, who she never knew. At camp they must have played together, sang, prayed when Binny read their bedtime devotions, told ghost stories and giggled in the dark long after lights out. And the other girls that summer, they'd been like sisters, yet she could recall them even less. If she could only remember their names—yet she'd remembered Binny and her braids. Lately her mind had been unreliable. She stood there wondering why, waiting for the picture to come around again.

Across the salon, beneath a bad etching of Westminster Abbey, Emily signed the guest book for both of them, half tempted to write Henry's name as well. He'd known Lillian better than she had. They'd served on the vestry together, and several capital campaigns, while Emily had been at best an acquaintance, trotted out at kickoff dinners and awards banquets with the other wives.

Lillian was flashy and outspoken, a confidence Emily, whose roots were humble, ascribed to having grown up with money. For decades Lillian had done cheesy TV commercials, dressing up as Abraham Lincoln or a tom turkey, often with one of the Steelers in tow, urging tristate area viewers to "come on down to Cochran-town!" She'd had work done, like Dolly Parton or a Hollywood star, and barely seemed to age, on-screen at least. Up close the effect was less successful, the skin of her face pulled too tight, her boobs too high. Emily would have said she wasn't intimidated by Lillian, yet the few times they'd met, she found herself struggling to make conversation, unable to forget she was in the presence of a celebrity, and then, recounting the evening to friends, casually dropped her name.

"Don't you worry about Henry working so closely with her?" Louise Pickering once asked, because their meetings sometimes went till nine or ten at night. The two were such opposites that Emily had scoffed at the thought.

Of Lillian, Henry said, "She's very strong-willed," which was not entirely a compliment, though he also called her smart and levelheaded, his ultimate commendation of respect. Emily could see how another man might be attracted to Lillian, but she would be too much for Henry. Even now, as a blithe exercise, she couldn't picture them embracing successfully, as if they were different species.

Kitzi, who was waiting in the snaking receiving line to pay her respects to Lillian's three sons, had visited her in Longwood after her first stroke. The all-knowing Joan had chosen her specifically, and she was flattered. Three days a week she drove out to Oakmont to sit with her and play gin rummy. Lillian was paralyzed on her right side, the corner of her mouth stuck shut so that she sprayed spittle and lisped. Having been such a public person, she was naturally embarrassed. The speech therapist hoped Kitzi's presence would encourage her to speak more.

At first, all Lillian did was swear. "Piethe of thit," she said, throwing down her hand. "Thith ith thtupid."

The stroke had taken everything from her, and she was bitter, holding it against the whole world, but gradually, week by week, as she grew used to Kitzi, she opened up.

"I hate thith plathe. I can't believe my family'th going to let me die here."

"They won't," Kitzi said.

"They'll do whatever Andy tellth them, and he wanth it all. I'm not kidding."

Andy was her eldest, a brat and a villain, his wife Lady Macbeth. The other two sons were useless. Lillian fixated on the idea of losing her empire so much that Kitzi wondered if it was a delusion ("You can always change your will," Kitzi advised), and then one night just before Covid hit, watching *Alone* or some other dumb show, she saw Andy dressed as a leprechaun doing her "Come on down to Cochrantown!" bit and backhanded Martin in the arm.

"Ow!"

"That's him!" she said. "That's the guy!"

"Who?"

Now, as the line moved up, she was about to come face-to-face with Andy Cochran and braced herself. What would Lillian want her to say to him?

The younger brothers and their wives were first.

She shook their hands. "I'm so sorry. She was an amazing woman."

When it was Andy's turn, he offered his. She opened her arms and he bent down to hug her.

"Your mother told me all about you," she said, and let him go. The look on his face was uncertain, as if he might have heard her wrong.

The wife was next. She opened her arms and held her close.

Pumpkin Eater

"So?" Arlene asked between hands. "How did it go?"

Susie shuffled, aware they were all waiting for her. They might have been in high school, trading gossip across a lunch table.

"It was coffee," she said. "It was good."

"This was Peter," Arlene said, so they'd all know.

"Did he look like his picture?" Emily asked.

"Pretty much."

"What's 'pretty much'?" Kitzi asked.

"Was he bald?" Arlene asked.

"No, he was not bald. I don't know, he was smaller."

"Shorter?" Emily asked.

"Thinner. Just overall a smaller person. He looked bigger in his pictures."

"Don't you have to give them your height and weight?" Emily, ever literal, asked.

"It was more his personality. He was very quiet. Reserved, I guess. I ended up doing most of the talking."

She feared she had babbled, going on about the Kenmawr and Oscar, and as she told Alyssa, she felt sorry for him. She'd chosen the Square Café because it was walkable and always hopping, but he was soft-spoken and the space was high-ceilinged and so loud that she could barely hear him. He mentioned Noh theater and studying Zen, and she assumed his quietude had something to do with the three divorces.

"What does he do?" Kitzi asked.

"He's retired from the post office."

"I thought he played the violin," Arlene said.

"He does, mostly bluegrass and Americana. He's in a band."

"Post office pensions are supposed to be very good," Emily said.

"He's also an actor," Susie said. "He's been an extra in a lot of things. He had a speaking role in *Mindhunter*."

"I don't know that one," Arlene said.

"It's a detective show," Kitzi said. "Martin watches it."

"He also volunteers as an usher at Heinz Hall."

"I wonder if I've seen him," Kitzi said.

Susie pulled up his best picture on her phone to show her, him in a tux at his oldest daughter's wedding.

"Don't recognize him. He's got nice hair. Very distinguished."

They all wanted to see and passed her phone around.

"He looks like an actor," Arlene said. "He has a thin face and a long head."

"Is he taller than you?" Emily asked.

"Yes, he's taller than me. He's intelligent and nice and interesting; he's just a little quiet." And thin, she didn't add. Vampire thin.

"Quiet's good," Kitzi said. "Better than loud."

She didn't say that Richard had been quiet at the end, and gave the deck to Kitzi to cut.

"So," Arlene asked, "is there going to be a second date?"

"There wasn't a first date." She took back the deck. "I don't know, we'll see."

Until then, she'd been leaning no, yet she'd defended him. He did seem kind, and thoughtful. Maybe he'd open up more in a nicer restaurant, or was that too much? She had a motherly urge to fatten him up. She tried to think of a place that wasn't too romantic but with good food. Maybe Casbah. She wasn't in any rush.

"Who paid?" Emily said.

She wasn't sure why it mattered. "We split the bill."

"Enough," Kitzi said, pointing at the deck in her hands. "Deal."

Big Bird Bucks

Columbus Day, Penny Rowland was still homebound, recovering from her bunionectomy, so Arlene went shopping for her at the Edgewood Towne Centre Giant Eagle. Built on the footprint of the defunct Union Switch and Signal plant, since losing the Kmart and the Eat'n Park—both frequent destinations for Arlene—and Covid wiping out the ill-timed Scene75 go-kart track and arcade, the plaza had become a reminder of how tenuous the economy was, both locally and globally. Radio Shack was gone, and Marshall's, AutoZone and PetSmart, the so-so Chinese place run by a mother and her teenaged son and the craft beer bar that lasted just a couple of months. All that remained was a Dollar Tree, the tiny state store (a uniformed guard at the door), a fancy sneaker place that had recently been the scene of a gun battle, and the newest arrival, a plasma donation center. Unlike Emily, Arlene had never feared for her safety there, but still parked close to the Jyggle's front doors, in the same stretch of lot where the men who drove the jitneys waited for shoppers without cars.

The list that Kitzi had emailed her was long, as if Penny was stocking up for winter, and as Arlene crossed off the items one by one, she was surprised by how different their tastes were. What did Penny need with a coconut, or these giant, hairy leeks? She drank almond milk and baked with quinoa flour. Candied ginger, lemongrass, figs—all products Arlene had passed by a thousand times yet never bought. Placing them in her cart gave her a feeling that she was missing out on something, her tastes staid and parochial, and by the time she'd searched the dairy aisle for goat yogurt and headed for the checkout, she was thoroughly depressed.

Twenty years ago, she would have been assured of seeing her former students working as cashiers and spend a few minutes catching up on their lives. Now only two of the regular lanes were open; the rest were self-checkout, a process Arlene found took longer than standing in line. The man in front of her placed the divider on the belt behind his order, and she began ranking Penny's groceries by weight, starting with the papaya juice and almond milk so there was no chance of them crushing her fancy English digestive biscuits and taro root chips. She was still pulling items out of her cart when the cashier started checking her through.

"What is this thing?" the cashier asked, holding up a leafy green vegetable.

"Kohlrabi, I think."

The cashier punched some buttons. "Nah."

She rang for the manager, giving Arlene time to catch up. When she finally emptied her cart, there was a line behind her. She reached in her purse for her advantage card—the free Big Bird Bucks her reward for doing Penny's shopping—but her wallet wasn't there.

Her first thought was that someone must have stolen it from the cart while she was shopping. She checked again, then looked on the floor around her as if it might have fallen out.

"I don't have my wallet."

The cashier stopped chewing her gum and gave her an open-mouthed double take she'd seen more than once from her students.

Behind her, a woman with a full cart abandoned the line.

"I can look in my car."

"I'll hold this for you," the cashier said, suddenly sympathetic. "But be quick."

She wanted to say she was eighty-nine years old. She was not going to be quick. As she passed down the line of registers, she felt people watching her as if she might flee.

The jitney drivers were playing music on their radios and visiting one another and paid her no attention.

Her wallet wasn't in the console or either footwell. She bent down to see if it had fallen under her seat. She checked the backseat as well, though it had no reason to be there.

She stood at her door and looked around the parking lot as if help might be coming. She'd lost her wallet—she had no idea how—and had no way to pay for Penny's groceries. It seemed impossible. She thought she should just go home but instead made the long walk back inside to apologize to the cashier, Nyesha, who'd started on someone else's order. Her cart sat off to the side, Penny's groceries already bagged, the almond milk and goat yogurt going warm.

"I don't know what happened."

"That's all right," Nyesha said. "Come back when you find it. Someone will take care of this."

"Thank you," Arlene said, because she seemed to understand.

She expected it to be sitting on the front hall table when she got home, or on the dining room table, or the kitchen counter, but it was nowhere to be found. She didn't want to tell Kitzi, so she broke into her emergency funds, hidden in an envelope under her silverware drawer insert, and headed back to the Jyggle. The cart was gone, and she had to do all of her shopping again. Her feet hurt, and her hands. Without her card, she would receive no discounts and no Big Bird Bucks, which seemed a waste.

She made sure she had Nyesha.

"Find it?"

"No," Arlene said.

"I've got a card you can use." She ran it through the scanner so at least she'd get her discounts.

"Thank you, Nyesha."

"It's probably at home somewhere. I do it all the time. My mama says I got baby brain."

"I'm too old for that, I'm afraid."

"You'll find it," Nyesha said, and, handing Arlene her receipt, told her to have a blessed day. Normally Arlene would have considered this vacuous religious claptrap, but today she was grateful and thanked her, saying, "You too."

Penny had to wear an air cast like a ski boot to protect her stitches and was sick of watching TV. Arlene moved a chair close to the open fridge so she could arrange things the way she liked.

"Thank you."

"Not a problem," Arlene said. "How is almond milk? I've never tried it."

"It's okay. Regular milk upsets my stomach."

Back home, she went into her office to let Kitzi know how much she'd spent. Last night she'd ordered some art supplies online, and there by the Warhol soup can mouse pad Margaret had given her, right where she'd left it, glaring as a hand grenade, sat her wallet.

"Dumb," she said. "Dumb-ditty-dumb-dumb."

At least it hadn't been stolen. There was that. She thought she should go to the bank to replace her emergency money, but she was tired. She returned the wallet to her purse, snapped the snap and set it on the front hall table so it would ready for the next time.

Masks

During Covid, Emily had tried to stay home as much as possible, having her groceries delivered to her front stoop and turning her flower beds out back into a victory garden. A war child, she prided herself on her preparedness and self-reliance. She had her own library and could hold out indefinitely, listening to Handel and rereading Agatha Christie, Angus dozing with his head on her slipper. The only place she missed going was church, and soon enough Calvary was streaming both the early and the eleven o'clock service. While viewing it online lacked the pomp and grandeur of being there, she could knit, and her chair was infinitely more comfortable than a pew.

Like the war, the pandemic also brought back the neighborly camaraderie she'd felt growing up in Kersey. While she learned to Zoom with Margaret and Kenny, sometimes she'd stand at her fence in her sunhat, spade in hand, and chat across the driveway with Marcia Cole just for some human contact. The Oldhams, never home before, waved from their porch when they saw her, and Noel the mailman still did his rounds. If there was no traffic on Grafton Street, she didn't mind the quiet. She was no lonelier than normal, she joked to Kenny.

For some reason it was harder on Arlene. Those first few months, she called Margaret so much that Margaret called Emily to ask if Arlene was all right. The three had always been an uneasy trio, with Margaret, an alcoholic, running to her aunt for sympathy (and money) when Emily was trying to hold to her bottom line. As Margaret never tired of reminding her, come Christmas she would be five years sober, as if she deserved special credit for it. Arlene had been Margaret's confidante and sole link to the family during her worst years, and it often seemed to Emily that she was too proud of her role in the whole melodrama, as if she'd been right all along rather than a contributing factor, but Emily wasn't allowed to say this. Margaret, against logic, was now a drug and alcohol counselor, and wondered if Arlene needed to see a therapist.

"She sounded depressed," Margaret said.

"I think we all are. It's frightening. Look at New York."

"Have you talked to her about it?"

"All we do is talk about it. It's the only thing in the world right now."

"I mean her depression."

Even if Emily believed in therapy, she didn't think she was qualified to treat Arlene. Possibly because she was inured to solitude—maybe even preferred it, constitutionally—she was impatient with Arlene making a show of her feelings when so many of their friends were locked down in Longwood, or worse. Patti Fields and Leslie Van Buskirk, two original HDs who'd sung with them, had died alone, so Arlene having to stay home was not the end of the world. And then, one day after lunch, eight or nine months in, for no reason, rinsing her single plate and tea cup at the sink, she thought how glad she was that Henry hadn't lived to see this and broke down in tears.

Last year, when things started opening up, she was cautious. She still had her groceries delivered and ordered her library books from their website, depositing her returns in the outdoor wall slot and picking up a stapled paper bag with her name on it from a table in the foyer. She wore a mask to walk Angus around the block, crossing the street to avoid other people. Kenny had to fly somewhere for his job, and while he said it was fine, she thought he was being irresponsible. The Jyggle reopened, and the library, and still she didn't go. Restaurants were serving people outside, and then inside again. Arlene and Susie went to Paris 66 for crepes and sent her a picture, maskless, the two of them grinning like idiots.

She had masks on the front hall table, masks in her purse, masks in her jacket, masks in her car. When she finally did venture out to the Jyggle, she was appalled at the number of people without them, young and old, and no one protesting. Masks were still recommended at most places, and the cashiers all had them on, but the state had dropped its mandate, the CDC's guidelines had changed. When she finally stepped inside the library again, no one was wearing them except her and the girl with the nose ring and fluorescent pink hair who led story time with the children, and ultimately even she abandoned Emily.

The first time she went out in public without a mask—walking Angus around the block in the dark—she felt vulnerable and illicit, an unease that faded, day by day, as she returned to her usual pursuits: church, bridge, her HD work. Even Longwood opened, finally. If Covid wasn't over, it had become just another virus like the flu. Her granddaughter Ella and her partner Quinn had both recently gotten over the Delta variant in less than a week, making it sound no worse than a head cold.

Now, the one place she still had to wear a mask was the hospital. She actually preferred the surgical masks they gave out, pleated and baby blue, made of softer paper, their straps easier on the ears. Today, visiting Joan, she wore one of her own from home to ride the elevator down from the parking garage, then took a new blue one from a box on the ledge by the pay station, tucking the stiff one into her purse. She stopped at the reception desk and gave the woman Joan's room number, then held her arm out, fist closed, for a wristband.

Here, nothing was over. The security guards, the orderlies, the other visitors—every person she passed in the halls wore a mask. There was something oddly nostalgic about it, as if they had all agreed to travel back in time. It was late afternoon, well after shift change, the cafeteria deserted. The walk to the main elevators was long. The first time Henry had been admitted to Shadyside, she'd lost her way, disoriented by the beige sameness and branching paths. Now, unhappily, she knew it by heart.

Joan was on the orthopedic floor in a corner room with a view of Rodef Shalom, Central Catholic and, towering above them both like a gloomy Gothic rocket ship, the Cathedral of Learning, where a lifetime ago Emily had walked into a class called The Geology of Western Pennsylvania and sat down next to a dashing sophomore just back from the war in Europe named Henry Maxwell. The view had sustained her during his illness, and even now she had affection for the building as if it were a monument to their young love.

She passed the nurses' station and kept on to the far end of the hall, open doorways leaking inane daytime TV and unsettling groans she did her best to ignore.

Joan's door was closed. Emily knocked and called "Hello?" before pushing it open to find the room empty.

The bed had been stripped, two pillows missing their cases stacked unsanitarily on the nightstand. The windowsill was bare, the flowers and cards that had crowded it gone, only a gray plastic pitcher with a straw.

It was Joan's room. The dry-erase board still held her name and information.

Emily's first thought was that she'd died and no one had told her.

She hurried to the nurses' station. There were only two nurses, both sitting at their computers with their backs turned.

"Excuse me, hello," Emily called, waving to get their attention.

One extricated herself from her rolling chair and came over. "Are you here to see a patient?"

"Joan Hargrove. She isn't in her room. Room 426."

"Are you family?"

"I'm a family friend."

"I can only release information to family."

"We're practically family," Emily said. "She's been here for weeks and now she's gone."

"I'm sorry. If you could have a family member call, we can let that family member know you were here."

"Her daughter's name is Darcy."

"Have Darcy call us and we can give her any information she wants."

In the past, faced with this problem, Emily would have called Joan. Now she called Kitzi, doubtful she'd have a solution.

"Are you still at the nurses' station?"

"Yes," Emily said.

"Do you see a big TV screen with a lot of names on it?"

"No. Yes. The print's very small."

"That's everyone on the floor. Find her room number and you'll find her name. Then go across and read what it says."

"I can't read it, it's too small."

"Take a picture of it with your phone. Don't let them see you."

The nurse was back on her computer, ignoring her. Emily pretended to be looking up Darcy's number.

"Got it?"

"I got it," Emily said, retreating to Joan's room.

"Now blow it up with your fingers."

"Wait a second." Because she wasn't good at it. "It says 'IVC.'"

"Are you sure? Look again."

"That's what it says: 'IVC.' What does it mean?"

"It means she's in surgery."

"Why would she be in surgery?"

"I don't know. Let me call Darcy and figure out what's going on."

Emily's job was to stay there in case Joan returned.

Maybe Darcy was teaching, because Kitzi couldn't raise her, and left a message. They'd just have to wait. Sitting in the bare room, looking out at the Cathedral of Learning, Emily wished she'd brought a book.

"Condition C," a recorded voice announced without alarm in the hall. "Shadyside 126."

Not cancer. Crisis, or cardiac, she couldn't recall. Three floors directly below her, in an identical room, someone was struggling to live, and here she sat, flustered by the onset of a migraine. It was almost six, dinnertime. Angus would be wondering where she was, the grandfather clock chiming in the still living room.

She was hungry, and thought of going down to the cafeteria but couldn't abandon her post. The door was open, and from time to time she stepped out into the hall, hoping to find an orderly rolling a groggy Joan her way.

It was dark out when Kitzi finally called, the red lights atop the Cathedral of Learning blinking. Darcy had talked with the doctors. Apparently Joan's oxygen level had crashed and they'd had to revive her there in the room. She had a pulmonary embolism in her collapsed lung, and while the surgeon was trying to fish out the clot, there'd been complications. She was still in surgery, and intubated, something she'd expressly forbidden in her advanced directive.

"I just talked to her this morning," Emily said.

"Darcy probably thought she was doing the right thing."

"So she's not coming back here."

"She'll be going to the ICU. It's going to be a while, so you might as well go home."

She didn't want to but knew Kitzi was right. Visiting hours were over in half an hour anyway, and there was nothing she could do for Joan. Still, riding the elevator down by herself, it felt wrong, as if she were conceding defeat.

There was no one on the first floor, the gift shop was closed. She paid at the parking kiosk and took the grimy elevator to her car, trudging up the ramp in the dank garage, then spiraling down floor by floor, stopping and pressing the flimsy ticket against the screen to make the gate rise. It was only when she was outside driving along Aiken, free, that she realized she still had her mask on and pulled it off so she could breathe.

Cat People

Susie had always been a dog person, messy and open-hearted, blessed with a tolerance for slobber and a massive backyard. She preferred big dogs and chose the happy breeds, known for being good with children—a series of goldens and Labs with a fat Brittany spaniel and sweet, goofy shepherd mutt thrown into the mix. Two at a time, always rescues, never the designer hybrids their Fox Chapel neighbors flaunted, bred not to shed. Richard, like his uptight mother, was a cat person. He didn't want the dogs in his Volvo, so the back of Susie's Highlander was perpetually matted with hair and stank when it rained. When one died, they observed a respectful mourning period before finding a replacement, worried the survivor and newcomer might not get along, but, maybe because of their age difference, it was never a problem. One snarl, one snap, and order was restored. Once the children were gone, though Susie wanted another, Richard didn't see the need—it would be easier to travel, he argued—and when Molly finally died, she cleaned out the dog closet, carrying a box of bowls and leashes down to the basement, where it sat until they broke up the house. As with so much of her life, all that remained were pictures, and yet, often, standing in Joan's kitchen, watching Oscar gnaw his kibble, she felt a motherly tenderness and wondered if she might adopt him if Joan ended up in Longwood.

She wasn't even sure she could have pets, yet the idea lingered, Oscar her roommate, her confidant, curled in her lap while she read, burrowed under the covers as she slept. He was the only one she saw every day, just as she was the only one he saw—twice, morning and evening. Inevitably they'd become friends. Now Oscar scurried to the door to welcome her, rubbing against her shins and vaulting onto the counter as she prepared his bowl, meowing at her as if asking where she'd been.

"Sorry, I had practice," Susie said. "I came as fast as I could."

She thought he must be lonely, and sometimes at night, out with Peter eating Indian food or just watching a movie by herself, she pictured Oscar in the dark, sprawled on Joan's pillow, and wished she could bring him home. She could sneak him in easily enough. No one would care. He could eat her spider plants and sharpen his claws on her old sofa. Joan would never have to know.

She was building up the nerve to kidnap Oscar when Joan threw her blood clot, bringing Darcy back east, exiling Susie to the Kenmawr. Late afternoons, she'd gotten used to walking over to Joan's as the sun set, and the twilit stillness of her place. Now not only was she afraid that Joan might die but that Darcy would take Oscar.

"I know it's silly," she told Arlene, "but I kind of miss him."

"This is Oscar you're talking about." Because the one time Arlene had sat him, he'd shit on the bed, then run away.

Susie showed her a picture she'd taken: Oscar perched on the rail of the balcony, peering at a finch on the bird feeder. "He's actually very sweet."

"I think you need a cat of your own."

"I don't want another cat."

"Does Peter like cats?" Arlene asked, as if she should know. "What if he's allergic?"

"It's not like we're living together."

Arlene seemed disappointed by the news, which irritated Susie. They all wanted her and Peter to fall instantly, madly in love and live happily ever after, an expectation she'd once entertained herself but now resented. Having failed at marriage, they were both careful. She couldn't honestly say they were friends yet. At times—seeing him across the mezzanine of the Benedum, waiting with her overpriced plastic cup of wine—he seemed a complete stranger, someone she would never know. He was a passable dinner companion, wasn't that enough?

Joan was stable but still intubated while the doctors gave her antibiotics to clear up a staph infection. Darcy spent most of the day by her side, monitoring her test results through the UPMC app and grading papers, tapping at her iPad. It was her fall break; if things didn't change, her TA would have to cover her classes, a prospect that clearly distressed her. Susie and Emily took turns spelling her so she could eat lunch, and while she seemed grateful, she declined their offers to run errands or make her dinner. Emily somehow got it out of her that she had a grown daughter living in Italy as part of an arts exchange program, but around Susie she was guarded, sensing—rightly—her interest in her mother's life. Susie had to stop herself from asking after

Oscar, though she knew he must be getting low on food, and so the two of them sat in silence as drop by drop the drugs seeped into Joan's bloodstream.

Wednesday, Darcy said her levels looked better. When could she breathe on her own? Maybe tomorrow, the doctors said, but Thursday came and went, and then Friday. Nothing happened on the weekend.

Tuesday, when the doctors finally deemed it safe to take her off the respirator, Joan could barely speak. Darcy had to stand and lean across the bed rail to hear her. She said she felt fine, she was just tired. Now that she was conscious, they thought Darcy would want to spend every minute with her, but the next morning Darcy announced she was going back to Austin tomorrow. Joan had told her it was okay, so they couldn't argue.

"I don't get it," Emily said.

"Maybe that's just how they are," Arlene said.

"I think they're very similar," Kitzi said. "Very logical."

"I think that's very generous," Emily said, and while Susie agreed, she was equally selfish, glad to have Darcy out of the way.

Now that she was better, the hospital wanted Joan's bed. She would do her rehab at a skilled nursing facility in Penn Hills—not the best place, according to Kitzi, who helped get her settled, but the best with an immediate opening, plus it was reasonably close. You never got your first choice. Everything was based on insurance. Medicare would cover a hundred days; after that, you paid out of pocket.

"It's not cheap either," Emily said—from her experience with Henry, Susie assumed, not knowing her daughter Margaret's full history.

If Joan wasn't going to be home for three months, it only made sense for her to take in Oscar, or was it bad luck, as if admitting she'd never return?

"Ask her," Arlene said.

"I don't want her to think I'm trying to steal him."

"She won't. I'm sure she'll be happy you're taking such good care of him."

It was true, she could promise her that, but when she drove out to Penn Hills and signed in and walked down the long, low hallway, passing maskless patients slumped and drooling in their wheelchairs, her nerve faltered. Above several doors, call lights blinked mutely, while from within the delirious beseeched the absent staff for help. By the vacant nurses' station, a slipper sock lay in the middle of the floor.

Joan's door was open, Joan propped in bed with a book, an oxygen line clipped below her nose. From the hall came a female shriek and a high-pitched keening, then a man swearing, telling them to shut up.

"That's Howard," Joan said, seeing her concern, and motioned for her to close the door. "It's not so bad, they're just understaffed. Covid. Most of the time it's quiet."

"How are you feeling?"

"Good. I'm keeping busy, doing my PT. I'm supposed to work on my core, so they have me doing a lot of leg lifts. They had me walking with a crutch the other day—that was fun. There's another tib-fib from Aspinwall they have me working with, guy in his forties, car accident, Scott. Nice guy."

The facility was a mix of long-term residents and people rehabbing. It had originally been a middle school, which explained the low ceilings and endless hallways. There was a courtyard where they could sit if the weather was nice, and a TV lounge that served ice cream at night. Not that she needed to be eating ice cream. The food was all starch. It wasn't Shadyside, but it wasn't awful.

"How is Kitzi getting along?" Joan asked. "She seemed a little frazzled when I talked to her."

"She's good," Susie said, wondering if the question was a loyalty test. "She has a lot going on."

"Don't tell her I told you this, but she'll try to do everything herself if you let her. So don't let her."

"She can be that way."

"I love her, but she needs to let go a little. How's Emily?"

"Good," Susie said, realizing, with relief, that she had nothing to report on her.

It was like Joan to focus on the practical, and when they were done catching up on club business, Susie saw her opportunity.

"About Oscar," she said, and paused, waiting for Joan to stop her.

"He's all right, isn't he?"

"He's fine. I'm just thinking it might be better for him if he had someone around so he wasn't alone all the time." Somehow, in trying to phrase the proposition gently, she'd described her own situation, and felt a flush of embarrassment, suddenly exposed.

Joan hesitated as if she disagreed. "What were you thinking, exactly?"

"I could watch him. At my place. Just until you're ready to come home."

Was she offended? Susie hadn't meant it as a criticism.

"I couldn't ask you to do that."

"I want to," Susie said. "I really like Oscar."

"Is *he* going to want to? That's the key. He's never lived anywhere else. He doesn't know anything else. I see what you're saying, though. That's very kind of you."

It's not, Susie wanted to say, because now she felt greedy, robbing her of yet another piece of her life.

"I suppose you can try it," Joan said. "If it doesn't work out, you can always take him back to my place."

"Thank you," Susie said, not sure if it was proper but grateful anyway.

"Make sure you take Mr. Chippymunk. He likes to use him as a pillow."

She hadn't known, and played along, feeling guilty.

Driving home, she made a mental list of everything she'd need. She'd never had a litter box before and worried it would smell. There wasn't room in the bathroom, maybe at the far end of the hall, but that might be too public. They were private animals, not like dogs, squatting in the middle of the yard. At least they tried to have some dignity—and again she saw the patients parked in their wheelchairs. They were never coming home, they were just waiting to die, and she thought of her own life, what was left of it, what good she might do with her time. She had no plans beyond being an HD and taking care of Oscar, and wondered if that was enough. It would have to be, for now.

She didn't stop at home. She went directly to Joan's, the guard at the gatehouse surprised to see her driving a car. Oscar thought she was there to feed him and leapt onto the counter. "You are going to absolutely freak out." She poured him half a bowl and packed up his food, distracting him, then went through the apartment, emptying his litter box and gathering his things in a blue Giant Eagle bag. His Chippymunk she found under Joan's desk, along with an eyeless squirrel and jingling red rubber ball. He followed her to the door, curious, and was waiting there when she came back up from the garage with his carrier.

At the sight of it, he bolted.

She knew where he'd be, and left the carrier in the hall. She knelt by the bed in the guest room. "It's going to be okay, I promise."

He was wary, making her wait until he finally came out and let her take him in her arms. In the hall, he stiffened, and she figured it might be easier without the cage.

"Are you ready for your big adventure?"

The stairs were steep. She was afraid he could sense how nervous she was and tried to slow her breathing.

"Okay," she said, "here we go."

Blimp in Landscape

The Steelers were playing the Ravens Sunday night, and all week the blimp plied the skies above the city, reminding them of Pittsburgh's true place in the universe. Arlene saw it first, coming out of the dollar store—a silver glint floating over Frick Park, its wallowing progress a giveaway. She stopped and shaded her eyes as if to salute, straining to hear its engines through the susurrus of traffic on Braddock. She didn't know why, there was something quaint and old-fashioned about blimps, their impractical, manatee-like clumsiness, that buoyed her. Though she'd never ridden in one, and likely never would, for a moment she forgot she was on her way to Mona Seifert's to deliver a bale of off-brand incontinence pads, imagining instead how peaceful it must be inside the cockpit, gliding over the bright, newly turned trees.

"Which one was it?" Kitzi asked at bridge. "There used to be just one, now there's a bunch of them."

"It looked like the real one. It was silver."

"I don't see why they don't just use a drone," Emily said. "It can't be cost-effective."

"It's advertising," Susie said. "It's working. We're talking about it."

"I'm not going to run out and buy a set of tires," Emily said.

"No, but when you do you'll know the name."

"I've known the name my whole life. I don't need a blimp to tell me it."

"But you're thinking of it now. That's synergy. Blimp, tires, football—it's all one thing."

"I don't watch football," Emily said, "so I guess I'm not going to buy their tires. I think a blimp is a bad way to advertise, especially something that's supposed to be safe. Remember the *Hindenburg*."

"That was a dirigible," Susie said. "Totally different thing."

"Plus, Nazis," Arlene said.

"It's the idea," Emily said. "Thing that explodes."

"All right," Kitzi said, hefting the coffee pot to stop them, "who's ready?"

Emily didn't actually mind football—she'd watch with Henry and knit, ignoring the play-by-play—she just couldn't resist needling Susie when she lectured them. Her politics reminded Emily of Margaret's, a fairy-tale world in which the rich were greedy and evil and the poor simple and good. Having grown up poor in a small town, Emily was skeptical. Like Henry, she prized integrity and consistency, neither of which Margaret was capable of, even when not drinking.

As with football, she had no opinion on the blimp. It had nothing to do with her beyond a moment's distraction, yet now when she glimpsed it—the next morning, off over the river as she walked Angus around the reservoir—she remembered her exchange with

Susie, and how she owed Margaret a phone call. Margaret had been lobbying her to come to Michigan for Thanksgiving, and Emily didn't want to go. She would give in, trading it for Christmas in Pittsburgh, as if that were any better. Kenny joked that they should all go to Hawaii, each of them picking a different island. It was easier for him, she thought, because he wasn't the problem. As much as they all might wish it—as much as Henry had wished it—she and Margaret would never get along. Why couldn't they reconcile themselves to the truth? Instead they'd go through the motions again, and at some point it would blow up. There would be scenes, and tears, accusations that couldn't be taken back. She dreaded the holidays, which was a shame, she'd so loved them as a child, but even then she and her mother fought like cats in a bag. When had she ever been an innocent?

Friday evening, after spending all afternoon sitting vigil beside Marion Gill in the ICU, Kitzi had just set Martin's plate on his tray table when the blimp came on the news, taking a group of disabled veterans on a flyover of the stadium. They showed one in a wheelchair at the controls, giving the camera a thumbs-up. The Wounded Warrior Project was offering half-hour rides for a thousand-dollar donation.

"I don't know if I'd do that," Kitzi said, fixing her own plate.

"Why not?" Martin said. "I bet the view's incredible."

"Would you?"

"Sure, if I had a thousand dollars lying around."

"The way it moves, I'm afraid I'd get seasick."

"You probably would."

As with so many of their conversations, it was mostly theoretical. There was no need for her to point out that Martin hadn't been on a plane in over a decade, when their flight from Myrtle

Beach had had to divert to Dulles so he could be rolled off, shirtless and hooked to a monitor, while everyone gawked at them. They kidded each other as if they were still that funny, indestructible couple from before then, their roles eternal, he headlong and adventurous, she queasy and timid, the motherly voice of reason. Now, eating her bland grilled chicken, she was tempted to say what the hell, let's do it, but they didn't have the money, she didn't have the time, and there was sure to be a waiver. It was probably fully booked anyway. The whole thing was stupid.

Saturday morning, Susie and Peter were waiting in line for breakfast sandwiches at the Bloomfield farmer's market when they saw the blimp heading downtown. After catching his band at Brillobox, she'd spent the night at his place, leaving Oscar by himself, something she'd vowed not to do. She'd been drinking Manhattans at the club and at some point—some other bar with a serious jukebox—had switched to tequila. Even with his sunglasses, the brightness hurt. Her hair smelled like cigarettes and she was wearing yesterday's clothes. They had sex for the first time in his bed and then half off it, laughing at gravity. Smashed, she'd overcome her self-consciousness, shucking her clothes with lusty abandon, and Peter, for his part, was eager and tender, kissing her over her heart afterward. He snored. She remembered trying to find the bathroom in the dark and almost falling into the tub. Now without a word he took her hand, the two of them a couple. When she was twenty she would have been thrilled. Instead she waited, dazed, her lower back aching, wondering how she could be so irresponsible. She would Uber home and feed Oscar, take a shower, sleep. She had choir practice at four, and Viv wouldn't let them leave until they knew the Buxtehude.

He squeezed her hand, and what could she do? She squeezed back.

Later that afternoon, Emily was raking leaves when the blimp hove into view above the Coles'. It was so low she could see the mooring lines trailing from the nose. She paused to watch it glide through the branches of the sycamore into open sky, Angus panting at her side with his tongue out, unsure why she'd stopped. She would call Margaret tomorrow and confirm for Thanksgiving. She'd be there only three days, and she'd get to see Sarah and Justin and the great-grandchildren. She needed to at least try. As viciously as they'd battled, her mother had never given up on her.

Of the four of them, only Susie didn't watch the game, popping a Vicodin and falling asleep on her couch beneath an afghan, Oscar nestled against her. Kitzi and Martin had been invited to a Steelers party in Point Breeze by some Calvary Camp friends and brought guac. Emily snuggled into Henry's spot on the daybed in the den, turned the sound down and read, glancing up every so often to check the score. "Get him!" Arlene shouted, stabbing a finger at her massive old Trinitron, because the Ravens were running right through them. The game itself was ugly—the Steelers were not good this season—but they could all admire the aerial shots of downtown, the buildings and the fountain at the Point tinted gold, the black, shimmering rivers. From above, the city looked impossibly glamorous, and though they knew it was an illusion, they were still proud.

The game started too late for Emily. She was more interested in her book, and put Angus out before closing up. Kitzi and Martin said their goodnights after halftime, leaving the bowl behind. Only

Arlene watched to the very end, exasperated by the final score as if she were part of the coaching staff, and then couldn't sleep.

The next morning, taking advantage of the weather, she painted *en plein air,* planting her easel facing Mr. Frick's bowling green. The light was clear, the trees dazzling. All around her, squirrels scampered, burying acorns. She was working on the fieldstone clubhouse when, through the rustling leaves, she heard the low drone of engines and found the silver dot high in the sky, heading east for Philadelphia or New York. It seemed a stroke of luck: she'd thought they would have taken off right after the game. Again, she pictured herself on board, floating serenely over the park, over the streets and alleys of Regent Square laid out like a satellite map, and the Parkway and the Turnpike and the rolling farmland beyond, free of her earthly cares. She stopped working on the fieldhouse and squeezed a bead of silver onto her palette, peering up at the blimp and then back at her canvas, trying to find the perfect place for it.

A Haunted House

One morning the week before Halloween, while Kitzi was frying Martin his three strips of turkey bacon, Jean called, sounding proper as always, wondering if Kitzi might be free to pop over.

"Why? What's happened?"

"I can't wake up Gene."

How was she so calm? "Is he breathing?"

Martin turned to her, concerned.

"He's breathing but he's not responding. At least, I can't get him to."

"Call 911."

"I did, straightaway. To be honest with you, I'd be more comfortable talking to them if you were here. To them I'm just some loony old bat."

It was true, even if she partly fit the description. "I'll be right there."

"Thank you, Kitzi."

"What happened?" Martin asked, looming while she tied her shoes.

She didn't need him getting upset and tried to be nonchalant. "He's probably just overmedicated. They'll give him Narcan and he'll be fine."

"Drive carefully," Martin called after her, as if she might kill herself speeding there.

"I will," she said, and then at Wightman she blew through a yellow.

The ambulance beat her, parked in the turnaround. The front door of the house was wide-open, and the porch was swarming with cats. As she climbed the stairs, a marmalade kitten in her path shied away, eyeing her.

Jean had been so private that stepping inside the house felt like a violation. Even before she'd breached the foyer, the smell hit Kitzi, a wave of ammonia and dung that made her clamp a hand over her nose and mouth. The entryway was piled on both sides with garbage—shoulder-high mounds of clothing, plastic bags and cardboard boxes, cracked storage bins and waterlogged books, a laundry basket full of dishes, a browned and broken lampshade, all of it covered with dust. Underfoot the path was slippery, matted with more trash, and she had to stop herself from reaching out and touching the mounds for balance. How did Jean manage it at her age?

She heard the squawk of a radio, and voices arguing, and was afraid she was too late.

"Jean, hello?" she called, picking her way through the filth. "It's Kitzi. I'm here."

The trench angled across a dark-timbered room with a water stain on the ceiling, in the very center a cobwebbed chandelier resting cocked atop the pile. If there was furniture under here, it was buried deep, and she wondered how much weight the floor could support. With every step something creaked, something shifted. She had the sense that at any second the floor would give way and she'd be trapped beneath an avalanche of rotting garbage like quicksand, bugs and mice crawling all over her, but plowed on, spurred by fear.

In the next room, the piano she'd heard Joan playing sat in a clearing, its top strangely clean.

"I don't want to," a man argued, coughing. "I know my rights."

The accent was Russian—"I don't vant to." It had to be Gene, and she was relieved. She plunged ahead toward his voice.

He was in what might have been a den, lying on a sofa fitted with sheets while Jean and two shockingly young female EMTs in ponytails and blue latex gloves stood over him. She didn't recall him being so small, almost childlike, with those short arms and that big head. He was wearing a baby blue monogrammed pajama top that swallowed him like a doll's dress. He looked withered. His face was gray, his beard wispy and limp. He wheezed, his lungs squeaking.

"We can't *make* you go, sir," the dark-haired EMT said, "but anytime there's an unexplained loss of consciousness, we're required by law to let you know the consequences."

"He almost died and he won't go," Jean said, and Kitzi thought of Martin, how stubborn he could be for no reason. He didn't care about dying. It was more important to be right.

"I feel fine." He coughed hollowly, his whole body jolting.

"Listen to them," Kitzi said. "Listen to your wife."

"Vhat are they going to do for me?"

"You need to get checked out. I'll go with you," she told Jean, touching her arm. "Shadyside?"

"Shadyside's the closest," the EMT said.

"I don't vant to go," Gene said, weakening.

"I don't care," Kitzi said, and shook her head to show him she meant it.

"I'm fine," he said, resigned, and the blonde went outside to fetch a backboard.

Standing there, waiting for her to return, listening to him breathe, no one said a word about the state of the house, and she was embarrassed for Jean, then scourged herself for being so trivial.

There was no easy way out. The EMTs carried Gene on the backboard like porters, scraping the sides of the trench, leaving a wake of trash. The cats on the porch scattered and then assembled again around Jean as if she might feed them. She and Kitzi stood aside as they transferred him to a stretcher and loaded him into the rear of the ambulance. Strapped flat, his face hidden beneath an oxygen mask, he looked even more helpless, like Martin on the jetway that time, his eyes pleading. She remembered thinking she wouldn't know what to do if he died. She did now, too well.

"We'll be right behind you," Jean promised as they closed the doors.

"So, what exactly happened?" Kitzi asked in the car.

"They're not entirely certain. They think it could be sleep apnea, but he's never been a snorer."

She wanted to ask about the drugs—to say how easy it was to accidentally overdose—but was afraid Jean might take it the wrong way.

"It's not his heart."

"They said everything checked out."

"Even more reason to get tested."

At the ER entrance they had to valet park, put a mask on and go through a metal detector, dropping their keys in a little bin offered by a bodybuilder security guard. Kitzi noticed that Jean didn't have a phone and thought in that house she really should. Though everyone was wearing a mask, Kitzi worried that the smell clung to her. Gene was already in back. They sat in the lobby for a good half hour before they took Jean in to see him, the nurse unlocking the door with a punch code. Kitzi, not being family, wasn't allowed, and stepped outside to call Martin and let him know she'd be a while.

"What was it?"

"They don't know. They're doing tests."

"Good luck with that," he said, having been through it too many times.

She told him to go ahead and get lunch. "We may be having takeout for dinner. Or leftovers."

"I like takeout."

She called Joan, figuring she'd want to know.

"He didn't want to go at first, but I kind of made him," she said, as if she were sorry she'd bullied him, when it wasn't true. Why did she need her approval?

"That's good," Joan said. "It can't hurt."

"I saw the house."

"It's sad, isn't it?"

Sad wasn't the word Kitzi would have used, and again she felt unkind.

"How's Jean doing?"

"She's upset but she's keeping it together. I wish I could do more for her."

"You're there, that's the important thing. *Come!* Hang on, someone's at the door. Well, talk about timing—it's Susie. You didn't have to bring food. It's Kitzi."

"Hi," Susie called from the background. "Sorry, didn't mean to interrupt."

"It's fine," Joan said. "She has things under control."

She didn't feel like she did, but accepted the vote of confidence. "I'll let you go."

"Let me know when you hear anything," Joan said.

"I will," Kitzi said, and then stood there a minute watching the cars on Aiken pass, wondering how often Susie visited her, before going back through the metal detector.

In the waiting room, time elongated. Watching the clock only made it go slower. She was hungry, but had no way to text Jean and find out how he was doing. On the far wall, totally ignored, a TV blared a talk show she'd never heard of. She scrolled through her emails, deleting and unsubscribing, reviewing the coming week's schedule, poking folks who'd volunteered to buy candy or drive people to their various appointments. She was surprised how quiet it was. Patients transported by ambulance went straight in through the bay, but most were driven by family members and processed by the staff, who sat behind plexiglass and called their names when a bed was ready. The one exception was a lanky Black man in a blood-spotted Chipotle apron who walked in with one hand raised above his head, wrapped in a dishcloth. It almost looked like a costume, reminding her that she still had to buy their pumpkins. She was getting loopy. She needed to eat something, and let the woman behind the desk know that she was going over to the cafeteria.

As she'd feared, it would take all day. Gene had pneumonia in both lungs and there was something wrong with his liver, it was producing too much of something, Jean couldn't remember exactly what (calcium, it turned out). They wanted to admit him, but couldn't until a room opened up. By the time they took him to the ICU and got him settled, it was past six and they were all exhausted. Gene said they could leave, but Jean wanted to make sure he got his dinner. Waiting for the elevator, she said she had a dreadful headache.

"I think I need a drink," she joked, and while Kitzi murmured in sympathy, she wondered if that might explain the house—or was that too pat, like blaming everything on some foundational trauma? She knew so little about her. It was an illness, not a symptom of another problem, and again she wished she could help.

Dusk was falling over the college, the chapel spotlit. The house was dark, and as she wound up the drive and slowed for the turnaround, cats scattered in her headlights. They slunk out of the high grass and slipped through the spiked iron fence, their eyes flashing. They stalked alongside the car as she parked, stood gathered in ranks on the porch stairs and railings like servants awaiting the return of their mistress, and while the idea was ridiculous, Kitzi had to fight the urge to lock the doors and take off.

She and Jean made plans for tomorrow. Visiting hours started at eight.

"You sure you're going to be all right?"

"I'll be fine, thank you."

"Can you see?"

"Like a cat," Jean said, and thanked her again.

They watched her as she got out.

"I see you," she teased. "I know, you're all starving."

It was not Kitzi's imagination. They parted for her, massed behind her back as she turned the lock and then followed her inside like the Pied Piper, a few stragglers dashing across the gravel and up the stairs before she waved goodnight and closed the door behind her.

Why do you need so many? Kitzi thought, crawling away, afraid she might run one over.

At home, Martin was waiting for her at the door and took her in his arms. His vest was rigid under his sweater. He'd ordered Chinese, he announced, as if to make up for her day, then sniffed her shoulder and let go.

"It's that noticeable." At the hospital no one had said a thing.

"You've got time to shower. If you want to."

"I was only inside for five minutes."

"How bad was it?"

"Bad. Does it matter? His liver's not working. He looked awful, and I don't think she's all there."

"I'm sorry," he said.

"I shouldn't have left her by herself. She has like fifty cats, no exaggeration." She shivered.

"Go take a hot shower."

She did, standing with her head bent and her eyes closed, surrendering to the warm pulse against her neck. Both lungs. So that's what double pneumonia meant. She'd never known. Joan would. All day she'd tried to stay positive, but now she couldn't stop thinking of Jean alone in the house and felt defeated. And tomorrow they'd do it all over again.

The Queen of Halloween

Arlene, Arlene, her mother used to sing, teasing, *the Queen of Halloween.* It had always been her favorite holiday, a fun excuse to become someone else. When she was teaching, she loved to dress up as a witch and then pretend she wasn't wearing a costume, acting confused when the children pointed to her broom. She stayed in character all day, setting her hat on the passenger seat as she drove home and handing out candy to the neighborhood kids with a mad cackle, only taking off her makeup as she got ready for bed.

It had been years since she'd done that, and while she still decorated, over time the effort had become too much. Though she festooned the porch with twists of crepe paper and cutouts of pumpkins and black cats salvaged from her classroom, she no longer had the energy to hang the black light that bathed the face of the house purple or to rig her stereo speakers on the stoop to blast a spooky sound effects record. The Vincenzos across the street had a sixteen-foot-tall skeleton from Home Depot and a blow-up Stay Puft marshmallow man that played the *Ghostbusters* theme all night long. Two doors down, the Sweeneys turned their yard into a cemetery, complete with a dry-ice fog machine. She wasn't trying to compete with them.

The one claim to fame she still held was that, unlike her neighbors, she gave out full-size candy bars. Emily thought she was crazy, spending all that money, but to Arlene the expense was worth it. It was not a day to be cheap, plus she had a reputation to uphold. Generations of children knew her. She liked to believe that when she died, the people of Milton Street would remember her, for one night at least. For now, to see the shock on their faces—the children's *and* the parents'—was enough.

She wasn't a complete fool, despite what Emily might think. She used coupons and her CVS and Walgreens cards, and scanned the Tuesday flyers for sales. The later you waited, the cheaper things were. Five for the price of three, three-for-two, two-for-one. She was buying for Barbara Parrish and for Penny and several other HDs who couldn't make it to the store, and had built up enough rewards that she was essentially getting hers for free.

Would three hundred be enough? The weather was supposed to be nice, so she grabbed another couple packs of Baby Ruths, a favorite from childhood. Unlike Emily, she only bought candy she liked. If there were any leftovers, she'd eat them herself, freezing them if she had to. Nothing would go to waste.

The day was bright and breezy, leaves racing in flocks across the street. She put on a sweater and filled her biggest mixing bowl with Butterfingers and Snickers and Hershey bars, stirring the candy with one hand as if folding a thick batter. She dragged the rocker from its spot to the top of the porch stairs and set a table beside it.

Trick or treat wasn't officially supposed to start till six, but dusk was coming earlier and earlier, the streetlights blinking on, the crows heading home over the trees. The toddlers were out before she'd even lit her pumpkins. They struggled up the stairs in their floppy costumes—tiny superheroes and princesses—and rather than have one fall, she got up from her rocker and went down to meet them, crouching low with the bowl so they could choose one.

"Happy Halloween!" she greeted them, but they only gawped at her, uncertain, their hands too small to properly grasp the candy, so she had to stand there bent double while they raked at it, making her back hurt.

"What do you say?" the parents asked, but the little ones were too overcome to understand, and Arlene just laughed.

"Happy Halloween!" she called after them.

The Vincenzos' skeleton was lit, their generator racketing, blowing up their marshmallow man. She was happy to see so many people out, and so many houses on their block decorated. The number of couples with strollers and babes in arms was a reminder that the neighborhood was getting younger—a healthy trend, even if it meant higher taxes. The world would go on without her, and that was as it should be. There was nothing morbid about the thought, especially tonight, when the dead were supposed to roam the earth. She'd lived her life, she'd tried to do right. She might not have become the great artist she'd wanted to be, but she couldn't regret anything now, when she had so little time left.

Night fell, and the older children mobbed the sidewalks, packs of them swishing through the leaves, parents hanging back with flashlights and plastic cups of wine. She sat in the rocker and let them come to her, holding the bowl in her lap. Witches and vampires, Steelers and actual pirates, and so many princesses. She was pleased to see a few were using pillowcases like she and Henry had. Some were so sincere in their thanks and others so rude they made her think of her students. Her last class would be almost forty now. She'd once kept scrapbooks—like a proud mother—following their progress through high school and on to college, celebrating their accolades, but had slacked off after a stretch when several had been arrested or murdered with no graduations or promotions to offset the litany of tragedies. It wasn't a surprise. Homewood and Wilkinsburg had always been dangerous places. In fifty years nothing had changed, and often, watching the news, she felt a dull sorrow, as if all her work, all her care, had been for naught, a kind of lie. It was not true, or not the whole truth—she had a drawer full of letters from former students to prove she'd made a difference—but at times like these, surrounded by the city's more fortunate children, she mourned the loss of innocence and wondered at the inequity of the world.

"Trick or treat!"

A new trio hustled up the stairs, jostling shoulder to shoulder as they rummaged through the bowl—a dragon, a masked superhero and the boy magician from the movies, whatever his name was.

"Thank you," the boy said, the other two echoing him.

"Happy Halloween!"

She went through the whole bowl in twenty minutes.

"This is my favorite!" one girl dressed as a squirrel in a deep-sea diving suit cried, clutching a 5th Avenue bar.

"Mine too," Arlene said. "You're welcome."

On they came, relentless, snaking lines passing in the dark like looters. The first hour, she had to restock three times. The Snickers were already gone, and the Three Musketeers. She hadn't even had a Milky Way. She thought she'd bought too much; now she was worried she'd run out.

"Just one, please," she had to remind an older boy, who muttered something under his breath as he walked away, his friends exploding with laughter.

She would not let it sour her, greeting the next bunch with the same jaunty "Happy Halloween!"

After the mad rush, a lull. The wind shifted, scattering the leaves, pushing a suffocating cloud of the Sweeneys' dry-ice fog over her, leaving an ashen taste in her mouth. From above the rooftops, out of the starry sky, a single peal from the Methodist church on Mifflin marked the quarter hour. It was colder now. She put on her jacket and ate both halves of a Baby Ruth, the sweet nougat returning her to her childhood, when, a team, she and Henry would venture far beyond their block, following Mellon Street all the way to the park and back, their pillowcases heavy with treasure they poured out on the floor of their room and then separated into neat ranks before surrendering it to their mother for safekeeping. They were too wound up to sleep, and lay in bed, going over which neighbors gave out the best candy, making even grander plans for next year. How happy she'd been then—it heartened her to remember it now. No wonder she loved Halloween so much.

Something was burning, making her sniff the air—one of her pumpkins, its candle charring the soft flesh of the lid. She pulled it off by the stem and set it on the steps, still smoking, a potential catastrophe averted.

Trick or treat was almost over, save one final invasion. Their block was known throughout the East End as a good hunting ground. The last half hour, the bulk of the traffic wasn't from the neighborhood. A steady stream of SUVs and minivans from Swissvale and Churchill and Wilkinsburg drawn by the beacon of the marshmallow man pulled up in front of the Vincenzos and dropped off loads of older children and teenagers, most larger than Arlene, many with no costumes. This was the one part of the night Arlene didn't enjoy, their mercenary greed, being too aware of the economics involved, but she stayed at her post, welcoming all equally until the bells struck eight, then blowing out her jack-o'-lantern and turning off the porch light to let the world know she was closed.

Along with a few 5th Avenues she'd set aside, she had a quarter of a bowl left over, and she was pleased. While she would never go out and buy herself a candy bar, she liked having them around as a treat. She counted the leftovers at her grandmother Chase's old dining room table, separating them into their respective piles, and made a note in her log: 293. Next year she'd have to buy more.

Her job done, following tradition, she wrapped herself in her down comforter and settled in with a scary movie, warming her hands with a cup of tea. *The Castle of Dracula*, in lurid Technicolor, the blood like house paint. She was sure she'd seen it before, but it didn't matter. The one benefit of losing her memory was that so many old things were new to her again. The black coach racing through the gloomy forest was familiar, and the roadside inn where they took shelter from the storm, the tankards of ale and blazing hearth, as if she'd been there herself, a strange déjà vu that kept her leaning forward, waiting to see what would happen. As they were about to reach the castle, an ad came on, ruining the mood, and there like a reminder (too late!) with his glasses and cape was the boy magician whose name she couldn't recall. She had to wait for the announcer to say it, and then shook her head.

"Harry Potter."

Fall Back

Every year Emily dreaded turning her clocks back. She could never remember which weekend it was, and was always dismayed when the local anchors reminded her a few days before. And why, for God's sake, did it take place at two in the morning? Intellectually she knew the days were the same, that twisting the knob of her watch had no effect on the earth's rotation around the sun, but practically the change was devastating. Sunday afternoon—already fraught, being the day she talked to Margaret—now gave way to darkness an hour earlier. As soon as the sky outside turned gray, Angus started lobbying for his dinner, parking himself beside Henry's chair and staring at her as she picked at the *Times* crossword. Though they were completely different breeds, he reminded her of Rufus so much that she often called him by the wrong name. She didn't bother apologizing for it anymore.

"Stop," she said. "It's not time. You have seventy-five minutes."

He retreated to his bed by the fireplace and lay with his head on his crossed paws, looking up at her glumly.

"Oh my. Mr. Pitiful."

Eventually she relented, feeding him and then fixing her own dinner early. It was fully night and it wasn't five thirty, which was wrong. She had to turn the back porch light on to find his poop, creeping across the grass with the scooper, trying to see past her own shadow.

The news itself was enervating. The big midterm election was Tuesday, and they were a swing state. The Senate, as Susie liked to remind them, hung in the balance, and maybe the fate of democracy, which struck Emily, a lifelong Republican, as an overstatement. Both parties had spent millions on attack ads that made every candidate look like a criminal. John Fetterman was a trust fund socialist. Doug Mastriano took money from a neo-Nazi. Dr. Oz didn't even live in Pennsylvania. She'd seen all the ads dozens of times, and she barely watched TV. Now they ran back-to-back-to-back, so she had to mute them and then missed the beginning of the next story. The whole thing was stupid. What kind of idiot didn't know who they were going to vote for? Why not use the money for something people actually needed?

After *60 Minutes*, she finished the crossword by the fire, listening to an organ recital from Utrecht. In the corner, the grandfather clock bonged eight, nine times, yet instead of appreciating the extra hour, she felt rushed. Should she stay up later to acclimate, even though she was tired, or go to bed early? The week before she and Henry flew to England, they had gone to sleep right after dinner to get ahead of the jet lag. It didn't work, the two of them napping every afternoon in the hotel and sleepwalking through Westminster Abbey like zombies. You couldn't fool the body.

She split the difference, putting Angus out and going up a half hour early with her book. She read until the sentences were just words and dropped off, starting with a shock, twisting her head from reflex as the book fell toward her face. She'd lost her place and patted the covers for her bookmark, stuck it in, a best guess. Tomorrow she'd read the same passages again and not remember them, but tonight it was too late.

At her age sleep was a delicate business, never entirely successful. The best she could muster, if she was lucky, was three or four unbroken hours. At some point her bladder would rouse her and she'd totter to the bathroom and sit. The trick was getting back to sleep, not lying wide awake and dwelling on her many shortcomings or replaying scenes from the past. Her battles with Margaret, yes, and Henry near the end, out of his mind and babbling nonsense when she was trying to say goodbye, but also things she'd never shared with anyone. When she was a teenager, Emily's mother used to lock her in her room as punishment; she was haunted by her voice on the other side of the door, asking reasonably, "Are you ready to come out now?" Her very worst nights, Emily paced that drab, sun-faded cell, recalling it in every detail and all of her teenaged promises of revenge while downstairs the grandfather clock chimed two and three and four.

Falling back only complicated her insomnia. Now when she woke in the dark, it wasn't two but one, and the night stretched endlessly before her like the sea. She had even more time to contemplate her failures, and when she did finally drift off, she had no hope of sleeping through till morning. At four she was up again, at the mercy of her thoughts, revolving and repeating until she had to get up and pee and take some aspirin. She switched positions and listened to Angus licking himself, finally yelling at him so that he moved out into the hall.

She didn't remember falling asleep. When she woke, the blinds were bright and Angus was curled up on the braided rug beside her. It was five thirty, an hour before her normal time, and she felt tricked. She lay there with her eyes open, looking at the sunlight reflected on the ceiling. Birds were chirping. She turned her alarm off and Angus padded over and rested his head on the covers.

"I know," she said. "I don't like it either."

She got up and weaved her way to the bathroom, exhausted. The clock for the floor controls was wrong, the tiles cold. In the shower she almost lost her balance and had to hold on to the grab bar. A minute later she dropped her shampoo, spooking Angus.

"You're fine," she said, then, "Sorry."

It was going to be a long day.

Trump Won

When Kitzi arrived at the JCC that morning, she wasn't surprised to find the guy with the van there, or Gracie Lapidus bundled up in her wheelchair, nursing a large coffee. After the madness of the last election, they'd been told to expect extra party workers. The county didn't use the word kooks, but the new handbook had a whole section on safety, including what to do in case of an active shooter. Though it was cold and the polls didn't open for another hour, the turnout disappointed her. She thought there'd be more of a crowd.

The van was a traveling Babel of signs and stickers. COME AND TAKE IT, one read, with the silhouette of an AR-15. THE MEDIA IS THE VIRUS. GOD, GUTS AND GUNS—LET'S KEEP ALL THREE. After Tree of Life, it seemed a provocation, tasteless. In his tan work boots and Carhartt jacket and camo ballcap, the man didn't look like he was from Squirrel Hill, but there was no law against that, and the van was parked beyond the fifty-foot limit, so he knew the rules. Kitzi waved to him and Gracie as she passed, doing her best to appear neutral.

"Morning, Kitzi," Gracie called, alarming her. She wasn't intimidated by the man, but she didn't want him to know her name either. It was easy enough to find their address online.

The front wall was all glass, built in a more innocent time. Inside, Sheila and Marcy were busy setting up the ADA table.

"How do you like our new friend?" Sheila asked.

"We'll see how long he lasts out there with Gracie."

"You think he knows what he's doing?" Marcy asked.

"I think he knows exactly what he's doing," Kitzi said.

She couldn't recall seeing a license plate. In Pennsylvania you only needed one in back. They had cameras that covered the whole lot, so he'd be crazy to try anything.

"Yes," Marcy said, pausing to make a show of her air quotes, "'crazy.'"

"I want to take a picture of him and post it on the site."

"Nope, you're fired," Sheila joked. "Go home."

"You're part of the deep state," Marcy said.

"How would you know?"

"Maybe it'll rain."

"We can always hope."

"He'll just go sit in his van."

"At least we'll get rid of Gracie."

"Not nice."

"Maybe he can take her."

Because of all the false allegations from the last time, there was a list of new protocols each ward's election board had to follow. She and Marcy witnessed Sheila checking the security seals on the bags with the ballots and then preparing the scanner and the machines. Everything required three signatures.

Out in the lot, more flacks had arrived, a mix of candidates' staffers and retirees, nearly all Democrats, like Squirrel Hill itself, gathered around Gracie, making the man appear even more out of place. He opened the rear doors of his van, and she wondered if the JCC's windows were bulletproof. It was like being trapped in a glass box. She wished they had a metal detector like the schools.

"Can we request a constable?" she asked.

"That's a good idea," Marcy said.

"It may be too late," Sheila said. "I can ask."

"Please," Kitzi said.

The soonest availability they had was after lunch, the county said. There was no guarantee. With all the protests, they were stretched thin.

"Looks like we're on our own," Sheila said.

Kitzi didn't want her to feel bad. Though it seemed obvious now, none of them had thought of it. Kitzi herself had been preoccupied with Gene's recent diagnosis—liver cancer—but that was no excuse.

"We'll be fine," she said.

"There's a security guard if we really need help," Marcy said. "It *is* the JCC."

Kitzi lifted out the hefty poll book while Marcy unboxed some fresh pens, testing them on a scratch pad. Sheila performed a last walkaround of the voting area and made sure they knew the new rules about spoiled and provisional ballots.

A line had formed outside, Gracie at the front, and standing right behind her, as if pushing her chair, the man from the van.

"Does he know he's not allowed inside?" Marcy asked.

"Unless he's voting here," Sheila said.

"I doubt that," Kitzi said.

Sheila had the custodian go to the door with her and unlock it, though there were still six minutes left. He stood behind her as she opened it a crack and poked her head out. From where they sat, Kitzi and Marcy couldn't hear what she was saying, but both Gracie and the man from the van searched their pockets and unfolded papers for Sheila to examine. The man dug out his wallet and handed her his ID. Sheila pulled her head back in, letting the door close, and brought the papers to the table.

She leafed through the handbook.

"What's going on?" Marcy said.

"They're watchers."

"What do you mean?" Kitzi said in disbelief. She knew exactly what it meant. They would observe Sheila and Marcy and herself to make sure they didn't steal the election.

"That's the stupidest thing I've ever heard," Marcy said.

"It's the law."

"It would be nice if they warned us," Kitzi said, still hoping Sheila might find some technicality to send him away. Gracie was annoying, but, like them, she'd been there faithfully, year after year. And *his* side was the one that had tried to steal the election. They still couldn't admit that Trump lost.

"What are they watching?" Marcy asked.

"Us," Kitzi said.

"Just do what you always do," Sheila said. "They have to stay outside of the guardrail. The only thing they're allowed to do is ask to see the list of voters 'at regular intervals, without disrupting the operation of the polling place.' If they want to challenge something, they have to go through the courts afterward. And they can't have any campaign materials on them."

"It's almost seven," Marcy said.

"Don't want to get in trouble for being late," Kitzi said.

"His name's Todd," Sheila said, logging his information.

"Where's he from?" Marcy asked.

"It just says Pittsburgh."

"What's the zip?" Kitzi asked.

"One five two three five."

"Penn Hills? Maybe Plum."

"Not from here," Marcy said.

"They're allowed to watch whatever polls they want. They can go from one to another all day long if they want."

"Let's hope so," Kitzi said.

They all had to sign off on the forms.

"What if I refuse to?" Kitzi said, but Sheila wasn't amused. "Can you at least pat him down?"

"Don't be a Todd," Marcy said.

"Let's be professional," Sheila said.

They were. They had been all along. To imply otherwise was an insult, and as Sheila let everyone in and escorted Gracie and the man past the table, he slowed and looked them over as if to show they couldn't fool him, and she had to stop herself from glaring back. Sheila installed them behind the guardrail, where they watched like pit bosses in a casino, and Kitzi was aware of her hands on the table. The accusation rankled. She would never cheat. He and his fellow Fox News zombies were the cheaters, gerrymandering districts and fixing the Supreme Court to do the bidding of the minority, storming the Capitol when they lost. She took pride in treating everyone who voted—Democrat, Republican,

Libertarian, Green, or Independent—equally. She cared about fairness and representation. He didn't care about any of that. All he cared about was winning. Now she did too, viciously, and it felt like a loss.

She looked up from the poll book and welcomed the first person in line, putting on an inviting smile.

"Name?"

How Old?

Mid-morning, as she had for years, Arlene walked the three blocks to the Wilkins Community Center to vote. Like Joan's nursing home, it had once been a school, and the high ceilings and wide halls and low water fountains took Arlene back to her own classroom. She signed her name, dismayed to see how her signature had deteriorated in the past six months, and a perky young mother led her to a touchscreen and showed her what to do, tapping arrows, zipping through the pages of the ballot too fast for Arlene to possibly follow.

"Remember, you haven't officially voted until you see the green confirmation screen. If you have any questions, I'll be right over there."

Arlene had used the machine before, she was certain—she was proud of her perfect voting record—and once she'd reacquainted herself with it, it was simple enough. She'd been waiting for months to vote for John Fetterman for Senate and Josh Shapiro for governor and Summer Lee for the House. All three were progressive

Democrats, champions of the underclass, while their opponents were nutty Trumpers like that lunatic Betsy DeVos who wanted to gut the public schools.

The judges' races were harder. Choose no more than four candidates. Choose no more than three. There were too many. She didn't recognize all the names and felt unprepared, and in the end, with only the smallest misgiving, she voted the straight party line.

The one referendum at stake seemed clear-cut: whether judges should have to retire at age seventy-five. Thinking of her own troubles, she agreed that it made sense to let younger judges decide the great questions of their day. It wasn't until she was back home, wearing her *I Voted* sticker, that she googled the referendum and discovered the current retirement age was seventy. She imagined she wasn't the only one they'd fooled, but it didn't make her feel any better, and later, when she saw on the news that it had passed—though Fetterman and Shapiro and Summer Lee had all won their races easily—she felt even worse.

"They got me too," Susie admitted at bridge.

"Good," Arlene said. "I'm not the only one."

"It was purposeful," Kitzi said. "It should have said, 'Should the retirement age be raised from 70 to 75?' I think a lot of people didn't know what they were voting for."

"That's what they were counting on," Susie said.

"I think it depends on the person," Emily said, shuffling. "We all know people in their seventies that are still sharp." She tipped her head at Kitzi.

"Did you know?" Arlene asked.

"I did," Kitzi confessed, as if she were sorry.

"I didn't," Emily said. "I voted against it, because I thought what you thought."

“So you canceled each other out,” Susie said.

“But not you,” Arlene said.

“I think it’s ageist,” Emily said. “Is Joe Biden too old to be president?”

“That would be a valid question if he’d run against anyone but Trump,” Kitzi said, cutting the deck for her.

“Amen,” Susie said.

“How old is too old?” Emily asked, and dealt.

They all recognized the question as rhetorical and fell back into the game, yet Arlene kept fretting over it and her vote on the referendum—not only then but for days afterward, the memory tweaking her at random, nagging as a forgotten password, as if it were further evidence of her decline, until it, too, disappeared.

Requiem

November, as was customary at Calvary, a requiem Mass replaced their usual Evensong. It seemed fitting, as the days grew shorter and the weather more dispiriting, to mourn the end of yet another year. Pittsburgh was gray, the sycamores along Fifth skeletal, and when it rained and night fell in the middle of rush hour, they needed a little extra faith to keep going.

They all had their losses, and if time made them easier to bear, the dead were also more remote and harder to recall, a silent slideshow of old memories unchanging as the past. Emily and Arlene had been alone for so long. It was the fate that awaited Kitzi, and while she vowed that she would sell the house after Martin died rather than inhabit an empty shell, she wasn't certain she could leave everything she knew behind for a box of an apartment in Maxon Towers or the Morrowfield, no matter how cozy. Susie, who had done exactly that, was still surprised to wake up in a new place with a cat and now some mornings a strange man, as if her other life had never happened. She missed not Richard but her garden and the woods beyond, the deer and turkeys silently passing through the birches as she watched from the window over the sink. Gone, all of it, the children grown, the house sold. There was no going back.

Emily, as always, wanted Bach, the Mass in B minor, its austere grandeur a comfort. Calvary's organ was perfect for it. "I wouldn't mind Brahms."

Susie knew it was Fauré but made them guess.

"We just had Brahms," Kitzi said, though it had been five or six years. They had to count backward. Vaughan Williams, Palestrina, Puccini . . . "I've always liked the Puccini. You don't hear it enough."

"It's always Verdi," Arlene agreed.

"Oh God," Emily said, "anything but that."

"Viv's not going to do Verdi," Susie said.

"It's going to be something weird and French," Emily said, and Susie had to suppress a laugh they all caught.

"Or, French," Kitzi said.

"Berlioz," Emily said with certainty. "Very weird, very French."

"Nope, not Berlioz."

"Duruflé's too modern," Kitzi said, "or is he?"

"Is it Fauré?" Arlene asked.

"It is. Well done." She tried not to act too surprised, Arlene having confided her struggles, and thought how strange the brain was.

"He's the only one I could think of with a requiem."

"He's French," Emily said. "I don't know if he's weird."

"I'm excited," Kitzi said. "It's been ages since I've heard it. I sang it once as an undergrad."

"It's very moving," Susie said. "Supposedly he wrote it right after his parents died."

Emily pictured not Notre-Dame de Paris or the white-domed Sacré Cœur but her own mother's and father's matching headstones in Kersey Cemetery. It had been years since she'd visited to tend their graves, overgrown with weeds and wildflowers. It was too far for her to drive now, and she realized as if it were a new thought that she'd probably never go again. What kind of offering was that?

No one spoke, each of them reflecting on their dead and the intractability of the past. That was the problem with getting old, Emily thought. After a point you outlived everyone who truly knew you. There was no one left to remember her aunt June. Soon there would be no one who knew Henry.

"It'll be good," Susie said. "The kyrie's gorgeous and the baritone who's doing the Libera me is amazing. We're going to have horns too."

"That's always nice," Arlene said.

"Is it going to be taped?" Kitzi asked.

It was. Everything was now. Viv had grand plans for the choir, hoping to make a name for them beyond Pittsburgh, as Chatham Baroque had. Emily was skeptical, and they debated which had a larger following, baroque or choral music, ignoring the fact that both were prohibitively small and no one bought CDs anymore. Viv was trying to put together a tour of Europe where they'd perform at the great cathedrals, a possibility Susie had imagined as glamorous until Kitzi said that was what the Allderdice glee club did. Every fall there was some nerdy sophomore ringing their doorbell to sell them candy bars Martin couldn't eat.

With dusk coming so early, the service started at five sharp. They'd need to be there by 4:30 at the latest to get a decent seat. It wasn't the nightmare that Christmas Eve was, but the place would be half-full.

"I'll drive," Kitzi volunteered.

"Thank you," Emily said, before Arlene could object.

"Maybe after, we can get a bite to eat?" Susie asked.

The other three hesitated, though only Kitzi had an excuse.

"That would be lovely," Emily said. "I can't tell you the last time I was out for dinner."

"Where should we go?" Kitzi asked, to show she was game.

"How about Casbah?" Susie suggested, and as they weighed their choices, the day became something to look forward to even more.

The question was what to wear. There were so few special occasions now that didn't involve a funeral, and while the requiem was somber, it was also a concert, the highlight of Calvary's fall calendar. When she and Martin had subscribed to the symphony, Kitzi would buy with an eye for how an outfit would look in the gilded lobby of Heinz Hall. She still had all of them in the guest-room closet, shrouded in Footer's dry cleaning bags, their pink tags safety-pinned to the cuffs, but when she picked through them they seemed dated and dusty. Had she really thought she could get away with these wild prints, and why was there so much velvet?

With Martin to look after, and Jean and Gene, and trying to visit Joan out in Penn Hills, she didn't have time to do any serious shopping, and ended up grabbing a black wool sweater dress off the rack at the Talbots in Shadyside. Her good coat would go with it, and her patent leather clutch, and her Tiffany earrings. Her mother's gold brooch was too much. She smoothed her stomach in the mirror, turned right, then left, looking over her shoulder. It would have to do.

"Whoa," Martin said. "Someone's got a hot date."

"Not really."

"You look nice."

"Thank you."

She felt bad leaving him behind, and had to regroup in the car, sighing before she backed out of the garage.

"I feel underdressed," Arlene said when she picked her up, though beneath her puffy L.L.Bean shell she was wearing a charcoal midi dress instead of her usual cardigan and slacks, and an amber pendant Kitzi didn't recognize. She'd had her hair done, the henna unnaturally dark, making her face look pale.

"You look nice," Kitzi said. "I like that pendant."

Emily sat in the back. She'd also had her hair done. Hers was gray but lacquered with spray and stiff as spun glass. She'd chosen a camel cashmere coat, plain black turtleneck and pearls.

"Elegant swellegant," Arlene said.

"Look who's talking," Emily said.

"For a bunch of old broads, we clean up pretty good."

"My shoes are already killing me," Emily said. "These used to be my favorites."

They weren't the first people there, but close. The rear of the church was dark as a barn, as if the power had gone out. In front, the lights were low, the candles flickering, making the sanctuary feel cozy. Two music stands and microphones stood by the chancel rail, bracketed by twin urns of lilies chosen by the Altar Guild. Kitzi thought Arlene and Emily would want to sit together, but as they genuflected to turn into their pew, Emily let Kitzi go ahead of her so she would be in the middle, like a mother with a child on each side. Across the aisle, surprisingly alone in his tweed jacket and Yale tie, his ear plugged with a beige hearing aid, Harold Cunningham examined his program. No one had heard anything about Mimi, and as the crowd filled in around them, they hoped someone would remind him to turn off his phone.

"There's Penny," Emily said. "She seems to be walking just fine."

"Do you see Helen anywhere?" Kitzi asked.

"There," Arlene said, leaning across her and pointing, "next to the Chamberlains."

"Oh, good," Kitzi said, because she'd heard she'd had Covid.

As they waited, craning around to see who else they knew, the organ purled and broke into the grave opening bars of a prelude by someone named Joseph Jongen. It was placid and pastoral—pleasant enough, Emily judged, and made a note to look him up when she got home.

Arlene, gazing up at the darkened vault, only half listening, thought how odd it was that she'd been here eighty years ago, and pictured the girl she'd been, in her knee socks and pigtails, Henry swaddled in her mother's arms. The other day, taking her lunch into the dining room, she'd noticed she was walking hunched over and wondered when that had started. Just now, getting out of the car, it had taken her several tries to stand up, holding on to the door for leverage. Lately her balance hadn't been great, and Emily suggested she might consider using a cane—there were some very stylish ones now—and while she was probably right, on principle (not out of pride, as Emily thought) Arlene didn't want to give in to this incremental weakening. That girl had learned her lessons well. She believed in the promise of eternal life, and thought of death as inevitable, a release. Now she worried about how she would get there.

Beside her, watching the shades of the choir in their black cassocks gathering in the dim vestibule, Kitzi imagined Martin fixing his dinner, and Joan alone in her room, and Jean sitting with Gene in Shadyside's ICU. He'd lost weight and had to have his lung drained every few days. The doctors wouldn't say it, but he was going to die, and then what was Jean going to do? Though Kitzi knew better, she felt responsible, as if by fully dedicating herself to Jean she might solve all her problems—move her out of that house to someplace clean with a piano and just a cat or two. The task was daunting, if not impossible, and she marveled at how Joan had managed all those years.

Donald Wilkins lifted his hands from the keyboard and the prelude stopped, leaving a sudden silence broken by a cough. Pages rustled. Emily checked her watch.

"Before we start," Viv's disembodied voice intoned, God-like, from the ether. "Tonight's performance is being recorded for broadcast, so please silence all electronic devices. Thank you."

"Broadcast to where?" Emily whispered to Kitzi, as if Viv might hear.

Across the aisle Harold Cunningham sat, still as a stone.

Arlene tapped Kitzi on the shoulder. The two horn players, in matching black tails and white gloves, were lurking in the near transept like a pair of extras awaiting their cue.

The organ rumbled a warning and the congregation rose. The introit was low and tenebrous, *molto lento.* As one they turned to observe the crucifer and torchbearers and Father John and the long train of the choir as they marched out of the darkness and processed down the aisle, raising their voices against oblivion: *Requiem aeternam dona eis Domine, et lux perpetua luceat eis.* Rest eternal grant to them, O Lord, and let light perpetual shine on them. Susie, paired with Phyllis Shipley near the rear because of their slippery grasp of Latin, was aware of Emily and Kitzi and Arlene but kept her eyes on her score as she passed, trying to get the stresses right. In all the pageantry, the horn players had taken their places up front, and she and Phyllis split around them, mounting the stairs, filing into their respective stalls.

As they were settling before the kyrie, the lyrics struck her as strange and predatory. All flesh shall come to you. The physical was fleeting, she knew, yet she'd felt such joy in discovering she was still a carnal being, her body a source of wonder, and Peter's. Was it wrong, just pride?

She didn't have time to dwell on it. The horns blared a fanfare. The kyrie was starting, a sweet, lilting figure, plaintive at first, and then, with a major chord from the organ, bursting forth and soaring with the full force of the chorus. It was the most beautiful part, she thought, and the most hopeful, asking for mercy.

Emily, who considered the Fauré a warhorse, had lost interest and skipped ahead, reading the collect printed in her program, puzzling over the new translation: *Grant to the faithful departed the unsearchable benefits of the passion of your Son.* Unsearchable benefits made heaven sound like a pension plan, and as always, faced with change, she wondered who preferred this to the poetry she'd known her whole life.

Standing, they said amen along with Father John, then leafed through their hymnals for 624, *Jerusalem the golden, with milk and honey blest . . .* The horn players looked to Donald Wilkins, as if uncertain. He raised a finger for them to wait, then pointed. With a nod, the two launched into the intro, but something was off—a sour note making Emily raise her eyebrows and glance over at Kitzi and Arlene, both of whom were staring, aghast.

The horn players stopped, the one on the left leaning across and whispering to the other, whose face, as in a cartoon, had turned pink.

"Viv is not going to like this," Emily whispered, and Kitzi shook her head.

The players started again, and again the one on the right flubbed the note and they both stopped, setting off a buzz among the crowd.

The player on the left pressed a hand to his chest, and the other stepped back from his music stand and let him start on his own. His tone was clear and mournful, and after four bars Donald Wilkins joined him, and the choir and congregation jumped in, singing with a special gusto as if to compensate while the other player stood aside with his horn.

"What in the world was that?" Emily asked Susie at Casbah, first thing. "Didn't they practice?"

"He was a fill-in. The original guy called in sick."

"I used to have a nightmare like that," Arlene said. "I'm supposed to sing but I don't know any of the songs."

"He can't read music?" Emily asked.

"It was very last-minute. I guess he was a former student of the other guy. I felt bad for him."

"We all did," Arlene said.

"I expect they were paid for their services," Emily said.

"I'm not sure what happened with that, but I don't think we're going to see either of them again."

"How was Viv?" Kitzi asked.

"Viv was Viv," Susie said, with a grimace. "I booked it out of there."

"That's what they should broadcast," Emily said. "I'd pay to hear that."

"The baritone was very good," Kitzi said.

He was, they all agreed.

Emily, feeling extravagant, had ordered champagne for the table, and they toasted themselves, the core four.

"How's Joan doing?" Arlene asked, intense, as if it were urgent.

Kitzi, who hadn't seen Joan in over a week, hesitated.

"She's trying to stay positive," Susie offered. "Darcy's not coming for Thanksgiving."

"Why not?" Emily asked, and Susie raised both hands to show she wasn't getting in the middle of it.

"I don't blame her," Arlene said. "It's the end of the semester. I'm sure she'll be here as soon as she turns her grades in."

"Do we have any idea when she'll be out of there?" Emily asked.

"They have no clue," Susie said. "The doctor's never there. They don't even have her doing PT anymore."

"What?" Kitzi said, angry that she hadn't known.

"Something about Medicare only covering so much."

"She needs PT," Arlene said.

"She needs to get out of there."

"It's a pit," Emily said. "Every time I visit there's trash on the floor and no one at the desk."

"It was the only place that had a bed," Kitzi said.

"That should be our goal," Emily said, "to get her out of there. To Joan."

"To Joan." They raised their glasses and clinked.

"How's Gene doing?" Arlene asked gently, making Kitzi sigh. She'd hoped dinner would be a reprieve from HD business, but how could it be?

"Not well," she said, trying to imply by her tone that the real answer was long and complicated (she did not want to say it was cancer, as if it were some shameful secret), and was grateful when their server appeared with a platter of appetizers—olives and hummus and stuffed grape leaves and a smoky baba ghanoush they attacked with wedges of pita bread still warm from the oven. She'd forgotten how good their food was. She and Martin used to come here all the time. Now she couldn't recall the last time they'd gone out to dinner. It seemed they were always eating in front of the TV. He was becoming a recluse, wearing his sweatpants and playing games on his iPad, going whole weeks without leaving the house. She could see how it had happened to Jean and Gene. When you had no energy, it was so easy to fall into bad habits.

The champagne was done, and Susie, already merry, wanted to order a bottle of red wine. Kitzi would have loved a glass, but she was driving.

"Oh, you can have one," Susie said, holding up a finger.

"Maybe just a splash."

"That's the spirit. Arlene? Emily, yes?"

When the server poured a taste for her, Susie rolled it around the glass, dipped her head and gave it a deep sniff before taking a sip. "It's delicious, thank you."

"So," Emily said, once the server was gone, "how is Peter, if I may be so bold?"

"He is fine, and you may. We're going to see Gillian Welch Thursday night at the Byham."

"I don't know who that is," Emily admitted.

"She's kind of an old-fashioned country singer. She's not old—well, I guess she is now. She sings old-timey songs that she writes. New songs that sound old. Retro, I guess. Americana."

"Aha," Emily said. "Have you heard of this person?"

No one else had either.

"She's very good," Susie said in her defense.

"When are we going to meet him?" Emily asked.

"Stop," Arlene said, waving a hand, as if Emily were joking.

"Don't you want to meet him?" Emily asked Kitzi.

"It's Susie's business," Arlene said.

"I don't know if I think of him like that," Susie said.

The whole table came to a halt, all three of them looking at her as if she'd confessed to murder.

"Like what?" Emily asked.

"Like someone I need to introduce to people."

They gaped at her the way they'd gaped at the horn player, and she saw that she'd scandalized them. Alyssa said it made total sense that her first was just a hookup (if that's what it was), there was no shame, but that was her generation, far more practical and open about sex. She wondered how much Arlene had told Emily. At the time it had seemed harmless, just girl talk.

"Not yet, I mean. It hasn't even been two months."

"Maybe later," Arlene prompted.

"Maybe. Right now we're having fun getting to know each other." Which, she reflected, was actually true. She hadn't decided about Peter yet; it was too new, too confusing. The few times they'd had sex she'd been drunk or stoned or both, as if she were back in college, free of any real consequences.

"That's good," Kitzi said. "That's how it should be."

"We're only interested," Emily said, "because our own lives are so boring. Feed the dog, put the dog out, pick up the dog poo—that's my day. Not very glamorous, I'm afraid."

"How *is* Angus?" Susie asked, seeing a way out, and Emily obliged, inquiring about Oscar, which led back to the question of Joan and how hard it was to get through to the doctor who was supposed to be in charge. All the system cared about was the insurance money, Kitzi said; it was the reason the hospital wanted her gone and why she wasn't getting the correct PT. Everyone was getting paid, yet no one was responsible—a bleak conclusion, if true.

"Maybe they should put Viv in charge," Emily joked, saving them for the moment.

Moussaka, tabouli, falafel, lamb kebabs on rice pilaf. They'd ordered too much and couldn't finish half of it. Arlene acted as if asking for a box was embarrassing, when each of them was glad not to have to worry about lunch tomorrow. They were too full for dessert, though the baklava was tempting. The bottle was empty. They sat, chatting about the upcoming church bazaar and their various plans for Thanksgiving, and had to stop the server from refilling their water glasses. All that was left was the task of divvying up the check.

"It's taken care of," Susie said, setting off a chorus of protests, but she was adamant, and, anyway, it was done. "My neighborhood, my treat."

Grateful but still miffed at being tricked, they vowed to pay her back.

Outside, they waited in the cold for the valet to bring the car around. The night was clear, a crescent moon shining bright and precise above Calvary's steeple like an illustration in a children's book.

"This was nice," Emily said.

"It was," Kitzi said, and whether it was the wine or the lateness of the hour or how chilly the wind was, Susie wrapped her in a boozy embrace, and soon they were all hugging like old friends who might never see each other again, though they were all getting in the same car.

They agreed they should do it again.

The Escape Artist

Oscar liked to hide. Joan was right, he was a Houdini. Susie tried not to take it personally, it was just his nature. She was used to big needy dogs poking her with their wet noses and following her around the house, barking warnings at every little noise. Oscar was quiet as a ninja. He'd be snoozing on the couch beside her, or curled in a ball on the cushion of the rocking chair, and when she looked up from her cross-stitch, he was gone. He'd disappear for hours and then come sauntering into the kitchen as she was putting dinner together and sit at her feet, hoping for a tidbit, knowing she couldn't resist him.

This was her favorite time of day, when sunset tinted the clouds pink and the hallways of the Kenmawr smelled of curry and five-spice. She waited for the bells of Sacred Heart to strike six, it was their ritual, as if she were teaching him how to count.

"Who's ready for kibbles?" she asked, and he stared at her so fiercely that she had to laugh. The great and powerful Oz. "There you go, eat up like a pup."

Ozzy, she called him. Oswald, sometimes Waldo, or Wally, Wally Bear. Wally Bear, the bear with no underwear, she teased, and he was not amused. Wallace, she called him, because sometimes he was a Wallace, all seriousness.

He could be sweet. When her back was hurting and she had to stretch out flat on the floor like a corpse, he rubbed against her and purred as if he knew she needed comforting. She was convinced that she slept better when he shared the bed with her, and when he left in the middle of the night to go exploring, she lay there bereft, willing him to return. "Yes," she said when he finally did, "come snuggle."

With Oscar she was never alone. Mornings he was up first, stepping over her as she dozed, inspecting her face from an inch away to see if she was awake, and when she came home from Soup Group deliveries or visiting Joan, he was at the door to greet her. Peter had gone on tour with his band, informing her at the last minute, and some days when she felt lost and scattered, Oscar gave her purpose. The schedule she followed was so simple it was almost thoughtless. When it was dinnertime, she fed him. When his water bowl was empty, she filled it. When his litter box was smelly, she scooped his poop with a little plastic spatula and double-bagged it to throw down the chute with her other trash and returned to her apartment feeling a sense of completion. How quickly she'd forgotten the small satisfactions of taking care of someone. After Richard, she'd thought she was done with it.

They still had some adjustments to make. He didn't always go in his litter box, preferring her potted plants and her closet, specifically her shoes. Likewise, walking across her office or bedroom in her stocking feet, she might step in a wet spot. He terrorized her asparagus fern, batting its fronds like a prizefighter working a speed bag, strewing pieces across the bookcase and the floor. So far he'd left her grandmother's old velveteen couch alone, yet he climbed her custom drapes as if he were being chased, shredding them.

He could be brazen. One morning when she was on the toilet, he jumped onto the vanity and—looking straight at her—swatted her electric toothbrush into the sink. Another time he bolted past her as she was unlocking the door with her hands full and scampered down the hall, though there was nowhere to go. Fearing—hysterically—that the elevator could close on him like a guillotine, she dumped her bags and ran after him. The stairway at the far end of the hall was protected by an old metal fire door. She cornered him in the dead end, only to have him dash past her the other way. She lagged after him, commanding him to stop, calling his name as if he were a dog as he zipped into the open door of her apartment.

"You stinker."

He was not a dog. When she'd yelled at her dogs, they turned their heads, too ashamed to look at her. Oscar didn't care, sitting there regally, licking his paw. There was no point scolding him because he would never admit to any wrongdoing, just as it was impossible for her to stay mad at him. By dinnertime they would be reconciled, looking forward to a quiet evening together.

The one habit he shared with her dogs—the one she would never be able to break—was that he constantly wanted out. From his first day at her place, at all hours, he sat by the door and whined. Her apartment was on the fourth floor, so there was no easy way to put him out and let him in again. Technically, she wasn't allowed to have pets; if they found out, she could be evicted. Like any building of its era, the Kenmawr had mice, and occasionally she'd discover one left on the kitchen floor in tribute, a reminder that at heart he was a hunter, used to roaming free. She hadn't thought of it when she decided to take him away from his home, and felt bad. He crouched on the windowsill with his paws tucked underneath him, his head swiveling, tracking the squirrels as they crisscrossed the front lawn below.

"I know," she said. "I see them too."

Peter, who'd once had a budgie named Ludwig who flew away and never returned, thought Oscar might get lost if she put him out. Tonight Peter was in Milwaukee, crashing on a couch at the club owner's house. In the background, reggae boomed so loudly that he had to shout.

"You don't get a bed?"

"I'm lucky I get a couch!"

How old are you? she wanted to say but held off.

"What do you think I should I do?"

"I don't know, I don't know him that well." Which was true. The last time he'd been over, Oscar had hidden and then pounced on them in the middle of the night, a sneak attack, though, to Peter's credit, he laughed. "You know him better than I do."

"You're so smart," she said, because he'd handed her the answer: Joan would know.

"If I'm so smart, why am I on the couch?"

"I miss you," she dared.

"I miss you too. The upper Midwest in November. I don't know why I thought this would be fun."

"I don't know either," she said.

The next morning she left Oscar to his pursuits and drove out to see Joan, hooking on her mask in the cold before the receptionist buzzed her in. She set the bright fall bouquet from Giant Eagle she'd brought on the counter to write her name and time of arrival.

It was stifling inside and the ward smelled of scrambled eggs and urine. She didn't like to think the facility was a pit, as Emily put it, but each time she walked the gauntlet of the main hall, it was littered with trash and the call lights were blinking madly above the patients' doors, their wails beseeching the staff for help. Here, among the senile and dying, she felt obscenely young and healthy, near superhuman. Why was she repulsed? This was what awaited all of them, the body and mind's inevitable breakdown, just another stage of life, yet, undeniably, she was, and this failure—her cowardice in the face of others' suffering—angered her. A grimace hidden beneath her mask, she strode past their rooms as if she were deaf, clutching the bouquet in front of her like a shield, focused on the deserted nurses' station ahead, and was relieved to reach Joan's without having to speak to anyone.

"They're gorgeous," Joan said, taking the bouquet. "I think we can throw these mums away and use that vase."

Like the Joan of old, she took charge, giving orders, and Susie was happy to comply, though in the bathroom, tossing the mums, she noticed an open tube of toothpaste and no cap in sight, and the toilet desperately needed to be cleaned.

Joan looked better—more energetic, not as pale. She'd started PT again, and bragged that she'd walked all the way to the dayroom and back on crutches, a distance Susie had covered in less than a minute. Her cast was finally off. Before Susie knew what she was doing, Joan pushed down the covers to show her where they'd put the screws in.

The scars were still livid, pink as ham. Her leg was shrunken, the knee a bony knob. Her muscles had atrophied. She was on a high-protein diet, drinking Ensure with her meals to regain mass. Every day they were slowly increasing her range of motion. Her tendons were held on with staples; they had to be careful not to tear anything. The doctor said it could take six months or more to get her back to full strength.

"Or more," Joan stressed. "They can never say anything definite. That way they're never wrong."

"Did they say when you can go home?"

She blew a wet raspberry inside her mask. "Who knows. I've got another sixty-three days here on Medicare."

The number panicked Susie. It was barely two months, and she smothered the small, selfish part of her that wished it were longer.

"Oscar misses you."

"I doubt it. How's he doing?"

"Good," she said, and could have left it at that, except he was the reason she was there. She kept seeing him looking out the window at the lawn and yowling at the door. Like Joan's neighbors crying for help, he was not going to stop, and ignoring him only made it worse.

"He's actually driving me crazy," she said, and explained the situation, taking the blame for not expecting it.

"I'm sorry he's such a pain," Joan said.

"He's not. Really. He just wants to do what he's always done."

"Don't worry yourself about it. He's fine staying inside, especially with the weather turning. He's not a fan of the cold."

"I'm afraid if I put him out, he might not come back."

"I don't expect you to," Joan said. "You're already doing me a huge favor."

"How does it work when he's at home?"

"I just let him out on the balcony when he asks."

"And he comes back."

"Eventually."

When he was done gallivanting, he'd cry at the sliding door for her to let him in—sometimes in the dead of the night. It was easier in the summer, when she could leave the door open for him.

"He's got me trained," Joan said. "Don't let him do that to you."

"I think it's too late for that," Susie said, because already she was trying to figure out how she could make it work.

They had a good visit, catching up on HD gossip and commiserating over their lack of Thanksgiving plans, and though Joan seemed better, as always Susie felt guilty leaving. She braved the long walk down the hall, then waited for the receptionist to buzz her out before she could pull her mask off.

"Jesus," she said, alone in the cold again, frowning at a scattering of lipsticked cigarette butts spread around a bench, and as she crossed the lot a familiar depression settled on her. The heater of the Prius took forever to warm up. She sat a minute, buckled in, as if she didn't want to leave, when honestly that was all she wanted. It was wrong. It was too easy for her to escape this purgatory, to return to the world of the living and act like everything was fine. A couple of blocks, she knew, and she'd be fretting over all the meaningless crap on her list, Joan pushed to the side until her next visit.

"I hate this," she said, her bitterness surprising her, and headed for the exit.

Driving, as she'd foreseen, she concentrated on traffic and her next stop. She'd stayed longer than she'd planned and was running behind. To save time, she'd combined her visit with a string of errands in Monroeville, having mapped out the most efficient sequence in her head, but Rodi Road was a mess, and then when she got to the Giant Eagle they didn't have Penny's prescription ready. Rather than wait, she pressed on to Jo-Ann Fabrics (Helen, Anita) and then Wild Birds Unlimited (Martha Wise) before the pharmacy texted her, making her backtrack. Patel Brothers, Petco, Lowe's. In between she daydreamed of letting Oscar out on Joan's balcony. She'd have to watch the weather and pick a nice day. He hated his carrier, but there was no other way to take him down the elevator, unless she smuggled him in a box, which might be worse. Maybe Peter could help when he came back, bringing her car around like a getaway driver. There were security cameras, she was certain. Should they do it at night to be safe, or was she overthinking it?

"Yes," Peter said from Madison.

"Yes you'll help?"

"Yes I'll help, and yes you're overthinking it."

She waited a beat so he'd know it wasn't funny.

"I'm kidding."

"No you're not," she said.

"You're trying to do something nice for him. I think it's sweet."

Then why did it sound like a criticism? Richard used to laugh and call her a bleeding heart, tallying her charitable contributions at tax time. She already worried that she was doing the wrong thing. She didn't need someone else to make her doubt herself.

"Maybe the weekend after you get back," she said.

"I'm in," he said, too enthusiastic.

"You're just saying that to appease me."

"I'm not," he said. "Name the day and I'll be there."

She believed him, and yet when she hung up it felt like they'd argued—over what she wasn't clear, but the next morning, when Oscar yowled at the door, she pulled his carrier out of the closet. At the sight of it he retreated to the kitchen.

"You want to go? Let's go." She opened the little wire door for him. "Come on, right now. Let's do it."

He watched her for a moment from the cover of the dishwasher, then turned and loped down the hall.

She left the carrier on the floor. She didn't need Peter's help, she just wanted him to support her decision. Why did she always need to be reassured? She was sixty-three, too old to be afraid of making mistakes. It was sunny out, and she had to go over and water Joan's plants anyway.

She put one of Oscar's salmon treats in the carrier and went to brush her teeth, and when she came back the treat was gone and he was drinking from his bowl. He watched her as she crossed behind him, dug a handful of treats from the bag and sat down beside the carrier, patting the top to show it was okay. He didn't follow into the front hall but stopped at the edge of the kitchen tiles, the tip of his tail flicking. She held out a treat on her palm. After a flinch of a false start, as if thinking better of it, he snuck across the rug and took it from her, skirting away so she couldn't grab him. She held up another treat and placed it inside the carrier like a piece of bait. He stared at it fiercely—whether outraged or tempted, she couldn't say. She was sorry to stoop to such a low trick (she hadn't expected it to work, honestly), she almost wanted him to turn his nose up and stalk off. He crept toward the carrier, hunched low as if hunting something. She kept motionless, holding her breath as he stopped short of the door, stretching for the treat with one paw, and then, when he couldn't reach it, ducked inside.

He was almost in when she realized she was on the wrong side of the door. As she reached across the opening to close it behind him, he whirled and she slapped the door shut, fighting the catch with her free hand. Through the wire he caught her with his claws, leaving a fine white lip across her palm that filled with blood and only then began to sting.

"Mother!" she said, squeezing it, and then, softer, "It's okay," to calm him, because it wasn't his fault. Why had she thought he might go quietly? She had Neosporin in the bathroom and spread a dab over the scratch. She caught herself in the mirror and had to fend off the idea that it was a sign. It was too late, she was already bleeding.

She draped a towel over the carrier and scouted the hallway before taking the elevator down, watching the numbers change, sure it would stop at every floor. He was heavy and her hand hurt. There was a camera in the corner behind her, and she imagined this was how it felt to be a terrorist. In the lobby, a female student with a puffy coat and a violin case held the door for her, and then she was outside, walking to her car like any other day, not hurrying or looking around to see if anyone was watching her, just opening the door and setting the carrier on the passenger seat and belting it in, though she only had to go two blocks.

"Guess where we're going?" she asked, as if she might make it up to him. "Your favorite place in the whole world."

But then, in Joan's garage, when she let him out of the carrier, he shot beneath the Subaru and stayed there until she'd gone upstairs. He reminded her of Alyssa as a teenager, locking herself in her room. He could be mad at her, that was fine. She'd endured worse.

Before she did anything with the plants, she unlocked the door to the balcony and opened it a crack, letting in the cold. The street with its identical condos and mailboxes lay deserted as a suburb, a squirrel digging at the grass the only sign of life, and again she compared the unearthly quiet to the Kenmawr and couldn't stop herself from seeing the long hall at Joan's nursing home and had to shake her head to get rid of it.

She filled the watering can at the sink, flexing her hand, expecting Oscar to come sashaying past her any second, but he was being stubborn. She ignored him, going from room to room, talking to the plants as she tended them, gathering the brittle husks of leaves that had fallen on the floor and the windowsills. In the weeks leading up to the requiem, she'd been too busy to clean, and the place needed a good dusting—so did her own, before she had Peter over again, and she didn't know where she'd find the time.

Twice she ran out of water and refilled the can, doing Joan's office and the ivy in the bathroom. There was still no sign of Oscar. She was hoping he might have gotten by her, and when she was finished she set the can in the sink and went downstairs and looked under the car, and he was gone.

She checked his hiding places, in case. She was pleased, as if she'd fooled him. She stepped out on the balcony and looked up and down the street, but all she saw were a couple of squirrels at work. It was bright but chilly, and she slipped back in, leaving the door open for him.

To kill time, she covered the scratch with three overlapping Band-Aids and dusted, moving pictures and knickknacks that had become as familiar as her own, knowing she'd just have to do it again in a few weeks. When Oscar still hadn't returned, she vacuumed. She needed to get some lunch, but there was nothing in the fridge except some moldy old kombucha Darcy had left. He'd come back eventually, Joan had said. She wasn't worried.

She called Alyssa just to talk but it went straight to voicemail. She tried Joan but no one picked up.

She hadn't planned on being there that long. She was bored, sitting on the couch, playing Candy Crush, when the doorbell rang, almost making her drop her phone. Her first instinct was to pretend no one was home, except her car was in the driveway. Maybe a neighbor had reported her to security.

It was Bill with his cane and his wraparound sunglasses, dressed for bad weather in a black watch cap, wool peacoat and suede gloves. At first she thought he might have Oscar with him and was confused when she realized he was alone.

"I saw your car," he said. "I just wanted to see how your mother's doing."

"Good," she said, and it wasn't entirely a lie. "She's already walking with crutches."

"That's fast."

"You know her, go, go, go."

"I do. Please let her know we're thinking of her."

"I will. You haven't seen Oscar, have you? I put him out a while ago."

"I'll keep an eye out for him. I'm sure he's fine."

She thanked him, glad to have an ally, but as the afternoon wore on, she fretted, finally going out to her car and cruising the three loops of the Village, stopping to peer into the darkness under the perfect hedges, afraid of finding Oscar limp and mangled on the road. Bill was right, he was probably fine, and she decided not to tell the guard at the booth.

The forecast was wrong. It was cloudy now, like it might rain, and then, as if she'd conjured it, sprinkles dotted the windshield. She hadn't thought things through, obviously. She could just see Richard shaking his head, and hear Peter asking why she couldn't wait.

She needed to eat something, and after a second pass she drove home, microwaved yesterday's leftovers, grabbed her knitting, some tea bags and granola bars and raced back, waving to the guard, scanning the yards on both sides for any movement. The day had turned gloomy, a misty drizzle haloing the streetlights. Getting out, she could see her breath, and pictured him huddled under a shrub, drenched and miserable.

She should have left the garage door open a gap at the bottom.

"Stupid," she said.

Again she checked his hiding places in case he'd snuck in while she was out. Dusk was falling, and she switched on the balcony's overhead light, hoping it might serve as a beacon, but the bulb was yellow and weak. She felt foolish calling his name as if he were a dog or a child late for supper. She projected from her diaphragm, holding the note, trying to disguise the fear in her voice. There was no one to hear her, the whole street buttoned up against the murk, and she went back in. He would have to come home for his dinner, she reasoned, now that the sun was down. She positioned herself on the couch with a cup of tea, facing the door, a blanket over her knees for warmth. Normally she listened to podcasts while she knitted, but she needed to hear him, and sat with Joan's reading lamp at her shoulder, needles clicking, silently counting her stitches as the sky in the west grew darker, the glass slowly going opaque until all she could see was her own reflection.

The Eleventh Day

All afternoon, as she painted, Arlene waited for the mail. She wasn't expecting anything, its arrival was just a reliable part of her day, a welcome interruption, ever promising. Sometimes, along with the bills and grocery store flyers and come-ons for supplemental health insurance, it contained a nice surprise like a dividend check or a catalog she enjoyed—the Vermont Country Store or American Stationery. She'd already started her Christmas shopping, turning down pages when she found an item the children might like. Sarah and Ella were easy, the boys impossible, in their thirties and still playing video games. Last year, after bugging them for ideas, she'd given up and ordered from their Amazon wish lists, a bitter defeat.

It wasn't like Dale to be late, and she wondered if there was a sub. Often they didn't come until after dark or—very rarely but still annoying—not at all. It did no good to complain, they were so understaffed. Everyone knew the new postmaster was trying to sabotage the mails because Trump hated Jeff Bezos. There was even talk of getting rid of Saturday delivery, which confounded Arlene, who remembered when mail came twice a day, morning and afternoon. It wasn't her imagination, the country really did seem to be moving backward.

She was working on a still life, a plate of winter vegetables—a cabbage, a pair of hairy beets, some carrots—and every time she took a break she went to the front window, kneading her pigment-stained fingers, and checked to see if there was anything in the Vincenzos' box across the street. She was looking down at the matted grass of their lawn, the color of a wet tennis ball, when she remembered it was Veterans Day.

That's why there was no mail. She'd known, it had just flown out of her head.

A half hour later she looked again and remembered.

Right, she thought. Stop.

Plans

As she did every November since proclaiming herself finally and totally sober, Margaret invited Emily to Michigan for Thanksgiving but not Arlene, who she was actually closer with, and as she did every year, Emily brought it up over bridge as if it were a slight. While Arlene might have been embarrassed once, resentful of being cast as a figure of pity—the lonely maiden aunt rotting away in her apartment—they all knew it was really about how much Emily dreaded going.

"I'll be enjoying a nice, quiet weekend with Angus," Arlene said. "We're going to walk in the park and snuggle on the couch and watch football."

"That sounds more relaxing," Emily said. "Can I come visit you?"

"You'll have fun. You'll get to meet Sarah's new beau."

"See? You talk to her more than I do. I didn't even know they were going to be there."

"He's a chiropractor," Arlene told the table.

"He's divorced," Emily said, as if it were a flaw.

"Really?" Susie cocked her head, giving Emily a chance to retract the insult.

"*Very* recently." She made it sound scandalous.

"And?"

"He has three teenaged girls."

"No thank you," Susie said.

"That could be hard," Kitzi said.

"Will they be there?" Susie asked.

Emily looked to Arlene.

"I'm not sure," Arlene said. "I doubt it."

"Whether they're there or not," Emily said, "it's always an adventure with her."

Peter was still on the road, so Susie hadn't discussed Thanksgiving with him yet. She liked the idea of not cooking.

"You're welcome to come to our place," Kitzi said. "We're having Jean over for dinner."

"Thank you," Susie said, thinking there was no way she'd subject Peter to that kind of scrutiny.

"I wish there was more we could do for her," Kitzi said.

They murmured agreement. They were done playing, the day flat and gray outside, crumbs on the tablecloth. The coffee was wearing off, but it was too late for another cup.

"Is anyone going to see Joan?" Emily asked.

"I can," Arlene said.

"I might be able to," Susie said.

"I can make a plate for her, if someone can take it," Kitzi said. "I'm already making one for Gene."

Can he eat? Emily wanted to ask, because the last she'd heard, he was on a ventilator, but held off. She thought Kitzi had gotten too close to them. It was strange: they weren't even Calvary people, just a stray couple Joan had taken under her wing. No one else had even seen them.

The grandfather clock bonged three, the signal to clean up. They filed into the kitchen with their cups and saucers and dessert plates, setting them in the sink while Emily tried to unload the leftover cookies. It was cold out, and they pulled on their hats and gloves in the front hall.

Emily held the door for them.

"Have a Happy Thanksgiving," they called. "Good luck."

"Thank you."

"Wednesday at eleven," Arlene said, pointing, as if Emily might forget.

"Thank you for watching him."

"He's easy."

"I wish you were coming with me." She'd never said it out loud before, and it felt like a confession.

"I know," Arlene said. "I'll see her at Christmas. I think she needs you to see she's doing better."

"It's hard to trust her."

"She'd be the first person to agree with you."

"I haven't been there since before Covid. I haven't even seen her new place."

"That's why she wants you to come."

"It's always a new start with her, until it's not."

"That just may be the way it is," Arlene said. "For now it sounds like she's doing good, and that's something."

"It is," Emily agreed, and let her go, watching her old car leave a ghostly trail of exhaust floating above the street.

Inside, alone again, she thought it was easier for Arlene because she had less to forgive Margaret. Not just ignoring everything Emily had tried to teach her, but doing the exact opposite: running wild in high school and then dropping out of college, wasting decades burning through dead-end jobs and worthless men, her children basically raising themselves. Missing Henry's funeral and then showing up high that night, sobbing that he'd always been ashamed of her. Was Emily supposed to believe this was part of the disease?

She was too old to change how she felt. Now that Margaret was sober, she was supposed to let it all go, and if not, it was her fault.

She climbed the stairs and let Angus out of her bedroom. He went bounding down, waiting for her at the bottom, his little tail whirling in a circle. When she opened the back door, he flew across the yard to his spot in the corner and squatted. She stood at the window with her arms folded, looking up at the Coles' great oak, its bare branches black against the low sky. On the national news the other night there had been a snowstorm moving across the plains—whiteouts and jackknifed tractor-trailers—and for an instant she pictured the concourse of the airport jammed with stranded passengers. There would be nothing for her to do but get back in the car and go home. She and Arlene could have their own cozy Thanksgiving, watching football and walking Angus around the reservoir, making hot chocolate. But later, when the local news showed the weather map, the forecaster said warmer temperatures were on the way, and she understood there would be no reprieve.

Tuesday night she packed Angus's bag and then her own, and Wednesday shed a few silly tears in the car after dropping him off. As her ticket recommended, she was two hours early. For entertainment she'd brought a favorite Agatha Christie. The gate area filled in around her, everyone talking on their cell phones. The flight was overbooked, and the agent made an announcement offering passengers a five-hundred-dollar voucher if they'd take a later one. The number tempted her, but she was done pretending she had a choice in the matter. Whatever mistakes she'd made, she would pay for them. She was in Group 3—she didn't need any extra help, not yet. She boarded and buckled her belt and waited for takeoff, trusting herself to fate.

Timing

The night before Thanksgiving, while Martin was cleaning up after dinner, Darcy texted Kitzi to let her know a nurse from the home had called. Joan had tested positive for Covid. So far she was asymptomatic, but there were eight other cases in her pod. They'd locked the place down.

"That's awful," Martin said.

"And she just had her booster. I bet it's the new strain. The vaccines are always one behind."

"I'm sorry."

"Maybe I can set up a Zoom with her. It's not the same but it's something."

Please keep us posted, she told Darcy.

She sent Joan a text but she didn't answer.

"She might be sleeping," Martin said.

"We need to get her out of there," Kitzi said, as if that were a possibility.

Though it meant less work, the change of plans threw her. She let Susie and Arlene know, floating the Zoom idea by them. She needed to get her turkey in early and take Jean to see Gene, so maybe late afternoon?

Susie was going to a Friendsgiving thing with Peter and sounded doubtful.

Arlene said she wasn't great at Zooming but she'd try.

She closed her iPad and sighed, aware of Martin watching her. "I just don't want her to be alone."

"You don't think Darcy talks with her?"

"You've never met Darcy. She's not exactly warm and fuzzy."

"You've told me. They get along all right, though?"

"Who knows. I know she's only been back here once this whole time."

From his silence she could tell she'd shocked him. While true, it was uncalled-for, and she apologized. "I'm sure she's busy."

"I'm sure," he said, absolving her, and asked what he could do to help.

"You're doing it," she said.

To make Jean feel at home, she was serving a trifle alongside her pumpkin pie. It needed to set overnight, so she shooed him out of the kitchen and put together her sponge cakes, slicing strawberries and churning half-and-half into whipped cream with the mixer while they baked. They rarely had dessert—they never had company anymore—and he hovered as she built the layers of the parfait and was surprised when she let him lick the spatula.

"Wow, what did *I* do?"

"Just wait."

In bed, as he slept next to her, she went over her menu in her head, worried that she'd forgotten something. The timing of the turkey was always tricky. They were going to eat early so Jean could see Gene and be home before dark, meaning she needed to put it in by eight at the latest. The potatoes and stuffing, the yams and green beans—everything else fit under that umbrella. The can of cranberry sauce was chilling in the fridge. They had slivered almonds and wine and three different cheeses for hors d'oeuvres, and the rice crackers Martin was allowed to eat, but she couldn't shake the feeling she was missing some key ingredient, and lay there in the dark, annoyed, puzzling over what it might be.

In the middle of the night she jerked awake as if his vest had zapped her: nutmeg. She wrote it down so she wouldn't forget, and in the morning rose early to go to the store with everyone else in Squirrel Hill.

There were two main brands of spices in the baking aisle, the more affordable McCormick in a plastic shaker with a red cap and the insanely expensive Spice Islands in glass. She tried the red caps first, one finger tracking the alphabetical shelf—mace, marjoram, mustard powder—but the space for ground nutmeg was empty. The glass had the exact same gap. The pumpkin pie spice was sold out as well. She asked an aproned stock person if there might be some in back. The man shook his head as if he'd been answering the same question all morning. She thanked him anyway, knowing it wasn't his fault, and stalked out to her car empty-handed.

Who would have it? she asked her windshield, dismissing the Market District in Shadyside and Trader Joe's, and thought of Joan's place, and then Susie. She was always making some vegetarian thing with weird spices.

She called, hoping she was awake, and was relieved when she answered. Her voice was a whisper, as if her phone were dying.

"Do you have any nutmeg I can borrow?"

"I do, but I'm not alone."

"Oh!" Kitzi said, "Sorry," trying not to picture the elusive Peter lying beside her. "I kind of need it now. Can I swing by?"

"Sure. Call me when you get here."

It was a holiday, there was no traffic, only joggers and dog-walkers. She parked by the front of the Kenmawr and Susie padded out in her puffer jacket and sweatpants and fleece slippers, her hair blowing all over. It was like a drug deal. She slid her window down and Susie handed her a rolled-up baggie.

"Say hi to Peter for me."

"I will. Happy Thanksgiving."

"Happy Thanksgiving," Kitzi said, and, driving away, imagined Susie closing her apartment door and climbing back into her warm bed, the whole day ahead of them.

At home, Martin had the parade on, new balloons and gaudy floats with country stars and casts of Broadway shows she'd never heard of doing their big numbers as she mixed the stuffing and prepped the turkey, sealing it in its basting bag to keep in the juices. She peeled and soaked the potatoes and the yams, blanched the green beans. She had everything timed and, item by item, checked off her list to mark her progress. Because of the nutmeg, she was twenty minutes behind schedule, and there was no way to make it up. Band after band clattered past Macy's, flags twirling. The hosts kept teasing Santa, his triumphant arrival with Mrs. Claus and the elves inducing a slight panic, and then in a blizzard of confetti the parade was over and the dog show was on.

She was just starting the pie crust when her phone rang, making Martin look over his shoulder.

It was Jean. She hesitated a moment before answering, as if it could only be bad news.

"Are you coming to pick me up?" She sounded flustered.

"At one o'clock," Kitzi said, enunciating so there could be no confusion. "I'm a little behind right now, so I may be late."

"I thought we were going to see Gene."

"We are, right after we eat."

"Would you mind terribly if we nipped over there now? I had an awful night. I don't sleep well when I'm here by myself, you know. The cats can sense things are off and make a racket, and when I finally did manage it, I had bad dreams. I'd feel better if I could see him, for my own peace of mind."

Across the room, Martin watched to see if she'd give in. As if she had a choice.

"Of course," she said. "We can do that."

She turned the turkey down to 200. The beans wouldn't keep, but everything else could wait.

"Do you want me to take her?" Martin asked, which, while logical, wasn't helpful.

"It's fine. We'll just eat later. She's got herself worked up. Which I totally get."

"It's good of you to take her."

"That's why I get the big bucks," she said, untying her apron, and bowed over the back of the couch to give him a kiss. "Happy Thanksgiving."

In the car again, she shook her head at the wackiness of it. Why had she thought they could have a quiet day?

Chatham's campus was deserted. As always, the house looked haunted, the blinds drawn, weeds sprouting in the turnaround. She had to get out and ring the bell and stood there waiting while Jean navigated the maze inside. She and Martin had never formally met. Remembering what he'd said about the smell the other day,

Kitzi hoped Jean was wearing something appropriate, and was relieved, when the door opened, letting a brace of cats escape, to see her face was made up and her hair knotted in a neat chignon, showing off her long neck. Kitzi had been silly to worry. With her striking height and perfect posture and posh accent, Jean could be imposing. Even now there was something theatrical about her, as if she'd just walked offstage. All the same, in the car Kitzi sniffed the air discreetly, but could detect only a hint of potpourri.

"Thank you for indulging me," Jean said. "I had the most awful nightmare, you can't imagine."

About Gene, Kitzi almost said. "I'm sorry."

She waited for Jean to describe the dream, but she was watching the stream running alongside them. At the bottom of the hill it disappeared into a culvert under Fifth Avenue, never to return. Across the street the soot-blackened Presbyterian church aimed its stone spire at the sky.

"What do you think?" Jean asked casually. "The doctors never tell me anything."

"I know. They're terrible at communicating."

"They won't even tell me what stage he is. They just say 'advanced.'"

"They don't want to be wrong."

"Every day I wake up and I think this could be it. I hear the phone ring . . ."

"I know," Kitzi said.

"I understand he's not getting better. Why can't they say that?"

"I think they think they need to be positive for the families so it doesn't look like they're giving up. They're trained to solve problems and project confidence. They're used to being successful, so it's hard for them to admit when they've failed."

"I just want them to be honest with me."

"The nurses will give you straight answers sometimes. They know what's going on more than the doctors. The doctors are there for rounds and that's it. It's the system. They have too many patients they need to see. It's how they get paid."

"Should I ask how you know this?"

"What did Joan tell you?"

"Nothing," Jean said.

"I've been doing this a long time. Not a lot has changed, which is a shame."

"They could do better," Jean agreed.

Because of the holiday, parking was free, the gate at the exit raised. There were whole rows of open spots. She chose one right by the doors, no need to take the elevator for once. They masked up, nodding to the guard behind his podium, the sole person they encountered downstairs. The café was closed, the gift shop dark. They rode the south elevator to the ICU, where the nurses were too busy hustling between rooms to greet them.

Gaunt, his jaw furred with a downy, mouse-colored beard, Gene lay intubated, attended by IVs and screens. Jean pulled a chair up to the head of the bed and rubbed the back of his hand with her thumb, whispering as if he could hear her. The whiteboard on the wall confirmed what Kitzi suspected: he weighed around ninety pounds. After standing at the window and looking out at the bare treetops and apartment buildings for a few minutes, she left them alone and retraced her steps to the family lounge, where the football game was playing soundlessly to a room of empty chairs. On a round table in the middle sat the remote, pointed toward the set. She had no idea how long they would be, so there was no sense calling Martin and telling him to turn up the oven. It was past one, the turkey had at least two more hours to go, and then there was Joan's Zoom that nobody wanted to attend. In this room where lives would never be the same, her plans seemed even more insubstantial, as flimsy as Gene's chances (as Martin's heart), and she turned off the TV and texted Joan, not expecting a response, and was surprised when her phone dinged.

Miserable, Joan wrote. Tight chest. Hurts to swallow.

Her headache was so bad that she couldn't read. All she could do was lie there and watch mindless TV.

So, no Zoom then. It was easier, Kitzi supposed. The whole day was hopeless.

Try to rest, she wrote. Jean says hi.

She wanted to give Jean all the time she needed but couldn't sit still, thinking of the turkey in the oven and the potatoes waiting on the stove, and after watching the clouds dragging their shadows across the hillside and the buses lumbering down Fifth as long as she could stand, she abandoned the lounge and headed back to Gene's room. Compared to a normal floor the ICU was quiet, sealed off from the hospital proper, and before she reached the door she could hear Jean talking with one of the nurses and stopped.

She sounded calm, and rather than eavesdrop, Kitzi retreated, peeking around the corner of the nurses' station. When the nurse finally emerged, Kitzi acted as if she was just coming to check on Jean.

She was standing at the foot of the bed, looking down at Gene with her arms crossed as if she were cold. For a moment she didn't notice Kitzi, then, without taking her eyes off him, gently nodded. "Right. I suppose we should go."

"We don't have to."

"I could stay all day. It's better I don't."

Kitzi only half agreed but didn't argue with her. Jean took his hand, pulled down her mask and gave him a kiss on the forehead and gathered her things, sniffling. At the door she looked back.

"Thank you," she said as they waited for the elevator.

"Of course," Kitzi said.

As they rode down, she thought Jean might reveal what the nurse had told her, but she just rubbed her nose with a knuckle, leaving a wet spot on her mask. Maybe she was in shock, the news too much to absorb. It wasn't until they were driving—the car being more private, perhaps—that she said she'd asked the nurse some questions.

"What did she say?"

"Nothing good."

"I'm sorry."

"She was honest, at least."

"That's good."

"I wish they would have told me before. I might have managed things differently. Now there doesn't seem to be much of a choice, if I understand correctly."

Again, uselessly, Kitzi said she was sorry.

Was it better to know? At least then you could make plans. She couldn't expect Jean to see beyond his death, as if it were the end of the world. Already Kitzi was trying to figure out what to do with the house and the cats and the car in the barn. Where would she go? Kitzi could see them being neighbors at the Morrowfield or Weinberg Terrace, sharing a folding grocery cart and an Uber to the Giant Eagle, waiting in the lobby for Susie to take them to their eye appointments.

"Do you need to stop at home for anything?" she asked.

"If it's all the same, I'm afraid I don't feel very social at the moment. Would you mind just letting me off?"

Yes, I do, Kitzi wanted to say—the turkey was in the oven—but understood. It would be hours before dinner was ready, the afternoon a torture for all of them.

Jean apologized, and Kitzi reassured her. "Maybe I can bring you a plate later."

"That would be lovely."

Except the place was filthy. Where would she eat, at the piano?

At the sound of the car on the drive, cats came running from all sides.

"Do you want me to stay?" Kitzi asked.

"I'll be fine." She gestured to her brood. "They'll look after me."

Kitzi thought it odd, though she'd heard Emily say the same about Angus, and Joan about Oscar. People were sentimental about their pets; they'd project anything onto them. In this case it was just the scale that made it seem strange, and when she got home she didn't repeat it like a joke to Martin, who, to his credit, said he was sorry and offered to take her out for Chinese.

"Too late," she said, tying on her apron. "We're doing this."

She'd hoped to eat early so Jean would be home before dark. Now, with everything that had gone wrong, she was shooting for halftime of the second game. The turkey was resting, the stuffing done. She was just scraping the roasting pan to make her gravy when her phone dinged.

Before she could get it, it dinged again

It was from Arlene: What time is the zoom?

And then Susie looped in: I can make it if it's before six.

She had to laugh. It was either that or cry.

"What's so funny?" Martin asked.

"My friends," Kitzi said.

Partisans

Sarah's beau, Tim, was losing his hair and liked to argue politics, neither of which Emily found attractive. While he was a doctor of sorts, he was divorced and older, and he wore a sporty watch like a trophy. By dessert she'd decided that Sarah, who'd inherited her good looks and Henry's sweet nature, could do better.

"If the Democrats win both runoffs," Tim said, "which could very well happen, they flip the Senate."

"Even if they do," Margaret said, "they can't get anything done without the House, and unless someone gets assassinated, the Supreme Court's going to be 6-to-3 for the rest of our lives. RBG totally screwed them."

"Talk about a flip," Tim said. "We went from her to Amy Coney Barrett."

As the sole Republican at the table, Emily understood this extra dig was for her benefit. While she disagreed with the late justice across the board, she respected her as a woman, and didn't appreciate the mocking tone, but, outnumbered, thought it best not to engage. Just because Margaret was sober didn't mean she'd be civil.

Sarah kept quiet as well, pushing back her chair and asking if she could take Emily's dessert plate.

"I can get it," Emily said, and helped her clear, carrying the dishes into the kitchen while Margaret and Tim aired the usual sour-grape liberal complaints, as if the laws were somehow different for them.

"Sorry," Sarah said. "He's just nervous. He really wants to make a good impression."

On whom? she wanted to say. "They seem to be getting along."

"She's been good lately." She crossed her fingers. "He hasn't met the bad one yet."

"Let's hope he doesn't."

"I warned him."

"He must really love you."

"That's the test, isn't it—will you deal with my crazy relatives?"

It was supposed to be a joke, and an easy one, universal and told without malice, but later, washing her face before bed, Emily recalled their exchange with a stab and felt indicted, as if it applied not simply to Margaret but her as well, since Margaret was her responsibility. The reason she and Margaret fought, she'd come to believe, was that they were so alike—quick-tempered and unforgiving. Her own mother had been the same, prone to shaking Emily by the shoulders, screaming into her face from inches away. Once, when Emily snuck a dab of icing from the rim of a mixing bowl, her mother spun and cracked her hand with a wooden spoon, splitting open her knuckle, then cried when she confessed to Emily's father. "You two have to find a way to get along," her father said, as if he had no part in their war. Likewise, Henry had absented himself from her and Margaret's struggle, taking her side on principle yet providing no support or understanding. Of all her regrets in life—and, alone so much of the time, she'd faced every last one—these were her greatest.

While she and Margaret had tried several times to negotiate AA's Step Nine, it was too late to amend the past. She had to be content with today, with tonight and this brief visit. Despite the political diatribe, overall, dinner had gone well. She'd gotten to meet Sarah's beau. There had been no explosions, no tears, no profane accusations thrown from the stairs, no slamming doors or recriminations, no shame, and for all of these she was thankful. She closed her door, propped up her pillows and settled into her Agatha Christie, the memory of her mother at the sink and Emily—three or four—reaching up to take hold of her apron intruding on the scene she was reading. She fended it off, only to have it return, so that at the same time she was looking out over the raging sea from the terrace with the other well-heeled guests of the mysterious Mr. Owen, searching for the mailboat, she was by her mother's side in their kitchen in Kersey before the war, too young to understand any of what was to come, the two moments circling, merging as her tired eyes tried to process the same string of words that made less and less sense until she realized she couldn't finish the sentence let alone the page and, grunting, already half-asleep, she closed the book and turned out the light, banishing both.

Two Out of Three Ain't Bad

The Friendsgiving Peter had promised her wasn't at someone's house, as Susie had assumed, but a brewpub in Sharpsburg called Ethyl that had once been a gas station. The floor was poured concrete, the tables picnic tables, and it was loud. Besides his stoner bandmates Bernie and Max, she knew no one. The crowd was younger, drawn from the local music and restaurant scenes, the vibe what she might describe as bohemian if not outright Goth or Emo (Alyssa would know the difference), hip thirty-somethings with shaved and layered hairstyles and elaborate tattoos. They probably thought she was somebody's mother.

Peter and Bernie and Max were discussing a drummer they wanted to audition, and her mind wandered to Kitzi's Zoom, and Joan, and Arlene watching Angus, and Oscar, home alone. She had to ward off feeling maudlin, with the holiday. They'd pregamed at Peter's with spicy margaritas, and she noticed she was drinking her pale ale too fast. If she wasn't careful, things could get messy, and Ethyl wasn't the place.

It didn't feel like Thanksgiving. The bathroom reeked of weed, and everybody was dancing. The DJ was spinning cheesy singles from her girlhood—Kenny Loggins and Toto and the *Grease* soundtrack—as if they were campy and cool now, each selection making her shake her head. It became a game, trying to name the golden oldie.

The punchy intro was familiar, a boring 4/4.

"Mock!" Peter called, along with half the crowd.

"Ye-ah!" Bernie and Max responded.

"Oh God, no," Susie said.

"Ing!"

"It's so dumb."

"Ye-ah."

"Bird!"

"Dumb and Dumber," Peter said.

"Ye-ah."

"It's great," he said.

"Yeah!"

"Is it?"

"Ye-ah."

Before she could protest that she was too old, he pulled her onto the floor, leaving Bernie and Max standing there. He took her hand and spun her, then spun her back again, catching her against him, the two of them nose to nose. She shouldn't have been surprised at how easily he moved. He was a musician, used to feeling the beat. At weddings she had to shame Richard into dancing. It was nice to be asked for once, by someone who actually knew how.

They stayed for "Jessie's Girl" and "Maneater," which Peter turned into a silly pantomime, pretending to run and hide while she bared her teeth and clawed the air, sure that she looked like an idiot.

Back at the table they drained their beers.

"Another?"

"We should get something to eat," she said.

"Besides me, you mean."

"Yes," she said. "That is what I meant."

Outside, permanently parked against the railroad tracks, its windows fogged, sat an old Greyhound bus converted into a food truck. Because these were chefs cooking for other chefs, they had turkey or tofu tostadas with a chestnut–cornbread stuffing and cranberry gelée, a chive mashed-potato churro, and fried pumpkin pie on a stick to finish—each dish clever and delicious, but, like the party, not at all what she was expecting. The plates were the kind you might find in a grade school cafeteria, beige plastic sectioned like a pie chart. She sent a picture to Alyssa with the caption: Idk.

Fancy, Alyssa replied, 🦃 ♡.

After dinner they put on their jackets and went outside and climbed the right-of-way up to the tracks and got high with Bernie and Max and one of the bartenders, glancing both ways for trains while drinking in the view of the river, then came back and danced some more. The oldies were gone, replaced by what she assumed was trance—spacy, looping synths underpinned by a gentle, steady pulsing. The weed was stronger than the homegrown she was used to and she felt like she was floating over the scene, remote, her mind silent. The song went on and on, a relentless groove that stretched forever. Peter was sweating, laughing. Her back hurt, but she didn't want to complain, and when they finally took a break, she dug in her purse and washed down four Aleve with a swig of beer. At some point they'd switched to an IPA, and her mouth was sour. What she wanted was a cup of coffee; instead, she settled for a glass of ice water from the bar. When she returned, the table was passing around a bottle of Fernet like a band of pirates. To prove she was one of them now, she snatched it from Max and tipped it up while they cheered. It was bitter as grass and she stuck out her tongue, making them laugh. The houselights dimmed and the crowd shrieked, the DJ pushing the beat so the whole room shook. Peter took her hand, and she followed him out into the chaos of bodies, closing her eyes and surrendering to the music, knowing she'd regret it tomorrow.

His Nibs

Arlene had watched Angus before, whenever Emily flew to visit either of the children, and while she honestly enjoyed his company (she still missed her fish), with Covid it had been a few years, and she'd forgotten how demanding he could be. He had his own schedule, rigid and totally different from hers. Even on the grayest day, he rose with the sun, ready for his breakfast well before she was awake. In the dimness he scratched and licked, making horrible slurping noises. He stretched, shaking off sleep, his tags jingling as if on purpose. The floor creaked as he moved about the room, then stopped, so close that she could hear him breathing. She opened her eyes and he was sitting there, staring at her. He whimpered as if he were injured.

"You are pitiful," she said, rolling over, but he was adamant. "I hear you. Let me turn my alarm off—if that's all right with you."

After her shower, he was waiting outside the bathroom door with his ears perked, on high alert. The more he tried to hurry her, the more she dawdled. She did her best to ignore him as he watched her get dressed. As soon as she sat and pointed her toes into her slippers, he ran for the stairs, stopping at the top as if he were leading her.

"Go ahead," she said, "I'm coming," and he bounded down, spinning at the bottom to face her, his tongue out, his stubby tail wagging.

It was this manic intensity that annoyed her, his urgency shamelessly self-centered. He was like a child, all raw need. She fed him every day, yet he raced for the back door as if he were starving, mussing the rug so she couldn't open it.

"Get off," she said, tugging one corner so the door swung free, and he shot across the yard, barking.

"Stop!" she called. "No one wants to hear that."

To his food she had to add a soft chew and half a pill for his hips tucked into a peanut butter–flavored pocket that left her fingertips greasy. When she let him in, he galloped for his bowl and attacked, frantic, gulping it so fast that he gagged, hacking, before diving in again. Even after he'd finished, he returned to the bowl, obsessively lapping the chrome as if he might have missed a crumb, his tags dinging against the rim, until she had to pick it up.

Now he had to go outside again so he could come back in and get his treat (though he'd done nothing). If she was busy with something else, he stood in her way, glaring as if it was his right.

"You're welcome," she said. "Now can I get my breakfast?"

He was such a beggar. Emily knew better than to give their dogs table scraps. It was Henry who was the soft touch, sneaking Duchess or Rufus something from his plate on the screen porch at Chautauqua. Since he'd been gone, as if in tribute, Emily had relaxed the rules, spoiling Angus with potato chips and peanuts and the crust from her sandwiches, one reason the vet said he needed to lose weight.

"Don't even think of it," Arlene said as he eyed her raisin toast.

He left to cruise the kitchen; she could hear him licking the floor by the dishwasher.

"Come," she said, and he zipped in, thinking she had something for him.

She raised her hands to show him they were empty.

"You're fine," she said. "Lie down. You're all done till dinnertime."

He ground his snout and shoulder against the couch as if he were itchy, first one way and then the other, leaving his oils and hair everywhere, and plunked down, claiming it as his.

"Thank you."

He was a rescue picked up on the streets of Cleveland; he was always scrounging. On the kitchen window she had a see-through bird feeder, a recent Christmas present from Margaret, and he ate the fallen seeds, shells and all. She found them, undigested, speckling his poop.

Saturday morning she caught him eating something in the yard—gnawing on it like a stick—making her come out in her slippers and tell him to drop it.

He kept chewing.

"Now!"

He did, fleeing from her as if he was in trouble. It was brown like a cigar or a candy bar, and, coming closer, she saw it was a piece of his own poop that had frozen overnight, glistening with saliva and scarred with toothmarks.

"In the house!" she yelled. "Go!"

He cowered on the porch, flinching when she opened the door, because he knew.

She didn't have a metal scoop like Emily, just a roll of bags that didn't protect her from feeling the hard, cold turd through the thin plastic. She winced, grimacing as she twisted the neck and tied it in a knot. From then on, she watched where he went and picked it up immediately, still soft and hot, rather than risk another Tootsie Roll incident.

It wasn't just food. He craved her attention as well, always underfoot. When she closed her book, he jumped up, trying to anticipate where she was going. As she made for the basement door, he weaved in front of her, looking over his shoulder, only to stop short so she almost tripped over him.

"I can't walk when you're standing there," she scolded, and he crouched, flattening his ears. "Move! Get out of the way!"

He was terrified of the basement stairs because they had no risers, as if he might fall through, and waited for her in the hall. He was her shadow. He had to be in the same room with her, and she wondered how Emily stood it. He thought he was a guard dog, barking at every little noise—the mail, a dish clacking in the cupboard, another dog barking a block away. He reserved a special hatred for the UPS truck, charging the front door whenever he detected its engine, even if it was just driving past.

"Stop! I can hear it. We like the truck. It brings us things."

Now he wanted her approval, sidling up to her after she yelled at him, looking for any sign of forgiveness. She knew he didn't mean to be bad, he was just needy, and ultimately she gave in. From a lifetime of watching married couples, she thought this was what it must be like to have a husband.

She liked him best when he was asleep, at peace. He lay with his back against the couch while she painted, its familiar bulk making him feel safe, and every so often she glanced over and caught him smiling, as if he were having a happy dream. Sometimes he ran in his sleep, whimpering, his face twitching, a growl starting low in his throat, erupting in a bark that woke him. He looked around, dazed, then subsided again. His snoring tickled her, she didn't know why. She observed him with a mix of admiration and envy. This was how she would paint him for next year's present. She took pictures with her phone, zooming in from across the room so he wouldn't lift his head and ruin it.

He loved the park—they both did. All she had to do was say the word and he jumped up and whirled in a circle. He was frantic, prancing and rearing on his hind legs as she struggled to clip on his leash.

It was Saturday, their last full day, and the whole world was out and about. She didn't trust her balance enough to take him on the trails that crisscrossed the sides of the hollow (the new bridge still wasn't open, the main path below cordoned off), but she was fine on level ground. He was good; he didn't pull. They made a circuit of the bowling green and the picnic grove across from the museum, pausing to sniff every shrub and signpost. He never seemed to run out of pee. He was surprisingly friendly with other dogs, letting them sniff him and sniffing them in return, his tail wagging. "He's so handsome!" the owners said. It was just the breed—everyone loved Scotties. Parents pushing strollers asked if their children could pet him, and Arlene was proud to say they could. He sat patiently while they grabbed at him.

"He's a wee good laddie," one father said, trying on a Sean Connery burr.

"He *can* be," she said.

The park was a sneaky way of tiring him out. When they got back, he drank a whole bowl of water and plopped down by the couch. It was past three, the sky overcast, and she decided to lie down herself. She took off her shoes and lay on top of the covers, curled away from the gray light of the window, her pillow cool on her cheek, and soon she was in the pottery studio at Allegheny, and Joan was there, baking something in the big kiln, except it wasn't ready yet, and then she was in a canoe by herself on Lake Chautauqua, the water absolutely still around her as if it were morning, the shore an unbroken forest, no sign of their cottage, no docks or other boats, and then she was in a jungle, following her fellow explorers along an overgrown path, hacking at vines with machetes, though she had no idea where they were going.

When she woke, he was sleeping right beside her. Hearing her stir, he lifted his head, rolling an eye back at her, and settled again with a grumpy puff of a sigh that made her laugh. She couldn't imagine Emily letting him on her bed, but she must have, and rather than kick him off, she closed her eyes and lay there listening to him breathe, trying to remember the last time she'd slept with someone. Probably a regular from her ski club, Curt or Bucky, bombed on Mateus and Irish coffee and Black Russians at some condo in Vermont back in the casual seventies. She'd never been successful at love, or just once, briefly, with Walter, their happiness so intense (illicit, doomed) that she still felt the loss, the rest forgettable lapses. She preferred sleeping alone, unencumbered, and was surprised at how cozy it was having Angus there, the two of them spooning as the day waned outside, the wind chasing leaves down the street. With a pang she recalled it was Saturday, the long weekend more than half over, as if she had somewhere to go on Monday. She'd have to look at the calendar.

She had her alarm set for five, but well before that her phone dinged, and, thinking it might be important, she rolled over to check.

Arlene, the message said, this is Joe Biden.

"For God's sake," she said, rousing Angus.

She deleted it and turned off her alarm.

"All right, mister."

He lay there, one front paw raised, and she rubbed his belly, then thumped it like a drum.

"Okay, get down," she said, and he did, preceding her to the stairs.

That night, as she readied herself for bed, she expected him to hop up, but he turned a few circles and folded himself down on the rag rug as usual. She told herself she wasn't disappointed. It was possible he'd join her later, like that afternoon, when she was asleep, and if he didn't, it didn't mean anything. Even he had his routine. She turned out the light and rolled on her side, one hand under her pillow. The bed was her grandmother Chase's, a full-size—in family lore, where her mother had been born. There was more than enough room for him if he changed his mind, but when she got up in the middle of the night to use the bathroom, he'd moved to the foot of the bed, near the radiator, where he stayed till morning.

Sunday there was no time to go to the park. Emily, making her getaway, had chosen a flight that arrived before lunch, so Arlene fed him and went to the early service—the start of Advent, Calvary draped in royal purple—then came back and packed his things. He watched her as if he knew, not doing his dance when she reached for his leash.

"Guess who's coming," she asked brightly. "Your favorite person in the whole world."

The flight was on time, there was no weather between here and Detroit. As promised, Emily called her from the baggage claim.

"How is his nibs?"

"He was a perfect gentleman."

"I doubt that," Emily said. "Thank you for watching him."

"He was very good."

"I appreciate it."

The Steelers were playing on Monday night again, so there wasn't any traffic. He heard Emily before she did, scrambling up from his spot by the couch and racing for the door. Arlene went to check, but the street was empty.

"False alarm, buddy," she said, just as Emily's Subaru turned the corner. "I stand corrected."

As Emily took several stabs at parking, he whined and leapt at the doorknob, his tail whacking the radiator, making it ring.

"Slow down, Mario Andretti," Arlene said. "You're going to give yourself a heart attack."

He wasn't listening, focused solely on Emily, and when Arlene opened the door he bolted for her, barking, capering at her feet and rolling on the ground, showing his belly as she bent down to pet him.

"I see you," Emily said. "Yes, I missed you too. Yes, I know. All right, that's enough. We need to thank Aunt Arlene for taking care of you."

"How's Margaret?"

"Good. *Very* good, actually. I got to meet Sarah's new beau."

"And?"

"I think they're serious."

"What's he like?"

"You'd like him. He's very opinionated."

"Not a Trumper, huh?"

"She seems to care about him, that's what matters. Stop. Yes, we're getting in the car. Thank you. We'll talk."

"I want to hear everything," Arlene said, and stood with her arms folded against the cold, watching them load up and go.

Inside, she locked the door behind her and set about getting some lunch. There was football on, but the Steelers weren't playing till tomorrow night, and she unfolded her tray table and sat on the couch, eating her half a sandwich and a cup of soup, not really watching, letting the commentators and the sound of the crowd fill the room. Margaret was fine, that was a blessing, and Sarah in love. She would see them at Christmas—not too far off.

She'd gotten used to saving the last bite of crust for Angus, and smiled at the force of habit. He'd trained her well. As she was doing the dishes, a squirrel hopped onto the back porch. It sat upright, flicking its tail, eating the fallen birdseed. "Git!" She rapped the glass with a knuckle, and the squirrel jerked its head around, dropped to all fours and scampered away.

The game went on, like the day, gray and monotonous. She toed off her slippers and draped a blanket over her legs and soon she was horizontal, watching the TV sideways. She hadn't planned on working and felt lazy for wasting the afternoon. She had five weeks left to shop, five weeks till she saw all of them, but right now time was moving so slowly. The throw pillow her cheek was resting on—the whole couch—smelled of Angus. When she ran a hand over the cushions, his hair stuck to her palm, long black threads. She needed to vacuum, another job she was putting off.

"Not today," she said, rolling the hair between her thumb and fingers into a bristly ball, and tossed it toward the coffee table. It fell short, one more thing for her to pick up, and she thought of Angus vaulting onto her bed, the two of them spooning. Now the house was empty and she was free to do nothing. She had to admit that, like Emily, he could be a pain in the drain, but she kind of missed him.

Advance Directive Planning

Everyone expected Gene to die. Kitzi had been preparing for it since they'd intubated him, so when Jean called, sobbing, to let her know the doctor had taken him off the ventilator, she assumed it was a matter of hours.

"I'm sorry," she said, imagining how hard it must have been for her, and wished she'd been there. She was trying to let her know it was the right decision when Jean broke in.

"No, sorry, what I'm trying to say is, he's breathing on his own. I should have mentioned that to begin with, I suppose. Apologies. They're thinking the trouble with his lungs may have been Covid."

"Where are you?" Kitzi asked, confused.

"I'm home. I was hoping you might run me over there so I can see him."

"Of course."

She'd been in the middle of making the HD schedule for December on an Excel spreadsheet, and saved everything.

"What's going on?" Martin asked.

"It sounds like Gene's rallying. We'll see. It's probably just temporary."

She didn't mean to be cruel. These eleventh-hour rebounds were common, the body making a last stand, and, unfairly or not, because of their house she didn't trust Jean's judgment. He had advanced liver cancer. Getting over Covid might have cleared up some complications, but it didn't fix the real problem. Last week he'd looked awful. She couldn't imagine he'd improved that much in a few days.

Jean was waiting for her on the porch, the cats notably absent. When she got into the car, Kitzi could see she was wearing magenta lipstick, the purple striking against her white hair and pallid skin. Her eyes were pink from crying, and from time to time she removed her glasses to wipe away a tear with the back of her hand.

"What else did they say?" Kitzi asked.

He was breathing on his own and his red blood cell count was almost normal (not the white), that was it. Kitzi could see she wanted to believe this might make a difference and didn't contradict her. She knew from experience how tightly you clung to the smallest scrap of hope.

"I'm sure he feels better," Kitzi said. "It's no fun being on one of those things."

But in his room in the ICU, he didn't look better. Though he was off the ventilator, he wasn't conscious, curled like an infant beneath the blankets with an oxygen mask over his mouth and nose, his face tinged a grayish-yellow. The whiteboard said he'd lost weight. It was listed in kilograms, and automatically she did the math—85.6.

There was no doctor on the floor to explain, and rounds were over. All the nurse would say was that Gene was stable and resting.

They tried his oncologist's office and got their voicemail. Kitzi had a UPMC app on her phone that Jean could use to see his test results. Among the blood cultures and metabolic panels there was one titled ADVANCE DIRECTIVE PLANNING that gave her a number to call to set up an appointment with a social worker.

"Not helpful," Kitzi said.

"No," Jean agreed, as if she'd already weighed her situation.

They stayed until the nurse looked in and promised she'd let the doctor know they wanted to talk to him—an offer they had to take at face value. They thanked her, said their goodbyes to Gene and retraced their steps to the elevators, flattened and dissatisfied.

"I thought he'd be awake," Jean said in the car. "I was hoping I could speak with him."

Not knowing what they'd told her, Kitzi couldn't gauge if this was wishful. What wasn't, in her position? Kitzi understood. The truth could be too much; at the same time, she didn't want to lie. She needed to be careful. Maybe tomorrow, she wanted to say.

"I know," she said, and while Jean seemed to accept her answer, again Kitzi thought she was the wrong person to comfort her. Since Martin's problems started, she saw disaster everywhere, her imagination prey to a crippling fatalism, as if she'd lost confidence in the world. She couldn't reassure herself, let alone someone else. How did Joan do it?

"We can go early tomorrow," Kitzi said, "and try to catch them at rounds. How does that sound?"

"You don't have to do that."

"I think that's *exactly* what we have to do."

They made a pact. They would be there at the start of visiting hours and stay as long as it took to get the answers they needed. It was practical, something Kitzi could actually do for her, even if, in the end, nothing good would come from it.

Der Christkindlmarkt

Each holiday season, beginning with Light Up Night, the Christmas Market took over PPG Place downtown. Every year they saw it on the news, rosy-cheeked tweens in earmuffs gliding around the towering tree at the center of the ice rink, the rustic vendors' stalls bedecked with pine boughs and fairy lights as if Pittsburgh were Munich or Vienna. Like the Arts Festival, it was an open-air craft fair—catnip to them, devout knitters and picklers, lovers of funky jewelry and scented soaps—and an opportunity to get their Christmas shopping done in one swoop. And food! Carts hawked Belgian waffles and sausages and pierogies and pretzels and roasted chestnuts and strudel and wassail and glühwein and hot chocolate, and there was a biergarten with an oompah band playing carols. Like the hall of trees at the Carnegie or *The Nutcracker* at the Benedum, it was a tradition. They'd always wanted to go, yet, whether because it was too cold out or they were too busy getting ready for the holidays or their husbands weren't interested, none of them had ever been.

"We're going," Susie said. "Let's pick a date before the calendar fills up."

"And sooner rather than later," Emily seconded. "If we wait too long, we'll get too busy. I haven't even started on my cards yet."

"You're still doing cards?" Kitzi asked.

"Not a lot."

"The pageant's the eighteenth," Susie said, because she was in charge of the shepherds.

"How about the fifth?" Emily asked.

"That's next week," Arlene said, meaning it was too soon.

"Mondays aren't good for me," Kitzi said, consulting her phone. "How's the seventh?"

"That's a Wednesday," Susie clarified.

They glanced around the table, surprised there were no objections.

"What time?" Arlene asked, as if that could be a problem.

"Night," Emily said, definite. "We want to see the lights."

Should they eat dinner there? Only Kitzi resisted, the rest of them enticed by the prospect of not having to cook. She hated leaving Martin on his own. Lately she'd been doing it too often, but gave in. She'd fix him a plate.

They all agreed, none of them wanted to stay out late.

"What's late?" Susie asked. Everything was a negotiation with them. It was hard to reach consensus when they were so set in their own routines, but ultimately she got them to commit.

"Mark it down," she said. "I'm driving."

"Can you fit us all in?" Emily asked, because, of their cars, Susie's was by far the smallest.

"We'll find out. I'm joking. Actually it's very roomy."

At home, she was glad she'd pushed them. They needed to do things besides play bridge. Maybe it was because she was from the suburbs, but it seemed to her that they took the city for granted, or maybe, being older, they'd lost their sense of adventure. It was one reason she liked Peter, he was always taking her somewhere new. While she was thinking of the market, she reserved parking, locking them into the time slot. Her calendar said there was a full moon that night, which she took as a sign.

As for the pageant, her shepherds were a mess. Instead of well-trained members of the children's choir—the stars of the show, working with Viv—they were an ungainly mix of Sunday school students. The youngest couldn't remember their lines, and the oldest thought the whole thing was a joke. Saturdays they practiced walking down the aisle in a group and hitting their mark as the angel delivered its tidings of great joy. Even that was beyond them, they were so distracted, pinching and poking each other with their crooks, staring off into space and yawning. She read the part of the angel and had to break off her speech to remind them that they were out in the middle of nowhere in the dark and they'd never seen an angel before: it was like seeing a ghost, so they should be terrified, which led to one of the older boys pretending to faint, his staff clattering on the floor, getting a laugh. "Good!" she said, "let's keep that," but then the others started doing it too—copycats—and she waved her hands and made them all go to the back of the church and practice their entrance again.

Saturday she also had practice for Lessons and Carols—Viv, as always, very demanding—which made for a long day, and then when she got home and fed Oscar she saw on the news that it was supposed to snow Wednesday. Another sign, she thought, imagining how pretty the stalls would look, until the weatherman hedged, saying it might be sleet or even freezing rain, depending on the track of the storm, so they needed to keep an eye on it.

"At least it wasn't a shooting," Peter said, because there had been one at Light Up Night several years before that scared people away.

"What's worse, a shooting or black ice?"

"Can you reschedule?"

"I already paid for parking."

"Rolling the dice," he said. "I like it."

"It's not like we're going to Antarctica."

She contemplated texting everyone but didn't want to spook them if the forecast was wrong. It made more sense to wait. They could talk about it at coffee hour—except the next morning when she filed by their pew, projecting "Prepare the Way, O Zion," Arlene wasn't there, the seat next to Emily empty.

"She said she wasn't feeling well," Emily said after the service, nibbling a lemon square. "I'm going to take her over some of that good tomato bisque from Soup Group after this."

"I hope it's not that stomach bug that's going around," Kitzi said.

"It didn't sound like it. More like a chest cold."

"I hope she feels better by Wednesday," Susie said.

"They're saying three to six inches now," Kitzi said.

"Which means we won't get any," Emily said.

"I already bought parking, so . . ."

"We shall see," Kitzi said.

"I didn't know you could do that," Emily said, equally noncommittal, and Susie thought she was foolish for paying in advance.

She called Arlene later that afternoon to see how she was doing.

"Okay," Arlene said. She sounded fine, just a little gravelly. "I don't think it's Covid, knock wood. I don't know where I could have gotten it from. I haven't left the house in days."

"It's probably just a cold that's going around. Be glad it's not that stomach bug."

"That's supposed to be bad."

"Rest, hydrate. Emily said she was bringing you some soup."

"Thank you, she did." And then, as if she'd divined the reason for her call: "The way I'm feeling, I don't know if I'm going to be able to make it Wednesday."

"Wednesday's a long way off."

"I don't want to get everybody sick."

"Don't worry about it," Susie said. "We may get snowed out anyway. Or iced out."

"That's true," Arlene said.

"Feel better," Susie said, and let her go.

She checked the weather—still crummy. Oscar was watching her as if he could read her mind, and she tossed his Chippymunk down the hall. He retrieved it and sat beside her, grooming it with his tongue like a mother.

"You are a very strange animal," she said, earning a glare.

There was still a chance Arlene could get better, and that the weather could turn, but then Monday Kitzi texted and said Gene was back on the ventilator and she needed to be available for Jean, which left just her and Emily.

"I knew this was going to happen," she told Peter.

"I'll go with you. Let's go."

"You don't want to go to a craft fair."

"Not really. I would, though. You said there was beer."

"The whole idea was for the four of us to do something fun together."

"People get sick." He could be so reasonable, that Zen acceptance of everything. It was the trait of his she liked the least.

"It's okay," she said, "I'm done with it. It's my own fault for getting my hopes up."

Emily said she was still game, but the offer felt like a sop, lukewarm, and rather than drag things out, or, worse, attempt to reschedule, with a group text Susie canceled their trip to the Christmas Market, eating the parking.

When she got up on Wednesday, the sky was blue and she felt a furious and useless vindication. The front didn't arrive until lunchtime, tiny flakes sifting down like sand. All afternoon, sleet ticked against her windows, a thin crust of ice gradually encasing tree limbs and power lines, causing a bad accident on the Fort Pitt Bridge just before rush hour, leaving commuters stuck in their cars. The T wasn't running, and there was video of a bus sliding sideways down a hill in Baldwin. They couldn't have gone if they'd wanted to, Kitzi pointed out, as if this was a piece of luck. Susie could have argued that the weather didn't change a thing, that they'd already decided themselves, but why? As Emily said, there was always next year.

Helping Mrs. Mexwell

She needed a tree, a real one, not the fake kind Arlene took apart and stored in a box in her basement. It wasn't just the smell, though Emily loved that too. A tree brought back memories, each homemade decoration a story—Margaret's origami doves and Kenny's Popsicle-stick stars crusted with glitter. Everybody was coming for Christmas, and she wanted the house to look as it had when the children were little—eminently achievable, since nothing had changed besides her kitchen appliances.

Jim Cole had already strung the outside lights, a task Henry had ceded to him only after falling off a ladder. Now Jim was Henry's age then, though still trim from his obsessive bicycling. She tried not to impose on him and Marcia too often. In this case she had no choice. Kenny wasn't coming until the twenty-second. The train platforms Henry had built over sixty years ago waited downstairs, too bulky for her and Arlene to carry, but there was no point asking Jim and Marcia to bring them up until she had a tree.

For decades she'd found nice ones at the School for the Deaf, soft-needled Douglas firs trucked down from Quebec by a pair of brothers who parked a trailer by their basketball court and kept a fire going in a barrel, but during Covid they stopped and never returned. Since then she'd had to scavenge. Last year, on Arlene's recommendation, she bought one from the Boy Scout troop in Edgewood but it must have been old, because within days it shed its needles and by Christmas looked sickly. She really had no idea where to look. She didn't want a tree from Home Depot or Lowe's, and the nurseries out past Monroeville charged an arm and a leg. She also had to coordinate with the Coles, choosing a day they'd be there to help, another hurdle, since, when it was nice, Jim would take off and go biking.

She hated waiting.

It was hard, not being strong enough to do things herself. She took pride in being independent, and then a stubborn jar lid could defeat her.

One thing she could do was the mantelpiece. Every year the Friends of the Library sold swags fashioned from pine boughs, and every year, as a long-standing member, Emily ordered two for the mantel in the living room, as well as wreaths for the front and back doors. They weren't cheap, but they were fresh and smart looking, and the money went to the community fund. Invariably, in the hubbub around Thanksgiving, she forgot about them, so it was a nice surprise when she received the email saying they were ready for pickup.

She had books on hold too, a bonus. The Subaru was cold from sitting in the garage, and she was glad for her heated seats. Traffic on Highland was light, the road dry. Her goal, as on any weekday, was to get back before school let out.

Along with the greenery sale, the Friends held a holiday craft fair in the auditorium, rows of folding tables with local artists displaying their wares. Though she was tempted, she didn't have time to browse, and breezed through, pretending to admire the goods and avoiding eye contact.

In the far corner by a pair of French doors, a table with a metal cashbox served as the checkout. There was no line. A volunteer she didn't recognize wearing felt antlers and a snowflake sweater sporting blinking Christmas lights ticked her name off a list and handed a chit to a second volunteer who ducked outside to retrieve her order. The price was higher than Emily remembered—she'd cut her own greens when the children were little, Henry sawing down their tree himself in the snow and dragging it back to the car—and with her usual misgivings she handed over her credit card.

"Sorry," the volunteer said. "We don't take American Express."

She dimly remembered doing the same dance last year. Blunted, she dug in her purse. "Do you take Visa?"

"We do."

Another woman in a coat was waiting behind her. Emily gave her an apologetic nod.

"It's not going through," the volunteer said. "Let me try tapping it, sometimes that's easier, I don't know why."

She pulled the card out and, holding it by one corner, raised it like a wand and ceremoniously lowered it until it touched the body of the machine.

"It doesn't like that either."

"Did you try swiping the stripe?" Emily asked.

The woman tried to explain that the chip reader prevented the stripe from working, which made no sense to Emily.

"It's not expired, is it?" the woman asked. "No, 5/26."

"It's practically new."

"Let me try the chip again."

There was another person in a line now, a young mother with a sleeping baby in a bjorn. Emily tried to apologize to her as well, shrugging as if it was absurd. They knew her. She'd been a Friend of the Library for fifty years.

"It says there's a hold on it."

"What does that mean?"

"It means it won't take it. It could be fraud. It could be stolen. You'll have to call them and find out."

"This is ridiculous," Emily said, feeling attacked. "The whole reason for the chip is to stop this from happening."

"Do you have another card?"

"I have an American Express card which you don't take. Honestly, this is the dumbest thing."

"I'm sorry," the woman said, opening both hands to show there was nothing she could do. "You can pay cash."

Emily looked at her as if she were insane. She held out her hand for her card. Before she even opened her wallet, it dawned on her—by the same mysterious power that helped her solve the crossword every morning—that she had her checkbook.

"Will you accept a check?"

"Of course," the woman said, suddenly chummy, pleased they could reach a solution.

"Perfect," Emily said. 'What do I owe you again?"

The box was far too large for her, and the other volunteer lugged it to the car, standing with it propped on her thigh while

Emily popped the back. Normally Emily would have tipped her, but after the battle she'd just had, she thought not.

Driving home, still puzzling over her card being declined, she tried to recall the last time she'd used it—the Waterworks Giant Eagle, probably, except it had never left her hands. Two weeks ago, she and Arlene had gone Dutch at the crepe place. She could see her card tucked into the leather bill folder, and imagined the server ducking below the register and taking a picture of it with her phone. She'd bought cookies for bridge club at Prantl's, and port at the state store, plus she'd been doing a lot of Christmas shopping online. Really, anyone could have it.

The first thing she did when she got home was call the number on the back.

A recording answered and began asking her for information, each successive question provoking her further.

"Agent," she said. "Agentagentagentagentagent."

"All of our representatives are currently busy. We apologize for the inconvenience. Due to excessive call volume, wait times may be longer than normal. Your wait time is: *twenty-six* minutes. Please press one to leave a message, or stay on the line to be connected with the next available representative."

She stayed on the line, sitting there bristling at the tinny hold music, her sighs amplified by the earpiece. She could go out to the car and cut open the box and start bringing things in one by one, but she was afraid she'd be disconnected, and then, when she finally got through, she couldn't make out the man's name on the other end.

"Thenk you, Mrs. Mexwell," he said, clearly not American. "What may I help you with today?" The line was crackly, there were other voices in the background, and for a moment she was afraid it was a scam like the ones she'd seen on TV, even though she'd called the number printed on her card.

After verifying the information she'd already punched in, he said there was some activity on her card that had been flagged as suspicious by their fraud protection department. He needed to ask her specifically about two transactions made last night. The first was a charge for $1.13 at a McDonald's in Wilkes-Barre. The second was at a BestBuy in Scranton for $2,484.96. Could she confirm that she'd made these purchases?

"I did not," she said, as if she were on the witness stand.

"Thenk you, Mrs. Mexwell. I will let our fraud protection department know that these were fraudulent charges."

"How did this happen?" she asked, thinking someone must have either stolen her passcode or forged her signature, and that they were probably on camera at these places.

He would only say that the fraud protection team at Visa were glad they'd identified the problem early and that she wouldn't be charged for the purchases. She should receive her new card in the mail in two to three weeks. She could go ahead and dispose of her old one.

"May I help you with anything else today, Mrs. Mexwell?"

"No," she said, wishing she knew his name. "Thank you. You've been very helpful."

"It is my pleasure, Mrs. Mexwell. Have a good day."

While she was speaking with him she was calm—the effect, perhaps, of his officious diction—but once she got off the phone, her anger returned, along with the shame of acting badly at the library, where people knew her. One by one she brought the swags and wreaths in, Angus trailing her dutifully, and arranged them in their customary places, but the unpleasantness had cast a pall over the day. She needed to get started on her Christmas cards and pack all of her presents that had to go in the mail and figure out her menus for the week. And she still didn't have a tree.

Snow Much Fun

Drowsing, in the middle of a dream set in their old house on Mellon Street (her clothes, strangely, Victorian, as if it were a period piece), Arlene woke to an insistent beeping like a truck backing up that she identified—but only after a prolonged moment of confusion, understanding that she'd fallen asleep on the couch again—as the smoke alarm. Above her, smoke hung in veils from the ceiling, acrid as burnt plastic, a gray scrim shot through with sunlight from outside, and she scrambled to her feet, coughing, her movements stirring the fog around her, and dashed for the kitchen, where a flame surged beneath a charred and empty pot. The black handle had melted and stuck to the stovetop like a slug, the only thing that stopped her, in her panic, from grabbing it with her bare hand. She used a hot pad to turn the burner off and moved the ruined pot to the sink.

"That was not smart," she said, as if someone else had done it.

The alarm wouldn't stop no matter how hard she waved the dishtowel at it, and finally she had to stand on a chair and pull the battery out.

In the rustic Pennsylvania Dutch spoon rest sat a soup spoon holding a shallow puddle of what appeared to be hot chocolate. She had no recollection of putting it on, but she must have—and long enough to boil off the liquid. The missing time was as terrifying as the fire, and as she went around the house, propping open the storm doors and raising the windows to air the place out, she tried to formulate a plan to prevent it from ever happening again and came up with nothing.

Near the end of her life, her grandmother Chase had mixed up her words, asking Arlene or her mother for a violin to blow her nose. She confused Henry with her dead son Henry, killed in the First World War. They shared a bathroom at the end of the hall, her dentures soaking overnight in a glass beside the sink. She wasn't supposed to leave the house by herself for fear she would wander away (the police once found her on the trolley, headed downtown), and when Arlene and Henry came home from school she'd be lurking in the front hall, waiting for them to open the door to make her escape. Arlene had feared her as if she were dangerous, an unpredictable, brain-damaged lunatic. Now, softened by self-pity, she realized how cruel she'd been, and wondered how the children would remember her.

The smoke still hung from the ceiling. Even with the windows open, there was no breeze, and she brought up a fan from the basement and set it to oscillate, dispersing the cloud. She lit a cigarette to help with the smell—electrical, like wires burning, or maybe just metal. The pot itself was melted. She ran cold water in it and let it sit a while before throwing it in the garbage. It was a shame; it was a nice size. She'd have to go over to Tar-jay, as Susie called it, and find a replacement.

"What a mess," she said, frowning at the taffy-like handle and dark scorch marks on the enamel. She wanted to lie down on the couch again, but dug under the sink for the can of Comet and a green pad.

She was able to get most of it off, and was just finishing when the phone rang.

"How goes it?" Kitzi asked, checking in to remind her that she was delivering gift baskets to the hospitals tomorrow.

Here was a chance to make a joke of it, self-deprecating and relatable. Who hadn't fallen asleep on the couch and burned something?

"Good," Arlene said. "How's Gene doing?"

"Who knows. He's on, he's off. If he was DNR, it would be simple, but he's full code, so every time he crashes, they bring him back."

"Is he conscious?"

"It doesn't matter, he's so zonked-out. I feel bad for Jean."

"That's hard," Arlene said.

She wasn't DNR because of her low blood pressure, and when she'd gotten off she realized that if it were a real fire she could have just pressed her Star Alert. She fished the pendant out of her blouse and held it in her palm like a talisman, the power to summon help a click away. She'd entirely forgotten she was wearing it.

In the days following her scare, she told no one, scrubbing the kitchen as if it were a crime scene. She took the drapes in to the dry cleaners and vacuumed the rugs. She blasted the couch and chairs with Febreze, going through a whole three-pack, and then, when that wasn't enough, placed holiday-flavored Glade PlugIns around the downstairs (she didn't trust herself with candles), so instead of fried wiring the house smelled of pine and cranberry and Christmas cookies, the mingled scents masking the evidence, the undernote of smoke so subtle that at times, with her slippage, even she was unaware there had been a fire. The only way someone might suspect would be if they came over to visit her, but, as she rightly calculated, there was no danger of that happening.

Surprise Inside

No one told her Trader Joe's sold Advent calendars for cats. She found out on her own, rolling her cart down the pet food aisle. She saw the bingo-like jumble of numbers on the box and stopped, her face betraying first confusion and concern and then honest astonishment. The picture on the front was a Christmas tree of cats. Behind each cardboard door waited salmon and dried seaweed treats in holiday shapes. It made absolutely no sense, and she knew she had to buy one for Oscar. They were on clearance because the month had already started, but honestly, as she bragged to Joan, she would have paid full price.

He could be so fickle. Sometimes when she opened the door he was there to greet her, and sometimes, like today, he was off in the back of the apartment and wouldn't emerge for hours.

"Yoo-hoo, look what I bought for you," she cooed, shaking the box at the hallway.

He came running, then sat in the middle of the kitchen floor, feigning disinterest, until she set the box flat on the counter and cut along the dotted lines for Day 1 with a steak knife. Even before she opened the door and pinched out the crinkly plastic bag, he was beside her, poking his nose in, his whiskers twitching.

"Can I help you with something?"

In the bag were three stars the color of a Tootsie Roll. They were larger than his normal kibble, and hard. He mewed and clawed at the plastic as if telling her to hurry up, and she tore it open and dumped the stars in his dish.

He sniffed them, tentative, though she could smell them from where she stood—a noxious mix of petroleum and fish oil. They were too big to get his jaws around. After batting one onto the floor, he tried turning his head sideways to pick it up, but couldn't, and she cut it into pieces for him.

He gnawed on it with his mouth open and his eyes squeezed shut.

"Like a rock, huh?"

He stuck with it, and soon he was chewing normally. He went back for another piece, and another. She cut up the other two, and when he was done he hopped onto the counter and rubbed his face and neck against the box.

"Okay," she said, "I guess we like seaweed."

He pawed the box.

"Nope, that's enough. Maybe later."

She set the box upright by the toaster so they could watch his progress. Over the next week they could catch up by doing one in the morning and one at night, but then, not ten minutes later, when she came back from flipping the laundry, the box was on the floor, a hole torn in its back, and Oscar was nowhere to be seen.

"Not cool," she said.

He hadn't gotten into any of the treats, and she took the box with her to search for him. The apartment wasn't that big; there were only a few places he hid when he was in trouble. She found him under her bed, hunched in the far corner where she couldn't reach him. She didn't yell. All she had to do was show him the box and he shied back as if it were cursed.

"That's bad," she said. "You don't do that. Shame on you."

She left him there and stashed the box on the top shelf of the kitchen cupboard, sad that she wouldn't be able to display it to count down the days.

She didn't see him again until dinnertime, both of them wary, like her and Alyssa after one of their blowups. He ate, and had a big drink. She didn't offer him a treat and he didn't ask for one.

The truce held. They were watching a documentary about Medicare and the cost of prescription drugs when a smell that had obviously come from him assaulted her. It was the same fishy stench of the treats, but hot and concentrated. He was oblivious, dozing.

"Oh my God," she said, holding her nose and waving a magazine to fan it his way. "Go. I mean it. Go fart somewhere else."

He jumped down and stalked off, stopping to glance back at her, more hurt than offended, and she thought that it wasn't his fault. New foods could be a challenge. It had been true with her dogs too, Beggin' Strips and Pup-Peroni making them gassy. She was the one who'd bought the thing.

Later, he woke her in the middle of the night, crying in the hallway. She held her breath, listening, but he'd stopped. The elevator whirred up the shaft; the doors rolled open, closed, and it descended again. The Kenmawr never slept. Someone several floors above her flushed, water rushing behind the wall. Then, for a long time, nothing. Blocks away, a bus dieseled past. She heard him slopping water in the kitchen and figured he was fine and let herself drift off again, dreaming, as she often did, of the woods behind her old house.

In the morning she saw why he'd been crying. He'd had diarrhea and hadn't made it to his litter box, leaving a mucky trail on the carpet dotted with undigested bits of the stars like chocolate chips.

"It's okay," she said, because she could see he was mortified. "That's my fault."

He stayed away while she scrubbed at the rug with a sponge and sprayed Renuzit on the stain. It had to dry before she could vacuum, so she went into the kitchen and took down the calendar. She had to pull off the top of the trash can to fit the box in, and then Oscar sat there meowing as if it held a body.

"Nope," she said, "we're not doing that," and yanked the bag out and carried it down the hall, opened the chute and stuffed it in. From the fourth floor it took a couple seconds to hit bottom, the impact, for once, unsatisfying.

"All done," she said.

The Animal People

Martin had just handed her his glasses and his shirt and was pulling on his hospital johnny when her phone buzzed.

It was Jean. Normally, Kitzi would have answered but they'd waited an hour for Dr. Guralnick's PA, and they were both nervous about this new set of tests. Martin wasn't the best listener, tending to accept anything the doctors said without question. He needed her there as a second pair of ears. As terrible as it sounded, she didn't answer Jean because she didn't want to be distracted.

"Let me guess," Martin said. "Joan."

"Close."

"You can answer it."

"It can wait."

Except Kitzi couldn't. As they sat there in the windowless examination room with its locked sharps box and hand sanitizer dispenser, the temptation to peek was too great, and she pulled up her voicemail. It was time-stamped twelve minutes ago; that's how long she'd held out.

The transcription called her Kitty, which she hated. Jean didn't want to be a bother but thought she ought to know the police were there, the animal people. They were inside her house right now, without a warrant. Did Kitzi know any lawyers?

She tapped Play and listened to it, not trusting the words. Who'd reported her? They didn't have any neighbors.

"Oh no."

"What?" Martin asked.

"They're going to take her cats. They're there right now."

"Oh no," he echoed.

"I bet it was one of the EMTs. No one else has been inside."

"Does she need help?"

"I'm sure she does."

"Go," he said. "I'll be fine."

"Let me call around first. You're always telling me to delegate."

Her first thought was Emily (she didn't trust Arlene), but Susie was the closest and had both been married to a lawyer and used one for her divorce. According to the schedule, she was delivering Christmas cookies to former HDs in nursing homes.

She didn't answer—it was possible she was driving—and rather than leave a message and wait for her to call back, Kitzi moved on to Emily, who was free, supposedly, though she didn't pick up either.

"Come on."

"Go," he said. "I've got my phone."

"I don't know how long I'll be."

"I'm not going anywhere."

"Ask her about the AFib and why it's not consistent."

"I will. Good luck."

"Thanks."

Before exiting the parking garage, she called Jean to see what the situation was.

"They say I don't feed them, and that's not true, I feed them every day. It's ridiculous."

"Are you being arrested?"

"For what, having too many cats? That's not a crime now, is it?"

Even if Jean would listen to her, Kitzi didn't have time to explain. "Stay there and don't say anything to them. I'm on my way."

How had she not predicted this? From the moment she stepped inside the house, she knew no one could live like that. They would take the cats and tear the place down and Gene would die, leaving Jean with nothing. Where would she go—a nursing home?

Flying up the drive, she pictured the turnaround jammed with police SUVs and Animal Control vans, a parade of gloved wranglers bringing out cages. Instead, there was a single compact car sporting a round county magnet on the door. On the porch, Jean and a Black policewoman with a military haircut, wraparound sunglasses and a clipboard were talking—the one thing Kitzi had asked her not to do.

"Hi!" Kitzi said, waving to show she was friendly. HUMANE POLICE, the woman's badge read. "I'm Kitzi, I'm a friend of Jean's."

"I was just telling Mrs. Sokolov she has one week to provide sanitary living conditions and proof of vaccination for her animals or she's going to be charged with neglect."

"A week." She glanced at the house as if it were impossible. "Her husband's in the hospital."

"So she said, and I appreciate that. If there's some alternate arrangements you need to make, now would be the time."

"I don't see why," Jean said. "They're perfectly happy here. They have everything they need. They have food, water—"

"Ma'am," the officer said, holding up one finger to stop her. "It is my judgment that that is not the case. This house is clearly unsanitary. Your friend here will agree with me. It may also be unsafe, that's up to Code Enforcement. As a mandated reporter, I have to let them know, so you can expect a visit from them as well. One week. I need to see tags and proof of vaccines for all of your personal animals. The feral ones I'm not concerned about. I understand a week is not a long time. If you need to make other arrangements, by all means make them."

She tore a pink sheet off her clipboard and handed it to Jean. "If you have any questions, the number to call is on there. You have a good day now."

Kitzi had many questions, but asked just one. "You said the feral cats don't have to be vaccinated."

"That's correct."

"How many of them are feral?"

"I don't know. Ask your friend."

Jean had no idea, but there was an easy way to tell them apart. The feral ones' left ears were notched to let Animal Control know they'd been spayed, so any cats with both ears intact were hers. She didn't know exactly how many she had, she said. She'd never seen the need to count them.

"What am I going to do? Do you think a lawyer would help?"

"I don't know," Kitzi said, looking over the notice, because that was another rabbit hole, and they didn't have much time. She could see, by a supreme collective effort, rounding up her cats and getting them vaccinated. The problem was the house.

"I think she's screwed," she told Martin that night. They were celebrating the stress test saying his ejection fraction had improved—his left ventricle getting stronger. If his numbers still looked good in February, he could get rid of the vest, and they'd allowed themselves a glass each of sparkling nonalcoholic cider.

"You said you wanted her out of there."

"Not like this."

"This may be the only way."

"Being forced to, great. What do we do about the cats? She can't take them all with her."

"Some places let you have cats."

"Cat. One. She doesn't even know how many she has."

"She can foster them out."

She thought of Susie watching Oscar, and Joan's apartment sitting empty, and before she could stop herself from picturing it, she'd moved Jean and her cats in, a clean slate.

"What's so funny?" Martin asked.

"We move her into Joan's. With the cats."

"No."

"It would be an experiment."

"Unh-uh." He shook his head.

"See how long it takes for them to destroy the place."

"I'm going to say one day."

"Not even. I think she lets them pee wherever. I just don't have a better answer right now."

"You've got a week."

"Thank you for reminding me," she said, and raised her glass for him to clink.

The Boonies

Joan was going to Longwood. A one-bedroom garden apartment that was perfect for her had opened up, and, aware of the demand, she grabbed it. She'd done it online, touring the place on her iPad, signing the contract electronically. They hadn't known she was looking, but weren't surprised. She was always thinking ahead.

Longwood, the next to last stop. With each passing year it loomed greater in their imaginations, like Death, or Heaven. As comfortable East Enders, inevitably they would have to either fight off or surrender to its respectable gravity. Emily saw it as a climate-controlled limbo, not quite real life. To Arlene it seemed like a country club without a golf course, the grounds impeccably neat. Kitzi, who'd volunteered there, couldn't reconcile the gap between the residents and the workers who took care of them, even as she dreamed of that very solution for Jean. Susie was too young, but thought she wouldn't mind being reunited with her Fox Chapel friends there in twenty or thirty years. It was like Florida, a land of no return. None of them expected to go without first experiencing some life-threatening crisis, and so, to a person, while they understood that Joan couldn't stay in her old place with her leg, privately they were disappointed, as if she'd abandoned them.

Once the semester was over, Darcy was coming back to help her move. She needed to be out of the condo by the new year, so it all had to happen fast. The apartment was smaller, and there was no garage, just an exposed parking spot. She couldn't take everything, and asked Susie to send her dimensions so she could choose which of the bigger pieces she wanted to keep.

"Oscar's going to love it," she said. "I'm having them put in a cat door so he can come and go as he pleases. The woods are right behind us, so he'll have lots of squirrels and chippymunks to chase."

"It sounds ideal," Susie said, jealous of her having not just Oscar but a patch of garden to tend. It was the time of year the new seed catalogs arrived, heralding the return of spring, along with Christmas cards from old friends, both recalling a richer, mostly happy past. She leafed through the pages greedily, circling perennials she thought would look nice, making Peter shake his head. The Kenmawr didn't even have window boxes.

"I hope you'll come visit me now that I'm out in the boonies," Joan said, as if they might forget her.

"Of course I will," Susie said, thinking it was unlike her, and mentioned it at bridge.

"I would if someone else drove," Arlene said. "It's a poke."

"It's twenty-five minutes," Emily said, shuffling noisily. "I can see why she said that though. She's used to being in the middle of things. She could roll out of bed into her pew. Is she going to get up early and drive in every Sunday?"

"Not in the winter," Arlene said.

"They have chapel there," Kitzi said. "It's very nice."

"It's nondenominational," Emily said. "It's not the same." She had a long list of reasons why she would never leave the city, with Calvary at the top. It seemed only natural as she neared her end that she should hold her faith closer. When she did entertain the idea of downsizing—Kenny and Margaret were always pushing her to sell the house—it was to a condo like Joan's where she could have her dog and her car and walk to services. She had the money, the worry was her health. Every time she climbed the stairs she knew eventually she'd have to move someplace single-level. If worse came to worst, she could always shack up at the Kenmawr and have Susie roll her over.

"It's something," Kitzi said. "Father John goes out once a month. There are a ton of Calvary people there."

"I'd miss the music," Arlene said, and they murmured agreement.

Emily was a forceful dealer, skimming the cards across the table. One shot off the edge into Susie's lap—the jack of clubs.

"I didn't see it," Kitzi said, blinkering an eye with a hand, and Emily kept on.

"I'm just glad she's getting out of that place," Susie said.

"Yes," Arlene seconded.

"Amen," Kitzi said. Being Joan's chosen successor, she wished Joan would have told her first, if only as a courtesy. Instead she'd received the same email as the rest of the HDs, part resignation, part valediction, urging them to continue their good work. She wasn't prepared for the finality of it. If she'd been unrealistic, thinking she'd simply hand back control to Joan with her notebook once she was feeling better, she didn't expect the transfer of power to be so casual and so complete. With no discussion whatsoever she'd become their new leader. It didn't matter that she didn't want the responsibility. It was hers now, and she would have to figure out how to bear it.

Emily finished and they picked up their cards and fit their hands together, Emily and Kitzi instinctively counting their points.

Arlene, Kitzi's partner, opened with a feeler of one club, took a sip of coffee and thought of the pot she'd melted the other day. She still hadn't made it over to Target for a replacement.

"So," she asked, "what's she doing with all of her stuff?"

Love, Emily

Among the Christmas cards in Wednesday's mail was a familiar red envelope addressed in her own once elegant hand to Luanne Beers in Delray Beach, Florida, stamped RETURN TO SENDER.

"No," Emily said, pouting. "Luanne. Oh."

Though she couldn't recall the last time they'd spoken—easily a decade ago—they'd been close in the fifties, when Henry and Luanne's husband, Rand, had worked at the lab at Westinghouse. She and Emily had both come from nothing, sharp small-town girls with ambition. In those heady, child-free days, they explored the city together, sharing clothes and dreams and secrets like sorority sisters. Every company picnic they drank G & Ts and made fun of the men playing softball, and every Christmas party they dressed up as Santa's helpers in fur-trimmed skirts and handed out gag gifts to the crowd. When Rand didn't get department head, he left to work for Rockwell in California. They rarely made it back to Pittsburgh. Luanne wrote, telling her about the children—their first had spina bifida, and underwent dozens of surgeries, only to die at forty-five—Emily reciprocating with tales of Margaret's and Kenny's struggles. After Rand retired, they invited her and Henry down to Delray, but with everything going on in their lives, they never had time, and for the last decade their only contact was a yearly exchange of Christmas cards.

She tried to recall Luanne's from last year but couldn't. She wasn't surprised she hadn't contacted her to say she was dying (Emily herself would not have thought to). It wasn't the first time this had happened. Her address book was messy with cross-outs.

It was also possible that she'd made a mistake. Hoping this was so, she went into Henry's office and opened the middle drawer of his desk to double-check.

No, it was the correct address. Delray Beach—she loved the sunny sound of the name. Why hadn't they gone?

She slid a nail under the flap and tore open the envelope, and there she and Angus sat, cozy in their matching red sweaters with the fireplace alight behind them. "Love, Emily," she'd written—no note, just a reminder that she was thinking of her. It didn't seem enough now.

Looking at the picture, admiring the regal tilt of Angus's head and her own queenly posture, she thought at least it was a good shot of them. It would be a shame to waste it, and she dropped the envelope in the trash and took the card out to the living room, propping it among the pine boughs on the mantel with the others as if it had been sent by an old friend.

Hundreds of Cats

Her plan was simple—round up Jean's cats and take them to get their shots—but when she started making calls, the veterinary hospitals she talked with said they couldn't fit them in before the end of the year.

"It's kind of an emergency," Kitzi said.

"Is it life-threatening?"

She explained the situation.

"You might try the Humane Society."

"That's who's making us do it."

The Humane Society couldn't take them either. They were understaffed and it was their busy season. They were swamped with holiday adoptions. The same with the Animal Rescue League.

"What are we supposed to do?" Kitzi asked.

"Maybe someone will have a cancellation. How many did you say you have?"

"Too many. Forget it."

It didn't matter, the house was going to screw them anyway.

"I was thinking," Martin said.

"This better not be a joke."

"How did you find my Covid shot?"

"Thank you," she said, pointing at him. When the vaccines were released, all the slots at the local Walgreens and Rite Aids had immediately been snatched up. Desperate to get him in, she started searching pharmacies outside the city by zip code, finally nailing down a time at a CVS in Beaver Falls.

The suburbs were full of kennels, except now they called them pet hotels. The higher-end ones had vet hours. She didn't mind driving.

"You're a genius," she said, giving him a kiss, because there was a cattery in Armstrong County that could take them late Friday morning. "Now all we have to do is catch them."

She knew the job was too big for just her and Jean, but she also didn't want to invade her privacy any more than necessary, and instead of activating the whole HD phone tree, she called Susie. Before she told her what the plan was, she warned her about the state of the place.

"No problem," Susie said, "just let me know when," and was there on Thursday with a mask and work gloves and hiking boots.

Jean had more than enough cages; the problem was they were buried under mounds of junk—storage bins and moving boxes and trash bags overflowing with clothes—so Kitzi and Susie had to dig them out.

"Careful with that," Jean said of a framed poster commemorating some long-ago concert. "The glass is cracked."

There was nowhere to put it all, and the footing wasn't good. Susie stumbled and fell with a yelp and scrambled back up again, slapping at her arms and legs as if they were covered with bugs.

Behind her mask, she looked panicked, and Kitzi wished she'd brought more hands. The cages were rusty, the bottoms matted with newsprint the cats had turned into a brittle papier-mâché. They pulled one free and a landslide of garbage filled the empty space, spooking a curious Siamese.

"How many cats can go in one cage?" Kitzi asked. "Eight?"

"I wouldn't put more than four," Jean said. "They don't like being crowded."

"Let's say six." She counted the cages, picturing how they'd fit in her car. "How many do you have, ballpark?"

Jean shook her head and looked at the trash as if it held the answer.

"More than twenty?"

"I really should know, shouldn't I?"

"I guess we'll find out," Susie said.

They bagged the newspapers and carried the cages outside into the clean air, where they looked smaller. Six might be pushing it, Kitzi thought. With the back seat down, she could fit at least five in her Honda, so thirty total. Some nights, coming home from the hospital, she'd seen Jean with at least that many. The question was how many were hers.

They hosed down the cages in the turnaround and set them on the porch to dry.

"That was the easy part," Kitzi said.

"Why don't we just notch all of their ears?" Susie said.

It did seem ridiculous, but Kitzi couldn't think of a better way.

At the rattling of a stack of mismatched cereal bowls, the cats materialized from their hiding places. Jean scooped kibble from a bag and filled the bowls, placing one in each cage. Unafraid, the cats flocked to the food, scurrying and pushing past one another for position. Six could fit easily, seven at a pinch. Twenty, twenty-five, and still they came, straggling across the gravel.

Kitzi counted thirty-seven. She would have sworn there were more. She was afraid they'd miss one—the officer seemed like a stickler.

As they ate, Susie used her phone to capture their faces while Jean discreetly closed the doors behind them, earning some mistrustful looks.

"I know, love," Jean said. "I don't like it either."

Cage by cage they went through Susie's pictures, Jean calling each by name, fishing out the notched ones with her long, pale hands until there were eighteen left—a spacious three to a cage.

"Is this all of them?"

"I don't see Clara, but I haven't seen her in weeks. They come and go, some of them."

"They all look pretty good," Susie said, as if she were surprised.

"I take good care of them, I do. I know the house needs tidying up, I'm not denying it. I just don't like being accused of something I haven't done."

"They need tags," Kitzi reminded her.

"And paperwork, I know. They never needed paperwork before."

Kitzi didn't want to lecture her. Jean had bigger things to worry about. "We'll take care of it tomorrow, I promise."

At her car, Susie said, "I didn't realize how bad the house was. She needs help."

"I think it may be too late for that," Kitzi said. "We do what we can do. Thank you for helping."

"Anything. Seriously."

"Want to take a ride to Armstrong tomorrow?"

"Sure," Susie said, and Kitzi was glad she'd asked her. It was a relief knowing she had someone she could count on.

The next morning, loading the Honda, she realized she'd underestimated how loud that many cats could be. When they understood Jean wasn't coming, they yowled, one setting off the others, a continuous round. Apparently they weren't used to riding in cars either, and by the time they hit Route 28, the interior stank of vomit and she had to lower the windows.

"Are you warm enough?" she asked Susie.

"I'm fine. Oscar hates the car too. I think most cats do."

They followed the river upstream, the sheer cliffs looming, giant boulders dwarfing orange signs warning of falling rock. How long had it been since she'd been out of the city? She'd forgotten the long views, the railroad bridges and little towns, the tank cars parked on sidings. She'd been so focused on getting things done lately, it was nice to let her mind relax, absently taking note of what passed.

"I think Arlene's losing it," Susie said.

"I know."

"Has Emily said anything?"

"She knows. I don't think there's much anyone can do."

They went on, the cats quiet now, hunkered down. At Ford City they crossed the river and 28 became a two-lane, worming back into the hills. It was hunting season, there were pickups parked in the ditches. The cattery was off Cornman Road, behind an old farmhouse. Just before the turn, they passed a line of white plastic-wrapped hay rolls spray-painted T R U M P in alternating red and blue, ruining her mood for a second, and then she was busy looking for the sign and the entrance and figuring out where to park.

The cattery itself was rough-hewn and new, a long, low-slung barn with a red metal roof and a fenced-in play area behind. There were two other cars in the lot, both with people sitting in them. The cattery was still following Covid protocols; only one client could be inside at a time. They were early, making the wait seem longer, but then, when they finally did go in, the vet—a woman not much younger than Susie, with a buzz cut and red cat's-eye glasses on a chain—had two assistants doing the paperwork, copies of which she presented to Kitzi in a pocket folder with her card.

The fee was under a hundred dollars.

"That can't be right," Kitzi said.

"We do these all the time," the vet said, waving off her thanks. "I hope you find good homes for them."

Stumped, all Kitzi could say was "We will."

"What does she think we're doing?" Susie asked in the car.

"I don't know. Maybe it was a case of Telephone. I didn't talk with her when I called."

She wanted to believe it was a simple mistake, a word misheard, an unthinking assumption, but as they retraced their way to Jean's, following the river back downstream, given everything, she thought she was probably right.

Catfight

Susie was working on a pair of socks that Emily would never wear when Darcy texted her from the airport to let her know she'd landed: Ty for watching Oscar.

Having spent her prime returning passive-aggressive backhands from Richard's ice queen of a mother, Susie understood exactly what she was asking. Not tonight—it was past nine, too late to pack him up and run him over—she was just softening her up for tomorrow.

Was it too early to pretend she was asleep?

She didn't believe Darcy actually liked taking care of Oscar, it was more about power and reclaiming territory, but—for her own sake, as well as Joan's—she wasn't going to fight her. She wasn't going to make it easy for her either. She silenced her phone, set it face down on the arm of the couch and went back to watching *Bridgerton*.

During the next break, she reached over and scratched Oscar's furry belly. He rolled on his back, ecstatic.

Screw Darcy, she thought.

He mewed at her as if he'd read her mind.

"That's right," she said. "Nobody likes her."

When her show was over, she checked her phone. No new messages. Darcy was probably still on the Parkway in her Uber. She could just wait.

She was almost finished with Emily's socks. All she had to do was bind them off, but her hands were tired and it was late. She set her yarn aside and switched off her gooseneck lamp, the cue for Oscar to abandon ship.

"Going somewhere?"

While she rinsed her wineglass and fit it into the dishwasher, he stuck his nose in his food dish and had a last drink. She closed the curtains in the living room, and by the time she turned off the lights he was waiting for her at the head of the hall. He had to go first, as if he were leading her. If she ducked behind the wall, eventually he'd come out and look for her. At the bathroom sink, brushing her teeth, she could see him lurking behind her in the mirror, and then when she sat on the pot he came in for a last head scratch. Again, he led her to the bedroom as if she didn't know the way, hopping onto the duvet and curling into a ball, watching her as she undressed. She wasn't so vain as to think he didn't do the exact same things with Joan, but while they were together she felt connected to him. She'd miss that.

"Okay, move over, Grover."

He liked to use her as a pillow, his head resting against her thigh a pleasing weight. It seemed impossible that tomorrow he'd be gone. The timing was awful. Friday they had dress for the pageant, and then it was Peter's big *Nutcracker* weekend, matinees both days. She'd be alone.

She checked her phone, and there was Darcy's old message.

Why drag it out? She'd known this was going to happen—he was Joan's—and yet it seemed unfair.

Np, she answered, he's a sweetie, set the phone on her nightstand and picked up her book.

She hadn't read two sentences when her phone buzzed.

She let it. Oscar lifted his head, then settled again. She read on, distracted, picturing Darcy in Joan's condo, and quit before she reached the end of the chapter, sighing as she replaced her bookmark and turned out the light. In the dark his body was warm against hers. Soon he was snoring but she couldn't sleep. Her legs were jumpy, and though she tried to keep still, she wasn't comfortable, curling her toes and shifting her hip, afraid she'd chase him away.

In the morning he was stretched out beside her, yawning and baring his claws.

She waited till she'd gotten dressed to read Darcy's message.

Lmk when you want to drop him off. Going out to see Mom in am.

"Nice," she said, because Darcy, by pretending that had been the plan all along, had leapfrogged her sensible arguments for watching him while they emptied the place.

She had to at least make her case. He can stay here as long as you need. Might be easier not having him underfoot.

Darcy was right on it, typing, He'll be fine here, ty. He's a helper cat.

You sure? It's np.

Appreciate it but want him to have a few more days here. It was his home too.

"Barf."

And it was only the fifteenth, they had two full weeks.

Oscar, at her feet, meowed for his breakfast, and rather than text something she'd regret, she went to the kitchen and filled his bowl with kibble and stood there watching him eat. She'd just bought him a new bag of food.

On the counter, her phone buzzed. Any time after noon is fine.

"Oh my God, chill."

She wasn't going to win this battle, and arbitrarily, knowing she was being petty—her afternoon was wide open—she tapped, How's 4?

No ty, just a thumbs-up like a middle finger.

Susie gave her one right back.

Hallelujah!

Saturday, while Calvary rehearsed for the pageant, Calvary United Methodist on the North Side hosted their annual Messiah Singalong, a Christmas treat Emily and Arlene never missed. Though the other Calvary's choir wasn't the juggernaut Viv's bunch was—the paid soloists were graduate students, the organist a guest—the church boasted exquisite Tiffany windows gifted by an otherwise forgotten robber baron. The concert started at four, doors opening an hour early so music lovers could enjoy the late-afternoon sun flooding the sanctuary with color. This being Pittsburgh, the weather didn't always cooperate, but the day was bright and promising, and Arlene, not the swiftest of drivers, left herself extra time to get to Emily's.

It wasn't far, fewer than two miles on streets Arlene had known her whole life, passing historic landmarks like Henry Frick's Clayton, which she'd led generations of students through, and George Westinghouse's former estate, where Tesla perfected his alternating current. Traffic was busy, last-minute shoppers flocking to Bakery Square in East Liberty, crossing off their lists. She'd taken out a boxed set of *The Messiah* from the library to bone up on the lyrics and sang along as she drove. *O thou that tellest good tidings to Zion, get thee up into the high mountain . . .* Her car was so low. She hated not being able to see around the big SUVs in ahead of her and gave them an extra cushion, which more aggressive drivers then used to cut in front of her, infuriating anyone stuck behind her. She followed along as a sinfonia opened with a burst of trumpets, staying in her lane, not paying strict attention, thinking of her painting of the cottage, hoping the framer in Shadyside would have it ready in time, and whether Emily would like the rustic barnwood she'd chosen ("Wonderful frame," Professor Aragon once said of the *Mona Lisa*), so she was confused when traffic stopped and she found herself at an intersection she didn't recognize.

SHERIDAN, the sign said, the word meaningless to her. The cross street was BROAD, equally foreign. She silenced the music so she could think, biting the tip of her tongue, but nothing came.

She was on her way to Emily's, that much she remembered. She must have missed her turn or gone too far, because, while the drab brick rowhouses and bare trees—like the cracked sidewalks and sagging chain-link fences—looked familiar enough for the city, she was lost.

When the light changed, the car behind her honked as if she were taking too long, and, panicked, by blind instinct, she made a right.

Sheridan was uphill and narrow, with chaotic parking on both sides. Above, a pickup truck was coming down fast. There was barely room for two cars. Instead of pulling to one side so they could both fit, it drove straight down the middle, honking, and she had to duck into a gap, the man at the wheel stabbing a finger at her as he passed, his mouth twisted with anger. It was only when a second car approached, blaring its horn and flashing its lights, that she realized she was going the wrong way.

"Sorry," she said, holding up a hand.

She used a driveway to turn around and coasted down the hill to the intersection. Thinking she'd backtrack and find where she'd gone wrong, she took a left.

Broad was a major street, its light poles trimmed with shimmering tinsel stars and bells and stockings. At the far end of a corridor of ugly new condos rose a great beige hangarlike shopping complex with parking beneath, a giant red bull's-eye emblazoned on its side: TARGET.

"Aha," she said, because even if she couldn't quite place the name, she knew she knew it, its meaning just out of reach. She was more intrigued than frightened, like a dreamer aware of being in a dream. All she had to do was wake up.

Seeing it as a safe haven, she pulled into the lot beneath the Target and parked. The red concrete balls by the entrance and the awful lighting—she'd been here before, probably many times. The knowledge was somehow comforting, and, struck by an idea, she dug in her purse for her wallet. She unsnapped it, and there, along with her driver's license and free senior bus pass, was proof: her red-and-white Target card.

She still didn't know where she was, exactly. Emily lived on Grafton Street. She could picture her house, but how to get there was a blank, as if her brain had erased that part of the map.

Her phone would have it.

"Silly." The answer was so obvious, sitting in her purse the whole time.

Once she saw the route they wanted her to take, the names came back to her from childhood: Larimer, Jackson, Highland. It was her old neighborhood; she'd roller-skated up and down those streets with her friends, Henry the brat tagging after them. From everything she'd read, her earliest memories should be the last to go. Now she was worried she might have something else and thought she really ought to get tested. Not that there was anything they could do.

Estimated time was three minutes. Even having no clue, she'd almost made it.

"But you didn't," she said.

Gradually the world returned, with its many connections. She knew the theological seminary on Highland, where her uncle had studied to become a priest before going off to the Great War, never to return, and the turreted Victorian mansions she and her friends had played hide and seek in, and Louise Pickering's place on the corner of Grafton Street, painted a tasteful mocha and dark chocolate by the new owners. Compared to East Liberty, it was striking how little had changed.

Emily was ready to go, opening the door with her coat on, so Arlene barely had a chance to say hello to Angus, who clamored by her side, bright-eyed, his tail whipping as they made their way to the kitchen.

"You be good," Emily said, giving him a treat, and they went out the back, tiptoeing across the stepping stones to the garage, where her Subaru waited.

"Thank you for driving," Arlene said, because after the debacle of getting lost, she was truly grateful.

"How is it out there?"

"It's Saturday," she said with a shrug. "It's always crazy."

Away in a Manger

The pageant was a disaster; that was part of its charm. The dropped lines and offstage prompts, the donkey braying and stealing scenes—any production starring children and animals was bound to have its unscripted moments. The sound was always a problem, certain characters muted and others booming, making it hard for the audience to follow the dialogue. Susie had tried to get AV to fix the levels in dress—unsuccessfully, clearly. Her shepherds had killed, the fainting bit earning a roar, but what everyone would remember was the lamb in Zelda Laughlin's arms peeing on her, the dark stain on her robe growing as she sobbed. She was only five, and with no hesitation Susie swooped in from the wings and carried her off, sacrificing her cassock as well as her back.

"Nicely done," Father John said as she passed on her way to the bathroom with Zelda, as if she'd made a great catch.

She was still fielding congratulations at coffee hour, which, predictably, was a zoo, the cookie table decimated, nothing but crumbs and decaf left.

"They know they're going to have five hundred people," Emily said, drinking tea instead. "It's not a mystery."

"It's probably not in the budget," Kitzi said. "It's the end of the year."

"Baloney," Emily said.

By the grand piano in the corner, sipping from a Styrofoam cup, talking with Father John and some of the vestry, stood Rabbi Myers from Tree of Life, who'd played Moses with a fake Santa Claus beard. Since the shooting, Calvary had opened their doors to the congregation, hosting the High Holidays in October, a gesture of solidarity they were all proud of—Kitzi especially, being from Squirrel Hill—though none of them had attended. He was a regular on CNN, an eloquent debunker of white supremacy. Like Moses, he'd led his people to safety during the massacre, a feat that lent him an air of heroism, rendering him unapproachable. Once, after rehearsal, he'd held the door for Susie, and she'd told Peter as if it were a brush with celebrity.

"Has anyone talked to Darcy lately?" Arlene asked.

"I was over there Friday," Susie said. "Why?"

"I just figured she could use some help."

"She was talking about hiring movers," Susie said.

"I was thinking we could help clean," Arlene said.

"That's not going to be for a while," Kitzi said.

"It should only take a day or two if we all pitch in," Emily said. "How are Jean and Gene doing?"

In such a public place, Kitzi needed to be delicate. She wasn't sure how much she should tell them about the house—the only real news—as if there were a chance it wouldn't be condemned. According to the orange notice Code Enforcement had posted on the door, Jean had two weeks to fix the long list of violations, which would never happen. After that, she'd be evicted. Kitzi was already looking at storage facilities, hoping they could salvage the pianos. She'd have to get a quote on the Rolls. Martin had started to look online but needed to know the specific model and year.

"Gene's still in Shadyside, still the same. I'm working with Jean on the house. The county's involved now."

"That doesn't sound good," Emily said.

"What about the cats?" Arlene asked.

"The cats are fine." She nodded to Susie.

"That's good."

"The problem is the house. If the house doesn't pass, the cats can't stay there."

"Where would they go?" Arlene asked, conveniently forgetting Jean.

Kitzi looked to Susie again. "I was hoping you could help me with that."

"I can."

"It's kind of a mess," Kitzi admitted. "We're just trying to take it one step at a time. The important thing is making sure Jean can see Gene when she needs to. The rest may be out of our hands."

"When did all of this happen?" Emily said, scandalized. "I must be out of the loop."

"Nothing's actually happened yet. They have to give us time to fix things, then they have to set up an inspection. Plus now with the holidays. It's not a quick process."

"It seems pretty quick to me," Emily said, satisfied that her displeasure had been registered. She still had yet to meet Jean, knew her only as a mythical figure who by some witchcraft held sway over first Joan and now Kitzi, who'd apparently chosen Susie as her lieutenant. Emily knew she should be more charitable but couldn't help feeling left out. An only child and a beauty, she wasn't used to being powerless, and she wished she'd pushed Kitzi to share the burden with her, ignoring the fact that she had neither the time nor the desire (let alone the energy) to take on anything extra.

"Let me know what we can do," Arlene said.

"I will."

"For Joan's," Susie said, consulting her phone, "the first is a Sunday, so try to keep that Saturday open. Maybe that Friday too."

"It seems a long way off," Emily said, "but it's not."

None of them could believe Christmas was just a week away. There was still so much to do. Susie hadn't even started on Alyssa's and Dwayne's socks. Emily needed to finalize her menus and put together her shopping list. Several of the children's gifts that Arlene had bought from Amazon were on back order; there was no guarantee they'd arrive in time. Kitzi had been so wrapped up in Jean and Gene lately that she hadn't decorated. The calendar was counting down, the days accelerating. Where had the year gone?

"All right," Susie said, because she'd been there since seven and her back hurt from standing. "I'll see you all in four hours."

"It is one already?" Kitzi asked.

"Congratulations again," Emily said.

"Yes," Arlene said. "They were very good."

The floor was a maze of tables and conversations. As they snaked through the crowd, looking for a wastebasket to dump their cups, at a busy intersection the rabbi yielded to Susie, gesturing for them to go first.

"Hey," he said, pointing at her and flashing his telegenic smile. "Good save."

Shocked and flattered—as if he were flirting with her—all she could muster was a head bob of a "Thank you" in passing, and kept going, Arlene on her heels.

When they reconvened by the doors, he was still stuck in the scrum, Jamie McMahon waylaying him.

Good save. She checked their faces to make sure they'd heard it too. Arlene gaped in amazement.

Outside, on the way to their cars, they replayed the scene.

"I'm surprised he recognized me with my clothes on," Susie said, and then realized how that sounded.

"Interesting," Kitzi said.

"I didn't know what to say."

"No," Arlene said, "you were right."

"What else could you say?" Emily asked.

"I don't know, something better than that," she protested, beaming.

It was strange, this exhilaration over such a small thing. It was just chance—or was it? At once she'd been seen, and singled out, her work appreciated, her essential goodness confirmed. After they'd gone, the feeling stayed with her. Walking back to the Kenmawr in the crisp winter light, she laughed, thinking Peter would never believe it.

Lessons and Carols

To all but the true aficionados, Lessons and Carols was an afterthought. That morning's pageant was the draw, families packing the pews to the very back, parents sneaking down the aisles to shoot video of their children sharing the stage with a geriatric camel and a brood of lambs making their debuts. Next week, both Christmas Eve services would be standing room only, the midnight crowd boisterous with old Calvary Campers and college kids home on break. Lessons and Carols was quieter, a respite before the gauntlet of the holidays—maybe the reason they loved it so much.

The mood was more contemplative—austere, even, the rare Anglican office eschewing Communion, based on the ancient Roman Catholic rite of matins, the daily devotionals sung by Benedictine monks in the silent hours before dawn. The ascetic life appealed to them, being for the most part solitary and celibate already, preoccupied by last things. Today they were foregoing the Steelers and Buffalo in the snow, a considerable sacrifice—for Arlene, at least. Instead of sunrise, they were standing vigil for the

Son, a pun Father John couldn't resist and Emily struggled with, taking the metaphor literally. The monks in their cloisters would always be rewarded—the sun rose every morning. It seemed like a cheat, too easy. Here, as they sang, night was falling outside, leaving them nothing to hold off the darkness but their faith.

"Where's Mr. Phonebone?" Arlene asked.

"We're missing a few people," Kitzi said, as if it were a surprise. She hadn't expected Harold and Mimi to be there—they were both getting over Covid; Arlene had just forgotten—but where were the Chamberlains and Polly Warner? She would have to make some calls tomorrow.

"No 'We Three Kings,'" Emily said.

"What's 'Jesus Christ the Apple Tree'?" Arlene asked. "I don't think they had apple trees."

"The Date Tree," Kitzi said.

"I don't want him to be a tree at all," Emily said.

"He'd be a sapling anyway," Kitzi said. "He's a baby."

"'It came upon a midnight clear,'" Emily said, and made a snoring noise.

"Stop," Arlene said. "I like it."

"Wake me up if I get too loud."

From the ceiling, like the angel guiding the Magi, came the voice of Viv warning them to silence their devices. Arlene was still futzing with hers when the organ pealed, bringing the congregation to its feet.

In the narthex, in a fresh cassock, Susie glanced over at Phyllis Shipley giving her nose a final blow and sticking the tissue up her sleeve for safekeeping. Since the requiem, the choir had been passing around a chest cold, its latest victim Viv herself. She'd hacked her way through the pageant in a mask, but trusted Cindy

Duncan to handle the lower profile Lessons and Carols. Without Viv to hector them, they chattered away like a class hazing a new substitute until Cindy raised a hand for quiet. She looked as if she might say something, a quick word of encouragement like Viv's rah-rah pep talks, and then the organ modulated and she was sending them down the aisle behind Father John two by two, careful to keep their spacing.

Compared to the morning, the place was empty, their footsteps echoing as they processed.

I look from afar and lo! I see the power of God coming and a cloud covering the whole earth.

Like the pageant, Lessons and Carols told the story of the Nativity by slowly gathering the characters, showing them wrestling with their skepticism at the beginning, then tracing their separate paths to Bethlehem, where the question of whether He was the Messiah would be answered. *Art thou He that should come?* Having just worked with the shepherds, what Susie didn't understand was how, after a single late-night visit from an angel—which seemed to be everywhere back then, like ghosts in Dickens—they never once doubted themselves. Even today, after the high of the rabbi praising her, she hadn't been able to get hold of Peter and sank into a mood. She needed to start on those damn socks, but her back hurt, and she ate a gummy and lay down on her stomach, setting her alarm for four. She dreamed of Oscar and woke up stiff and bereft, the sky outside gray. Though the matinee had to be over, there was no message from Peter. She tried him again and microwaved some pumpkin soup, checking her phone as she ate, and then later, waiting for the elevator, and once more as she walked across the lawn of the Kenmawr to church. It took so little to discourage her.

Arlene, closest to the aisle, caught Susie's eye as she passed, losing her place on the page for a second. The hymn was new to her and she had to concentrate. It wasn't just her; it was new to everyone. Like any good musical director, Donald Wilkins made a game of stumping them. Normally she would have appreciated it, but when the choir had filed into the stalls and turned to the first carol, she was relieved to hear the trusty opening bars of "Once in Royal David's City" and joined in with gusto.

Stood a lonely cat-tle-le shed, where a mother laid her-er baby, in a manger for hi-is bed . . .

This was what she'd come for, the easy comfort of the familiar. With the lights turned low and the candles burning and the altar decked with simple holly wreaths, Calvary looked the same as it had when she was a girl standing beside her mother and father and Henry, balancing an onionskin-paged hymnal on the pew ahead, using her finger to follow the words. At her age, now, she relied on that leap back to a richer, more innocent past to bolster her against the present. Lately time had been playing tricks on her. Often she was plagued by the idea, as in a dream, that she urgently needed to prepare for a looming task or occasion—watching Angus for Emily, or going out to dinner with them after the requiem—only to realize it had already happened, as if she'd been transported to the future, the weeks in between missing. Not Christmas, mercifully. This feeling was eternal and untouchable, beyond whatever was wrong with her, and as she sang, she lingered over the flickering candles and the wooden saints in their niches and the backs of her fellow worshipers, as if she might hold on to it longer.

They remained standing for the Bidding Prayer, Father John opening his arms: *Let us at this time remember in his name the poor and the helpless, the hungry and the oppressed, the sick and those who mourn, the lonely and the unloved, the aged and the little children . . .*

That's all of us, Kitzi thought, casting her lot with the helpless. She couldn't see how she was going to clean out Jean's house enough to save it, even if she could convince her to get rid of all her junk, which, according to Martin, a connoisseur of *Hoarders*, was doubtful. There wasn't enough time, and it would probably cost more than Jean had, and likely a good chunk of their petty cash. The alternative was to do nothing, which Kitzi thought might be the wiser choice—the reason she hadn't called any haulers yet—but one she feared she was incapable of making.

During the Lord's Prayer, Emily peeked across Kitzi at Arlene to see if she was reciting it with them, and she was, her head held high. While Emily liked to think she'd been aware of her memory problems from the beginning—the missed tricks and groping for words—she didn't know what to expect next, and was constantly looking for clues that she was getting worse. One of her greatest fears was ending up like Winnie McKnight in the locked wing at Longwood, unable to recognize her visitors. She'd be sitting in a bulky armchair, staring straight ahead with her mouth hanging open until Emily crossed the dayroom and said her name—smart, stylish Winnie, who'd been a shark at doubles and run the jewelry room at the church bazaar. She was in there for years, like a prisoner, eating when she was told to, growing heavier and heavier from the starchy diet so they had to bring her new clothes in bigger sizes until she finally died of congestive heart failure. It was Winnie as much as Henry who'd changed Emily's mind on euthanasia, an issue she now felt strongly about. She'd told the story more than once in Arlene's presence. As with so many things in life—too late—she wished she'd been more discreet.

Arlene noticed Emily glancing over to check on her—again, endlessly, and totally inappropriate here—and rather than stick out her tongue, as she wanted to, she kept going. She didn't have to remember, the words were indelible, apiece with the familiar rhythm. *Forgive us our trespasses, as we forgive those who trespass against us.* Did she have to include Emily? It seemed too soon. She was tired of being treated like the weak-minded aunt who might wander away, her face stapled on a phone pole like a lost dog, and yet, after her little misadventure, she had to admit it was a possibility. She could see herself on the Turnpike, driving to Stone Harbor or Ocean City, only the water stopping her. Every so often the new electronic signs that straddled the Parkway flashed a Silver Alert, listing a license plate, as if deputizing passing drivers to track down the doddering old cottonhead. One day that would be her, pulled over on the shoulder and placed in the back of a police car like a criminal, her name on the news for the whole city to see, her former students pointing at the screen. She didn't need Emily watching her for the smallest slip to feel shame. She was reminded every time she checked to make sure she'd locked her front door, or her car—three, four times, like someone with OCD. She couldn't be sure of anything anymore, but what hurt worse was that they saw her as unreliable, Kitzi leaving her off the schedule when she'd told her she was free. All she wanted was to be useful.

For thine is the kingdom and the power and the glory, for ever and ever, amen.

Father John asked them to please be seated, which they did, noisily.

The first reader was Gil Showalter, the senior warden, a good choice to open. Some readers were mumblers and could be hard to hear, but Gil knew how to project.

As Susie was trying to sit up straighter on the hard bench, holding her shoulders back, her phone vibrated beneath her cassock. Just once, signaling a text message, probably from Peter. It was a relief and at the same time a torture, since she couldn't look at it until the service was over. The rule was firm, and necessary. As much as she wanted to—not to answer anything, just to confirm it was him—she wouldn't do it if Viv were there, and she thought she should extend the same respect to Cindy.

As Gil went on about Adam and Eve and the serpent, her phone buzzed again, and she wondered if it might be Alyssa, except Alyssa knew she had Lessons and Carols tonight. Whoever it was, they'd just have to wait.

Gil finished and stepped down from the pulpit, and the choir rose, the congregation taking the cue, and Donald Wilkins led them into "Jesus Christ the Apple Tree." If the melody was childishly simple, setting it as a four-part round made it a challenge. Viv hadn't been happy with it in practice but wasn't feeling well enough to push them to perfection. Susie was glad Viv wasn't there now, because it was a mess, the altos tentative, the tenors blustery, burying them. She would hear about it from Cindy and dress them down next week. For now, they struggled through.

I'm weary with my former toil, / Here I will sit and rest awhile . . .

In the pews it was hard to follow the different parts. Few knew the song, and the organ drowned out the words. Around them, people stood silent. Arlene was the first to give up, humming along instead. Emily, who prided herself on being able to sing anything, quit after the third verse, Kitzi soon after that, closing her program and standing there between them, waiting for the chorus.

"Oh my," Arlene said later, as they dawdled by their cars.

"Yeah," Susie said. "That was a rough one."

"I don't see what's so Christmasy about it," Emily said. "Besides being about a tree."

"I can't tell you. Donald wants what Donald wants."

"Sleeps Judea Fair was beautiful," Kitzi said.

"*It came up-on-on a midnight clear,*" Arlene sang. "That was my favorite."

"It was all lovely," Emily said, "except the one."

"Of course that's all we talk about," Kitzi said.

It was human nature, Susie thought, walking across the lawn of the Kenmawr, careful of the tree roots. Peter hadn't been able to text her because someone had pulled the fire alarm halfway through the Battle of the Mice and they'd had to evacuate the place and then seat everyone again. The evening show had just started, meaning she wouldn't be able to tell him about that morning for another couple of hours at least. It already seemed a long time ago. The mood was ruined, and instead of how happy she'd been, now she saw the day as a series of missed opportunities—and a waste—when she knew it wasn't true.

15

Gene died Tuesday night—or, technically, since it was past midnight, early Wednesday morning. Jean had sat with him most of the day and there'd been no change, so Kitzi had taken her home. Around seven the ICU called to let her know he'd had a stroke, most likely caused by a blood clot, and Kitzi left Martin to do the dishes and drove her back over.

He looked the same, sleeping beneath a confusion of tubes attached to an oxygen mask, the blankets tucked up to his armpits, but the surgeon who spoke to Jean said she'd examined his scans and at that point there was nothing more they could do. They would make him as comfortable as possible—meaning they wanted to take him off the ventilator. The news didn't surprise Kitzi. She'd accompanied enough HDs there over the years to know the protocols. Even after the last month, Jean wasn't prepared.

"What's happening?" she asked, making the doctor explain it again.

His respiration was depressed, which was why he was on the ventilator. Instead of the sedative, they'd give him morphine. Eventually he'd stop breathing on his own.

"I'll be here if you need anything," the nurse named Lindsay said.

Jean looked to Kitzi as if it were her decision. "If we leave him like this, what's the point, is that it?"

"I think so," Kitzi said, trying to be reassuring.

"I was hoping he'd make it to Christmas, I don't why."

"I know," Kitzi said, to comfort her, but also because she'd heard the very same wish before from someone else, maybe in this same room.

There was a form the doctor and Jean had to sign, and then the doctor was gone, Lindsay taking over, exiling them to the family lounge so she could prep Gene.

When they returned, the lights were dimmed, and they could see the night outside. Without the steady exhalation of the ventilator, the room was silent save his heart monitor softly blipping. Gene looked peaceful, and Jean pulled her chair up against the bed and took his hand. She leaned over the rail, stroking his cheek and whispering to him.

The clock on the wall was digital, its red numbers glowing. Kitzi tried not to watch it.

Lindsay slipped in and checked the monitors. "Can I get you anything?"

"I'm going to step out for a second," Kitzi said, and Jean nodded.

In the lounge, before she called Martin to say she might be late, she thought she should let Joan know. On the table in the center of the room stood a fake Christmas tree, and as she chose a seat in the corner so she could plug in her phone, she remembered it was Maggie Woodwell who'd hoped Ned would make it through Christmas for the sake of their kids. She didn't want his passing to ruin the holiday forever, a fear Kitzi understood, but, cruel as it was, maybe because she'd almost lost Martin, she'd come to accept that death shadowed every day. She'd once thought she'd never get used to it, yet how many times had she waited like this while her friends said their final goodbyes? It was her specialty, it seemed. Ned Woodwell, and Marion Gill, Franny Blevins last Easter, Guy Peters and May Talbot. She'd reached ten when she recalled the marks totted up beside her name in Joan's notebook. Fourteen seemed low. Why was Joan keeping a running total? And what did it say about her that she'd never counted until now?

"Should I ask?" she asked Joan, when she'd filled her in on Jean. For a moment the line was silent, and Kitzi worried that she'd overstepped.

"Who does the hard jobs?" Joan asked. "That's who I want in charge. Was I wrong?"

"No," Kitzi said, picturing her choices. "Who did it before me?"

"Who do you think? It's what we do. What do you think of Susie?"

"For this? I don't know."

"You can't do it all yourself."

"Delegate, I know. So for Gene, McCabe's or Freyvogel's? I was thinking we could do a visitation next week. Who has a better chance of fitting us in?"

"The week after Christmas?" Joan said. "Good luck."

Beggars

If there was one thing Arlene and Emily knew, it was how to plan a funeral. They'd been doing it for decades, stealing ideas from friends' and neighbors' to make theirs the ultimate statement of good taste. The service, the music, the flowers, the food—no detail was too small to fuss over. In the bottom drawer of her secretary, Emily's handwritten instructions filled twelve pages, including an ever-dwindling list of guests. Arlene's was simpler: Rite I at Calvary and a private commendation graveside at Allegheny Cemetery, where she would lie to Henry's right and Emily to his left, their claims on him eternal.

In their blind devotion to the ideal, they merely assumed Calvary would be available, and Father John, and Donald Wilkins and the entire choir, all of whom they would happily pay the going rate, money not being an issue. (Emily had once flirted with hiring soloists, like the Dilworths had for Gretchen's, but worried that it might come off as ostentatious.) They also assumed the children would drop everything—as they would—to make the necessary preparations.

In Gene Sokolov's case, none of these assumptions applied. Gene had been an atheist, so there would be no church service, just a visitation at the funeral home. McCabe's was closed over the holidays, and the only date Freyvogel's could give them was the twenty-seventh, when a lot of people, including Susie, would be out of town.

"Beggars can't be choosers," Kitzi said, an inarguable truth Emily's mother had used to frustrate her as a girl.

It was already the twenty-second. Margaret and Kenny were coming tomorrow, and then it was Christmas weekend. Kitzi had given them a budget of five hundred dollars for refreshments, but every halfway decent place they called had been booked for months.

"How about Panera?" Arlene asked.

"We are not serving sandwiches," Emily said.

"They have salads too."

"Keep looking. There has to be someone who makes a quiche."

"They make a quiche."

"Someone nice."

"There isn't anyone nice left."

They weren't even sure how many people they needed to feed. They'd called the music department at Chatham to see if they could spread the word to Gene's old colleagues, but the college was on break and no one picked up. His obituary mentioned the visitation, only the *Post-Gazette* was on strike and no one with any sense read the *Trib*. Jean didn't have an address book full of friends and relatives she wanted to invite, and Kitzi was worried that it might be just them. Joan was coming, at least, making it a kind of going-away party.

Deviled eggs, meatballs, cocktail weenies in sauce, and brownies for people who wanted a sweet. A coffee station with water. It was discouraging. They weren't asking for anything special.

"We could do it ourselves if we had time," Arlene said.

"Don't," Emily warned her.

"I'm not finding anyone."

"I'm not either. I don't have time for this. Try Panera. See if they have a quiche."

"I know they do."

"Just no sandwiches," Emily said, but Arlene was already calling and had turned away.

Earthly Possessions

Gene's will was in a safe-deposit box at the Dollar Bank in Squirrel Hill. Kitzi didn't think there was any way Jean would be able to find the key, and was impressed when, after a brief search of her bedroom, she produced a small gray envelope with a tiny brass snap holding both the original and a duplicate.

"It may look a right jumble," Jean said, "but I know where everything is."

"I'm sure you do," Kitzi said, breathing through her mouth because of the stench.

According to the notice Jean had received, Code Enforcement would be coming to inspect on January fifth. With all Jean needed to attend to in the wake of Gene's death, Kitzi hadn't pressed her about cleaning the house, and each passing day rendered the hope more remote, as if Kitzi were sabotaging any chance Jean had of keeping the place just to spare her feelings. Kitzi liked to think she was being practical. That battle was lost long before Joan had chosen her to take over. She needed to focus on where Jean would go next, because as much as it would hurt her to leave, clearly she couldn't stay there.

"Watch, we're going to find out they're millionaires," she wanted to tell Martin, but was afraid of saying her wish aloud. If the house was condemned and Jean couldn't afford a place of her own right away, Kitzi planned to offer her their spare room. It was a conversation with Martin she was trying to avoid, if possible. He was already unhappy that she was coming Sunday for Christmas dinner.

"Do you know if he had life insurance?" Kitzi asked Jean on the drive over. "Maybe through the university."

"We both did at one time. It was a joke, one of us killing the other for the money, but I think it stopped after a while. I'll have to look. I thought of killing him, you know. With his pills. I thought about it often, even before he went in hospital."

She said it so casually that Kitzi gave her a concerned look. "You're not thinking of doing anything now, are you?"

"No." She waved a hand to banish the idea. "My babies need me."

"I like having you around too."

"I don't see why. All I do is make work for you."

"I think you're an interesting person. You've led an interesting life."

"I suppose you could say that. Gene was an interesting person." She sniffled and dabbed at her eyes with a tissue, blotting the tears before they could fall. "I keep thinking we need to go see him. I've gotten so used to it, it feels strange not to, like he's still there. He's not."

"You need to choose which recordings you want to play at the visitation."

"I can't, there are too many."

"I think people would like to hear the two of you playing together."

"The Brahms was always our favorite."

"I think we saw you play that at Chatham once."

"I'd think so. It was our big encore."

She brightened as they discussed Schumann, but when they pulled into the lot beneath the library and Kitzi wrestled the car into a tight spot beside a pole, Jean went silent again. She'd been up till three o'clock with Gene the other night and had to be exhausted—she was probably in shock—and here she was, ready to start the long bureaucratic process of erasing him and putting everything solely in her name.

Across Forbes, sitting tailorseat on the sidewalk by the old Isaly's, a torn flap of cardboard box advertising his hunger, a bundled-up panhandler shook his cup at them, forcing them to swerve wide as they passed. Kitzi might have remarked that in a few weeks Jean could be homeless too, and in that way broach the topic, but she kept walking, not making eye contact.

They would have time to talk inside. The tellers couldn't help them. Though there were six cubicles, only one associate was working, a younger woman who was occupied with another client and asked them to have a seat in the waiting area—two hard chairs and a table arranged with brochures.

"What else am I looking for besides the will?" Jean asked.

"Your own will, since you probably need to change it. The deed to the house, the title to the car. Any stock certificates or bonds in his name."

"Gene didn't believe in the stock market."

Disappointed but not surprised, Kitzi seized her chance. "What *did* he like to invest in?"

Diamonds, she was thinking. Gold. Real estate.

"Pianos," Jean said, as if it was obvious. "And some harpsichords. He couldn't resist a beautiful instrument. He had a wonderful ear, you know. It wasn't a problem until the college said they couldn't store them anymore."

"Where are they now?"

"In the house."

"Are they playable?"

"I'm sure they are. The one I compose on was built for Tchaikovsky."

"Interesting." If it was the one on the way to Gene's bedroom, it was in good shape, and aware that she was being crass, she wondered how much it would bring at auction. But then Jean would have nothing.

Done with her client, the associate ushered them into her cubicle, where Jean provided an expired driver's license and her signature. Kitzi wasn't allowed to go with them into the vault and sat wondering what else might be in the box. In theirs, Martin kept his father's collection of railroad watches, heirlooms without an heir, beautiful but useless. She had no clue what she would do with them, maybe offer them to a museum. It seemed a shame to let them go to waste.

When Jean returned, she was carrying several envelopes and a square maroon jewelry box embossed with a gold heraldic eagle. There was another client waiting, and the associate walked them out to the lobby, where they buttoned up their jackets and Jean tucked away her valuables before braving the cold and the homeless man, still rattling his cup as they passed.

"I found the deed *and* the car title," Jean said, back in the Honda, proud of herself.

"Did you notice if your name's on them?"

"I didn't think to look." She produced them for Kitzi to inspect.

They were both in Gene's name, which meant they would have to pass through probate. The funeral home had ordered extra death certificates from the county, but with the holidays, they wouldn't have them until late next week.

The Rolls was a 1993 Silver Spirit; she took a picture for Martin.

"I'm assuming you're the executor."

She scoffed. "Sorry, no. Gene knew how bad I am with that kind of thing, so he chose Francoise."

"Who's Francoise?"

"Our agent. His first wife."

"Ah," Kitzi said, trying to hide her surprise.

"She's in London. I let her know right off."

Why had she thought it would be simple? Maybe Francoise could help Jean find a place to live.

"What's in the box, if you don't mind my asking?"

"It's his medal from the Chopin." Beaming as if she'd won it herself, she opened the lid to show Kitzi a dull bronze disc bearing the composer's heroic face. On the reverse, etched into the metal, were Gene's name and the date, March 1, 1959. "He was eighteen. He played the 'Raindrop' Prelude and won, and the next day he defected. He didn't know a soul in New York. This and the prize money and the clothes on his back were all he had in the world. I was thinking we could display it at his visitation so people will remember how brave he was."

"That's a great idea," Kitzi said, feeling meager.

"And we must play the Raindrop. He did a really lovely version for EMI back in the seventies."

"Do you have a pen?" Kitzi asked, because she knew she'd forget if she didn't write it down.

"I do," Jean said, and handed her a gold one featuring the Dollar Bank lion.

Kitzi had been sitting right beside her in the cubicle and hadn't seen her pocket it, but she hadn't been watching her closely either. She wondered if that had anything to do with the state of the house, or was it just another mania, like the cats? And Francoise—so bizarre. She couldn't imagine Jean had always been this eccentric, and yet she didn't rule it out. To Kitzi, who considered herself boring and normal, she was fascinating in a very British way.

They turned before reaching Tree of Life and wound down through Woodland Road, past Chatham. As they pulled up to the porch, the cats came running. Kitzi reminded her about Sunday; there was no need to mention the disaster at Thanksgiving. Jean gathered her envelopes and Gene's medal and stepped out to greet her brood, cooing and bending at the waist to scratch behind their ears. She was like a teacher trying to pay attention to each of her students, praising them, saying their names. They weaved between her ankles; it was a wonder they didn't trip her. Kitzi watched her go, the door finally closing behind her, trusting she'd find a safe place to keep it all.

In Memoriam

Every year, both Emily and Arlene filled out a form in the church newsletter and made a donation to have Henry's name read aloud during the Prayers for the People on Christmas Eve. The lector said his name just the once, which they thought unfair, but it had become a tradition, and neither of them wanted to stop. When they'd first begun, Emily had asked Arlene how much she'd given, and was embarrassed to discover Arlene had outspent her handily. From then on they agreed to each give a hundred dollars, a truce they honored for Henry's sake.

Now, standing with Margaret and Kenny and Lisa and the grandchildren as they waited for Connie Dorsey to say his name, with a flash of panic Arlene couldn't recall sending in the form. After such a long stalemate, it seemed cruel to lose to Emily this way, yet at the same time Arlene was grateful to her. The important thing was that Henry be remembered.

"Loretta Marshall," Connie intoned. "Shirley Masterson. Henry Maxwell."

Arlene dipped her head and peeked at the children to see if it had registered. Kenny, who shared his father's jawline and cleft chin, nodded reverently, and she was pleased.

Who would make sure she and Emily were on the list? For all Margaret's talk of a higher power, none of them were churchgoers. They were long gone anyway, Arlene thought. Once she and Emily died, the children would have no reason to come back to Pittsburgh and likely be glad of it. The city that had been her world held nothing for them, a flat fact impossible to deny.

At dinner she thought she might make a joke of forgetting to send in the form, but the table was noisy and she was enjoying the children's company. It was rare to have them all together, sharing glimpses of their distant, mysterious lives. They were discussing Ella and Quinn wanting to adopt, and Sarah possibly getting married again, and Sam's new sales job with Pfizer, and by the time Emily brought out the almond torte, the moment had passed. Arlene wasn't even certain she'd forgotten, so why draw attention to her problems? No one would ever know.

Home, she changed into her robe and slippers and watched an old Audrey Hepburn movie under her comforter, but the question nagged, and at the next break she flung the comforter aside and went to her grandmother Chase's secretary and dug out her checkbook. She leafed through the ledger backward, and there it was, right after Thanksgiving, check number 3652 to Calvary for $100.00.

"Ha!" she said, as if she'd known all along.

Loveland

She would never get used to the West. The plains ran on for hundreds of miles, flat as a floor, then stopped at the Rockies. The scale of the landscape was inhuman, the mountains making everything seem puny. The drive from the Denver airport to Alyssa's place outside of Glenwood Springs was almost as long as her flight, giving them time to catch up.

"How's Peter?"

"He's good." She was too used to deflecting her friends, and felt she owed Alyssa an honest answer. "I don't think we've figured anything out. I think we're serious, but exactly what that means isn't clear."

"It's still new."

"I don't know if it is. I think maybe this is just how it's going to be, and maybe that's all we want for now. I don't know. It's different."

"Different is good."

"Sometimes. Sometimes it's confusing. Sometimes it's wonderful."

"That's good. Are you two compatible?"

"We enjoy each other's company, if that's what you mean. How's Dwayne?" she asked, and then it was Alyssa's turn to confess. Like Peter going on tour, Dwayne would take off for a week at Moab or Bryce with his mountain biker buddies, trusting Alyssa to understand. He wasn't uncaring, but sometimes he could be thoughtless. As much as Susie wished it otherwise, her worries were familiar. She liked to believe they were both liberated, independent women. Then why weren't they stronger? Why was their happiness always at the mercy of others?

Coming into Denver, they were going against the flow. It was like Pittsburgh, the airport was out in the middle of nowhere. The fields by the side of the road were pockmarked with gopher holes. The billboards touted lawyers.

"So I guess Dad is on a cruise," Alyssa said. It sounded like a question, as if she were feeling Susie out to see how much she knew. Alyssa didn't mention Cheryl's name, which Susie appreciated.

"He never struck me as the cruise type. Too type A."

"It's only for a week."

"Do I want to know where?"

"Probably not."

"The Caribbean would be too obvious, so let's go with that."

"Yup. Barbados today."

"Not very Christmasy, but I'm not surprised." She feigned indifference for both of their sakes. Richard had never taken her on a cruise, and though she knew they were terrible for both the environment and the local economies, she felt cheated. He spoiled

Cheryl in a way he'd never treated her. When they were courting in Boston, neither of them had any money. A bowl of pho was a big date.

"He said to tell you 'Merry Christmas.'"

"That's your father all right. He never changes. There's something admirable about that, I'm not sure what."

She expected Alyssa to defend him against her cynicism, and was disappointed when she held back, putting the matter on pause for now. It was a long conversation. They'd have time to pick it up later.

As they climbed the Front Range, the weather gradually deteriorated, snow squalls buffeting the windshield, and then, in minutes, covering the road. They crawled along like everyone else with their hazards flashing, Loveland Pass lost in the clouds. Short of the Eisenhower Tunnel, traffic was stopped—a normal occurrence during ski season, Alyssa assured her, but the number of tractor-trailers idling around them was worrisome. There were no cars coming the other way, the lanes trackless. Message boards warned that only four-wheel-drive vehicles were permitted past this point, arrows indicating turnouts like rest areas where people were supposed to attach chains. The minivan full of kids on their right wasn't four-wheel-drive, or the BMW convertible with the snowboard rack on the back, and they weren't pulling off. The snow was falling harder now, hiding the lines. It was almost five, the light fading behind the peaks. She imagined being stuck here all night, eating the biscotti she'd saved from the plane, drinking handfuls of melted snow.

"This isn't bad," Alyssa said. "The uphill's easy. Sometimes the down side can get a little hairy. They're probably plowing and salting before they let us through."

"They're not plowing this side."

"Yeah, I don't know what's up with that."

They sat with the heater on low. They had just over half a tank of gas. As she searched her purse for mints, a trucker in a Santa hat climbed down from his cab and trudged past them with a red cookie tin. She took a video to show Peter, adding the caption: *A says this isn't bad.*

When she hit Send, it failed. She had only part of a bar. She tried a photo but that wouldn't go either.

"We're pretty high up here," Alyssa said.

The taillights of the BMW went dark and the driver stepped out and stretched, rolling his head on his neck like a prizefighter. More people were getting out and walking between the cars.

Alyssa lowered her window and asked a woman with bright purple hair and a rainbow neck gaiter what was happening.

"Avalanche. Eastbound's totally closed. They're just starting to dig our side out now. Could be a couple of hours."

"Thanks." She rolled her window up to keep in the heat.

After a few minutes she turned the car off. "Are you warm enough?"

"I am. A couple of hours."

"Merry Christmas."

"Merry Christmas," Susie said.

The Giving Season

Knowing Jean would be alone for Christmas, Kitzi wanted to get her a present that had nothing to do with Gene or the cats or the house, something practical yet extravagant, and, above all, personal. The Tog Shop in Shadyside was her first thought, though she would have to fight for parking, ending up on the top floor of the garage. She pictured a cashmere scarf to go with Jean's good woolen coat, but everything she looked at was drab, and ultimately she settled on a pair of silk-lined black calfskin gloves from Italy. She couldn't be sure of Jean's size, only that her fingers were longer than her own, and made a best guess, keeping the receipt.

"What, are we adopting her?" Martin said when she showed him the gift-wrapped package.

"That's nice. I'd hope someone would invite me for dinner if I was alone."

"You could give her your mittens."

"Stop. Susie knitted those herself."

"Yes she did."

"I just want it to be nice for her. You don't have to make small talk, you can watch football, I don't care. You're going to like dessert."

"Are you making that trifle again? That was good."

"This is better," she teased.

Dinner was one thing. She still didn't know where Jean was going to go. Kitzi hadn't offered her their guest bedroom yet, hoping she'd come up with something on her own. So far she hadn't heard a word. The Rolls Silver Spirit, Martin discovered, was their stab at an economy car; there were dozens online around ten thousand pounds, so no real help. Supposedly, Francoise was working on the estate, but that would take months, and who knew what it involved? She could see Jean filling the guest bedroom to overflowing with garbage bags and kitty litter bins, setting off Martin. If only Joan wasn't selling her condo—but Jean would ruin that too. There was no easy solution, and so Kitzi busied herself with dinner, and Gene's visitation, pretending she'd have time to find a place for her later.

Despite all of her planning, after the debacle at Thanksgiving, there was no guarantee Jean would make it for dinner. That morning, when Kitzi had called to confirm, she'd reached their machine. Now, driving over, she prepared herself for another letdown, and was surprised to find Jean waiting on the porch, holding an oblong gold box topped with a red bow—probably a bottle of wine. The suede gloves she had on appeared to be men's, and Kitzi thought she should have gotten her a larger size. She hadn't wanted to insult her.

"What's this?" She lifted the bottle out by the neck enough to see it was a red. "You didn't have to get us anything."

"Please, you've done so much for us. For me—sorry. I'm not used to being a 'me.' I liked being a 'we.' I could blame everything on him."

"Thank you."

"I should let you know"—she paused as if giving her warning—"Francoise is coming for the visitation."

"All the way from London?"

"I told her she didn't have to. She never listens to me."

"I'll be interested to meet her." She wasn't sure how much hope she should invest in this news. She didn't want to seem too eager, but she was excited to finally have an ally, and glad that Jean wouldn't be alone anymore.

"She's a strange bird," Jean said, making Kitzi tilt her head skeptically. "Very spiritual. She went to India with the Beatles, if you remember that. Gene used to tell stories about her sleeping on Chopin's grave. For a while she was a bit of a darling, and then she wasn't, and I think that was hard for her. She's fine, she's sweet as pie, but if she starts going on about astrology, run."

"She sounds interesting."

"A little Francoise goes a long way, as they say. She took care of Gene after Natasha died, and for that I'll always be grateful."

"Natasha."

"His second wife."

"I didn't know he had a second wife."

"Awful story. Violinist. Killed herself. Francoise fed him and made him play every day. It wasn't a year later, she introduced us. She said she knew. And she did."

"That's wild," Kitzi said.

She already saw Jean's life as impossibly romantic, this only confirmed it. She wanted to tell Martin so he'd know she wasn't just some crazy old cat lady monopolizing her time.

Home, he opened the door before they climbed the porch stairs. Without her having to ask, he'd changed into his good clothes and was wearing shoes instead of slippers. He thanked Jean for the wine and took her coat, trailing them into the living room, where the mantel candles were lit and Kitzi's gift sat on the coffee table, along with a platter of smoked salmon and a stack of festive reindeer napkins.

He lurked like a waiter as they arranged themselves on the couch. "Champagne?"

"I won't say no," Jean said.

When he came back with the tray, the three of them clinked glasses. "Merry Christmas."

"This is for you," Kitzi said.

"Really, dear, you needn't have." She was careful opening it, as if they might reuse the wrapping paper.

"If they're the wrong size I can always return them."

"Let's see. They feel expensive. They're very soft."

She tugged one on, struggling, the leather stretched tight across her palm, not quite covering the heel of her hand.

"Too small," Kitzi said, dejected.

"It's always a problem." Jean set them on top of the box. "They're lovely, though. Thank you."

"I'll take them back," Kitzi said, and sipped her champagne, embarrassed for both of them.

"*I*," Martin said, addressing her, "have a present for you," and produced from behind his back a flat package the size of a bathroom tile, wrapped in familiar paper.

As she'd guessed from the shape, it was a CD: Schubert's Fantasie in F Minor for Four Hands, played by Jean and Gene. On the cover Gene had a Fu Manchu and appeared taller than Jean, regal in a sequined gown showing a demure hint of cleavage, her honey-blond hair feathered and blown out like Farrah Fawcett's.

"Where on earth did you find that?" Jean asked.

"And when?" Kitzi asked.

"Jerry's Records. They had a bunch of them. This one's signed."

Kitzi handed it to Jean, who put a fingertip to the plastic case as if she might touch Gene. "I remember this."

"Okay, you beat me," Kitzi said later, after she returned from dropping Jean off. Dinner had gone well, her sticky toffee pudding was a triumph. "I forget how sneaky you can be."

"I thought you'd like that." He had the dishes going and was wiping down the counters.

The gloves were still sitting on the coffee table. "They weren't cheap either."

"How much?"

"You don't want to know."

"You're right, I don't.

"Hey," he said, plopping down beside her. "Check this out."

He held the wine Jean had given them. It was a Pauillac, which meant nothing to her. "It's French."

"Look at the date."

"Nineteen eighty-one."

"You can't buy this anymore. The only one I could find online sold for a thousand pounds at auction, and that was a decade ago, when the pound was worth something. Makes you wonder what else she has in there."

"It does," she said, though after the Rolls, she'd given up on discovering buried treasure among the horde. There could be a whole cellar beneath the house right now and it wouldn't help. Knowing the bottle was expensive only made her gloves more of a disappointment, and she wished she'd gone with a scarf.

“Open it,” she said.

“Don’t you want to save it for a special occasion?” Because that’s what she did. When had she become no fun?

“It’s Christmas. It doesn’t get more special that that.”

“Okay,” he said, as if it were against his will.

After so long, wine could go bad, but the Pauillac hadn’t. She tasted cherry and plum and raspberry and chocolate and coffee.

“Holy God,” Martin said.

“I don’t know about a thousand pounds, but this is pretty good.”

“To Jean and Gene,” he said.

“To Gene and Jean,” she said, and they proceeded to drink the whole thing.

Sleeping Arrangements

The house on Grafton Street had three bedrooms and a den with a daybed—a squeeze even when the grandchildren were little. Now that they were grown, and some, like Ella, accompanied by their spouses, finding space for all of them was impossible.

It was rare that both branches came to visit at the same time. Normally they alternated holidays, Margaret or Kenny reclaiming their old room, the spare bedroom going to either Sarah or Ella, respectively, since they both had partners, with the boys, Justin and Sam, still single in their early thirties, relegated to the den. This Christmas was the exception, a planetary alignment occasioned by Emily visiting Margaret at Thanksgiving and Lisa's parents' house on the Cape being struck by lightning, leaving Emily to sort out their accommodations.

As if bound by the right of succession, she followed a strict seniority, offering Margaret her old room first, which Margaret, not having money for a hotel, promptly accepted. Next was Kenny, or rather Lisa, who, beneath the guise of wanting to make things easier for Emily, preemptively announced that she and Kenny would be staying at the SpringHill Suites in Bakery Square, as they often did, regardless of how many beds were available.

Sarah and Ella were trickier, requiring some delicacy. If Sarah was bringing her new beau Tim, she would have first dibs on the last bedroom. If not, it would fall to Ella and Quinn, the den being a pass-through, and unsuitable, in Emily's mind, for a couple, same-sex or otherwise. Margaret, monitoring their group text, volunteered to take the daybed if Tim came, an offer Emily ignored, reading Sarah's silence as a sign that the problem would most likely solve itself. In the meantime, she made Arlene aware that she could be hosting the boys and reminded her to test the air mattress.

She worried about meals. Like a chef opening a restaurant, she'd written out her dinner menus, filling Henry's old yellow pads with grocery lists, but had only the vaguest plans for breakfast or lunch. It was official, Tim wasn't coming, so there would be ten of them, including herself and Arlene. Ella and Quinn were vegans, Lisa newly gluten- and dairy-free. Emily loaded her cart with yogurt and bagels and cottage cheese and cantaloupe, avocados and cold cuts and olives and hummus and pita bread, afraid they'd have nothing to eat.

Margaret and Ella and Quinn would be driving, which meant Emily had to borrow a second visitor's parking permit from Marcia Cole. The rest of them were flying, and while they tried to coordinate their arrival times, Justin was coming from Seattle and didn't get in till after midnight Christmas Eve. He said he could take an Uber, but Margaret insisted on picking him up, and while the idea bothered Emily (in her drinking days, Margaret had wrecked several cars and had her license suspended), she couldn't intervene without seeming to criticize her and let her text pass without comment.

The day they were scheduled to arrive, she cleaned the bathrooms, stashing her eyedrops and hand cream and Listerine beneath the sink. She emptied the linen closet, making up their beds and setting out fresh towels. Angus followed her from room to room, unsure.

"Are you helping?" she asked.

In the den she had to rearrange things to lay out the daybed for Sarah and was thinking about her luck with men, unfairly comparing it with Margaret's, when, as if to rebuke her, she barked her shin on her mother's old sewing table, the wrought iron frame unforgiving.

"Cheese and crackers," she said, clenching her teeth. She hiked up her pantleg and there was blood. Her skin was so thin, see-through like rice paper. She limped into the bathroom for a Band-Aid and kept going, afraid that if she sat down she'd stop altogether. She still had presents to wrap.

All afternoon she could sense them coming, like a storm. She could prepare only so much, and when they finally did arrive with their roller bags and backpacks and winter jackets, bleary from traveling, she was overcome, and grateful.

It was the Christmas she'd wished for, all of them together (maybe for the last time), even if the weather didn't cooperate. It rained, Angus not wanting to leave the back porch to go pee, tracking his muddy pawprints across the kitchen floor. They played board games she'd never heard of by the fire, and the standing rib roast turned out perfectly. They all fawned over Arlene's painting of the cottage, even Lisa. Later, in Henry's office, with the door closed, Margaret gave Emily her five-year chip, a surprise that made them both cry, and Sunday, when it was time to go, Emily held her close. She hadn't always believed in Margaret and didn't expect the gift to be so momentous. Was it just that she was older, growing sentimental, or had they finally reached some understanding? That night, alone again, she took the chip upstairs and set it next to Henry's watch on her dresser, where she would see it every morning and evening, a reminder.

Monday they were gone, but the rain stayed. Someone had left a gob of blue toothpaste in the sink. The house was so quiet she could hear herself sigh as she put the rooms back together. She ran loads of sheets and towels and went around emptying the wastebaskets, resisting the urge to play detective. In the kitchen, the children had put away the dishes, and she had to stand on her step stool and rearrange things. No one had touched the bagels or the cantaloupe. The fridge was crammed with Tupperware. What would she do with all this food? Maybe Arlene would want some.

Now that Christmas was over, she needed to think about Gene's visitation, which involved a whole different set of preparations.

She called Arlene and stood at the front window, looking out at the rain falling on Grafton Street, the gutters running.

"Dang it," she said, because it always happened.

She'd forgotten the parking pass.

Marche Funèbre

They were afraid no one would show up, and had ordered accordingly. Laid out on a mahogany sideboard with paper plates and plastic silverware and individual packets of condiments, the spread from Panera dismayed Emily, and she wished Jean would have let them have it at Calvary, whose regular coffee hour put this to shame. What would Francoise say about these croissants, this quiche?

She and Arlene were the first ones there. The flowers had arrived, along with a few far-flung tributes, some still stapled in cellophane, including a tasteful spray of lilies from Joan. While Arlene set them around, Emily followed the funeral director through a maze of hallways to a locked closet where they kept the sound system. He wasn't a Freyvogel brother but a cousin, wearing a tailored suit, a chunky gold Duquesne class ring and newly shined shoes. He wouldn't let her touch the stereo, taking each CD from her and placing it in the carousel as if it were a special skill.

"We don't want it to be too loud," she said, but, back in the room, it wasn't.

"A lot of people like to choose their own music," he said.

Why had she thought it unusual? Now she saw it as an opportunity, and thought of what she'd choose for hers.

"That looks nice," she told Arlene, who'd started on the pictures.

"I was thinking we'd put the albums on the coffee table so people can sit and look through them." She'd wanted to do something chronological, beginning with baby pictures, but there were none. The earliest shot she could find was from a clipping of him winning the Chopin competition at eighteen, as if he'd never been a child. Kitzi had said he'd defected; only now did Arlene appreciate what that entailed. There were no parents, no siblings, no boyhood friends, only Gene bent over the keys, Gene taking a bow, Gene shaking hands with another man in tails.

"I think that's Rubinstein," Emily said.

Arlene looked on the back. "Good guess."

"I didn't realize he was such a big deal."

Sic transit gloria, thought Arlene, who'd never been and never would be famous, though privately she liked to think she'd had, in her day, her glorious moments.

In the hall, a clock chimed the hour. They only had the room from four to six.

"No one shows up to these things on time."

"Bad form," Emily agreed, straightening the pens by the guest book.

There were no windows, so they couldn't see if people were rolling into the parking lot. As they waited, Gene played one of Schumann's Kinderszenen—which, Emily wasn't sure. By the end, no one had come. Where were Kitzi and Jean? She feared they'd slapped this together too fast. It had all the makings of a disaster—too close to the holidays, when people were away and it was too late to change their travel plans.

Just then a pale young man wandered into the room, glancing around as if he were lost. With his dark suit and rigid posture, for a moment Emily thought he was another Freyvogel until he came over and introduced himself, offering a cartoonishly large hand. His eyes were an icy blue, his eyebrows so blond they were nearly invisible.

"Anders Jansen." *Yan-sin.* His accent made them concentrate. "I was a student of Professor Sokolov a long time ago. I'm so sorry."

"Thank you," Emily said, nodding as if she were Jean.

Though they'd never heard of him, Anders Jansen was indeed a concert pianist. He owed everything to Professor Sokolov, he said. A great man, such elegant technique, and so generous. Whenever he was playing and there was a question of interpretation, he asked himself: What would Professor Sokolov do?

They were fascinated but didn't have the chance to find out more about Anders Jansen because he was followed by several other students of Gene's—men and women both—as if a bus had dropped them off. They filed by Emily and Arlene in a kind of receiving line, along with a number of Chatham faculty who asked after Jean, making them explain that she was on her way, and here came Donald Wilkins, of all people, to pay his respects. Gene had once arranged for him to play the organ at the Thomaskirche in Leipzig, a thrill he'd never forget. As a Buxtehude and Bach aficionado, Emily was genuinely interested in the program he'd chosen, but, looking over his shoulder at the room, all she could think of was how crowded it was now, and wished they'd ordered more food.

The reason Kitzi and Jean were late was that Francoise was on a call with another client, pacing the length of the porch, ignoring the cats in her path. Apparently she was staying there. After Jean's description of her as a '60s icon, Kitzi expected a twiggy Parisian, a mod dresser as cool as Jean Seberg or Deneuve, clad in Prada and Yves Saint Laurent. She wasn't wrong about the clothes, or that she smoked and spoke rapid-fire French with a blasé disdain. What Jean neglected to tell her was that Francoise, like Gene himself, was a little person, a fact that, unfairly or not, changed how Kitzi saw her earlier celebrity and made her wonder about his second wife.

Finally, Francoise stopped and stowed her phone and crossed the porch to them.

"I apologize," she said in a polished British accent that threw Kitzi, as if she'd turned into a different person. "Sometimes it's the geniuses who need the most handholding, isn't that right?"

"God, yes," Jean said. "Sir Simon again?"

Francoise waved the question away. "You take the front—you've got legs. How far is it? I still can't believe I'm here. Mehlman said he might try to come."

"Isn't he supposed to be on tour?"

"He was in Vienna last night. I told him he didn't have to. Lei-Ling should be here, and Simone. *Entre nous*, Simone's pregnant."

"That's wonderful."

"A wonderful pain in my arse."

Kitzi had thought of Jean as being alone, but as she eavesdropped, she realized how large her circle was, encompassing the whole world.

The lot at Freyvogel's confirmed it, the valets hopelessly behind. She and Gene had taught at Chatham for more than forty years, and the moment she entered the room she was besieged by former students. They embraced Francoise as well; many of them were clients of hers, the visitation a reunion. Their shoptalk swelled, conversation drowning out the carefully curated music. From group to group, the news circulated that Mehlman might be coming. Had they heard his new Debussy?

As those in the know waited for him, their own special guest arrived—Joan, looking rosy, if thin, with Darcy pushing her in a wheelchair. Emily and Arlene found them in the crowd and they had their own HD reunion.

"They let you out?" Emily joked.

"You look good," Arlene said.

"No Susie?" Joan asked, and Kitzi explained that she was still in Colorado.

"Nice turnout," Joan said. "I'm not surprised."

Because she knew. What would they do without her?

She thanked them for helping Darcy clear out her apartment, and they promised to visit her at Longwood. The prospect rendered them silent, an awkward pause as they realized this was her farewell.

"I'm sure Jean would like to see you," Kitzi prompted, and as if they were her bodyguards, they parted the throng to make way for her chair.

It wasn't quite jealousy Kitzi felt as Jean bent over and held Joan, but a childish twinge at being left out, or left alone. As Darcy shook hands with Jean, Francoise kissed Joan on both cheeks, the two clearly familiar. At some point today, Kitzi had hoped to take Francoise aside and address Jean's living situation directly, and now here was Joan, who could help, but this wasn't the time or the place, and Kitzi stood there smiling as they shared stories about the old days.

In the middle of Jean's remembrance of Gene's hatred for a certain brand of piano, Francoise checked her phone and raised a finger. "Mehlman's here."

Word circled the room. Mehlman, straight from playing with the Vienna Phil. He'd taken the red-eye and grabbed an Uber. Tomorrow he was due in Munich.

"Here he is," someone said, and the whole room turned toward the door. For a moment Kitzi could hear the music before it was lost in shouts of welcome as his classmates surrounded him, crushing him with bearhugs, pounding his back. It was only when they ushered him to Jean that Kitzi saw him, a bushy-haired string bean with a beak of a nose and a stoned smile. In his blazer and jeans, he looked like a stand-up comedian, but they watched him like a rock star. He held Jean for a long time, whispering to her, then bowed low and held Francoise. He stood between them, an arm over both their shoulders, as if he were their progeny. People were taking pictures with their phones, which Kitzi thought inappropriate.

The department head, who Kitzi had met, sought him out to shake his hand, then, after a brief powwow, stood in front of the three, facing the room, and motioned for quiet as if he were their spokesman. White-haired and gnomelike, he wore a kippah and gold-rimmed bifocals, his eyes sunken in dark sockets. He took a piece of paper from his jacket pocket and unfolded it.

"Thank you all for coming. It's good to see so many familiar faces. Today we gather to celebrate a great man." Behind him Mehlman nodded his bushy head for emphasis. "Gene was more than a friend and colleague to me. He was my musical conscience, as I know he was and *is* to so many of us. In 1961, he and his wife, Jean, created our performance major, because he believed that performance matters, that the right note and the right inflection can move and possibly even transform us as people for the good. On behalf of Chatham University, it is my great honor to announce the establishment of the Yevgeny and Jean Sokolov Scholarship for Piano Performance, to be awarded annually to an applicant of exceptional promise."

Everyone clapped, ready to resume the party, but there was more.

"For their generosity, the department would like to recognize Professor Emeritus Jean Sokolov, Madame Francoise Delalande, and Benjamin Mehlman, class of '08. Thank you."

It called for a toast but there was nothing to drink, and Kitzi wished they'd let her know ahead of time—or was it something Francoise had orchestrated at the last minute? She expected they were using Mehlman's money to fund it, though she couldn't rightly ask. She hated to quibble, but she thought the idea misguided, or maybe it was the timing that bothered her. Did they not understand she was going to be thrown out of her house?

The professor's speech had touched Arlene. While she'd never told anyone, she'd daydreamed of her former students coming together to honor her, possibly with a sentimental gift—an engraved nameplate for her desk or just a personalized mug. All she'd gotten, her last day, was half a plain Giant Eagle sheet cake in the teacher's lounge and a modest Target gift card from her colleagues, which she spent on some household gizmo she could no longer recall (an air fryer, relegated to the basement).

Emily was still racking her brain, trying to reconcile this doofus with the Benjamin Mehlman whose Scriabin she'd heard on QED when, from the ceiling, the same three notes began repeating like a ringtone. The CD was skipping, stuck on a scratch or speck of dust—she should have tested them—and without excusing herself she wheeled and hurried down the hall for the closet, only to get lost, emerging, as in a dream, at a separate entrance leading to two smaller rooms ranked with folding chairs, and then when she did backtrack and find the right way, the closet was locked.

The skip, plinking on and on, cleared the room like a fire alarm. People clamped their hands over their ears as if their hearing might be damaged. Kitzi found the noise annoying, but thought they were being theatrical.

Darcy said she was taking Joan home. It was almost time to leave; they were going to lose the room anyway. Entrusting Emily and Arlene to clean up, Kitzi followed Jean and Francoise and Mehlman to the coatracks, where, as a group, they tried to decide what their next move was, a bar or restaurant close by, maybe somewhere with a piano. Kitzi, perversely, thought they should all go back to Jean's place.

In the end the department chair had them to his home, a perfectly restored robber baron mansion on Woodland Road with a roaring fireplace and vintage Steinway grand. Gene's students took turns playing bagatelles as if it were a recital, Jean and Mehlman watching like judges. To Kitzi's surprise and her clients' delight, Francoise drained her Manhattan and, perched atop a pillow from the couch, played a Chopin nocturne, taking an exaggerated bow and blowing a kiss to Jean.

"That was beautiful," Kitzi said in the gleaming kitchen, where Francoise had gone for a refill. In her arms, the whiskey bottle looked giant.

"You're too kind. No, I wish I had time to play. It's like the joke, how do you get to Carnegie Hall? Practice, practice, practice."

"I wanted to talk to you about Jean."

"Ah, yes." Francoise finished pouring and set the bottle on the counter with a clink. "What is Jean going to do? you mean."

"Where is Jean going to go?"

"That is the question. I'd hoped the university could do something, but no. I think they're glad to have done with her, honestly. She doesn't want to come and live with me . . . I offered. Not that I think she should right now."

"I'm worried that she won't be able to afford a new place."

"She can afford a new place," Francoise said. "She doesn't want one."

"I don't think she has a choice. Her problem's only going to get worse now that Gene's gone, and she won't have her cats."

"I'm sure you're right. It's going to be hard for her. I know you and Joan have tried to help. She's lucky to have friends like you." She took up the vermouth and continued fixing her drink as if the matter were closed.

Kitzi wanted to protest that she wasn't a friend—she wanted to ask her what the two of them should do—but Francoise had no more answers than she did and people were spilling into the kitchen.

Later, when the lights were low and the fire was almost out, Mehlman played the "Raindrop" Prelude in utter silence, improvising a coda, closing the night with an aching, low-down blues. Kitzi listened in the dark, privileged to be there, and happy for Jean, yet even before the last notes faded, she was ready to leave, and as she drove home after dropping them off, she chewed the inside of her cheek, feeling desperate, remembering what Francoise had said. Why did she think money would solve anything?

Stuff

According to Darcy, Joan had already taken everything she wanted. Her new apartment at Longwood was a one-bedroom with no garage, so she'd had to leave a lot behind, but none of them was prepared for just how much. Her condo was full of furniture as if she were still living there, the place in disarray, the kitchen counters piled with junk mail and cookbooks and cleaning supplies, the carpet strewn with paper clips and kitty litter and pennies, worn-out shoes and plants and extension cords. Joan had always been so neat, it felt like a desecration.

Darcy had moved her mother herself, without soliciting their help, a unilateral decision that struck them as arrogant. They were at an age where they dreamed of downsizing and living more simply, keeping only those possessions that sparked joy, so they could see not taking the dated sectional or the humiliating potty chair, but surely there was a place for this dropleaf table and this inlaid maple highboy. They were tempted to save these fugitive pieces for Joan, as if Darcy had tricked her into letting them go, when it was too late. She'd already contracted a charity called Brother's Keepers to cart away the larger furniture. In the driveway sat a rusty red dumpster. Their job was to fill it with everything that was left. Essentially, Susie pointed out, they were the cleaning crew. They needed to be out and the condo spotless by midnight on New Year's Eve. They had three days.

Darcy was still getting Joan settled at Longwood, so they had the place to themselves, which was strange. To stay out of one another's way, they each took a room, dropping an empty U-Haul box in the middle of the floor for donations and flapping open a garbage bag. The idea was to touch each item just once.

There was so much that it was hard to know where to start. It went against their frugal nature to waste anything, and most of what remained was in decent shape. They set their garbage bags aside and filled box after box for Goodwill rather than throw away a perfectly good bucket or washcloth someone could use.

The problem with this approach, Kitzi knew from *Hoarders* (and perseverating over Jean's place), was that it took too long. The closest Goodwill was in Monroeville. Susie was committed to recycling, but the drive ate up time, and after her first trip she stopped questioning every little thing and put aside only clothes they could donate at local drop boxes.

More upsetting and harder to discard were the personal items—pictures and letters and birthday cards Darcy apparently had no use for. One wall of Joan's office was covered with plaques and awards for her service that must have meant a great deal to her, displayed so proudly. They had her name on them, and though Kitzi knew no one would want them, tossing them in her bag, she felt bad for Joan, as if, without these tributes to remind them, people might forget all the good she'd done. The same with the folder of thank-you notes from families of former HDs, and their browned and crumbling obituaries. In they went.

Having spent time there, Susie was having trouble saying goodbye to the apartment. It had become a haven the way Oscar had become a friend, and now, like Oscar, it would be gone. Each time she lugged a bag out to the dumpster, she searched the sidewalks for Bill with his cane and sunglasses, hoping to have a last chat with him. She knew so few people in the city, she hated to lose even the most tenuous connection.

Arlene saw the job as a cautionary tale. Her own apartment was around the same size and just as full of junk. She could picture Emily rifling through her dresser and coming upon Walter's letters and the picture of them at Lake Tahoe, young and tanned and sunstruck, as beautiful as movie stars, their teeth a blinding white. That trip had been the end, when it was supposed to be the beginning. Walter was going to get a Reno divorce and then they'd get married. It was all in the letters. She'd never told Henry—she'd never told anyone, especially not their mother—and the idea that Emily would tell her story after she was gone alarmed her. She'd have to find a safer hiding place, maybe the attic.

By the second day, Emily had lost patience. Why were *they* doing this? It was a job for young people. At their age, just walking down the stairs to the garage was perilous—a fact Joan had proven. She blamed Darcy.

"She hired movers. Why didn't she hire cleaners?"

"Because we're free," Arlene said.

"We said we wanted to help," Kitzi said.

"I'm fine with helping," Susie said. "I thought she'd be doing at least some of it."

"You assumed," Emily said.

"I assumed," Susie said, as if it were her fault.

The last day, around eleven, Darcy showed up five minutes before the truck came for the furniture. It was unmarked, the top edge of the cargo compartment crumpled as if it had hit a bridge. They'd expected a crew of movers, but it was just two older Black men—one junkie thin with stumpy teeth—wearing matching fluorescent green T-shirts. Darcy signed some papers and did a quick circuit of the rooms to see how much was left.

"It looks good," she said, because after their initial doubts they were going to make it easily. "What does everybody want for lunch?"

"Not sandwiches," Arlene said, needling Emily.

"Can we do Casbah?" Susie asked. "It's close."

"Are they open for lunch?" Kitzi asked.

"They are."

It wasn't their only reward, besides knowing they'd helped Joan. Each of them salvaged something from the condo. Emily took a whole stack of towels she could leave on the back porch to wipe Angus's muddy paws. Arlene snagged a bag of sheets she could use as drop cloths and a small saucepan to replace the one she'd melted. Susie rescued the abandoned plants and a jingly ball she'd found under the guest bed to give to Oscar when she visited. Kitzi had the most, filling a box with Joan's HD files and a treasure trove of office supplies—all the highlighters and folders and ledgers and pushpins and binder clips she'd ever need.

Now that everything was out, the walls bare, the place looked impersonal, a blank space ready for its next occupant, as if Joan had never lived there. They were dirty and tired, but they were so close. Flagging, their hands aching, they dragged themselves from room to room, dusting and scrubbing and vacuuming until no trace of her remained.

What Are You Doing New Year's Eve?

When they were young, before they were married (Arlene too, pre-Walter), New Year's Eve had been important, a night for dining and dancing and romance. Like courtship back then, it was a formal ritual. There was nothing casual about it. As the song said, you were supposed to spend it with the one you'd chosen above all others, your appearance together in your very best signaling to the world that you were a couple, the kiss at midnight a public declaration of love. Finding the right date might take months, and if the boy you yearned for asked another, you went out with your friends or, in the most painful cases, stayed home.

Once they were married (but true of Arlene too), New Year's became an occasion to reflect on the past year and recommit to some ideal—not always realistic—of happiness and how it might be achieved, until, decades later, even the conceit of fundamentally changing oneself faded, the ceremonial countdown merely serving to mark the inevitable and tireless passage of time.

They were frazzled after emptying Joan's, and stayed home.

Ever since Henry had died, Emily saw no reason to stay up until midnight. She felt grubby and took a shower, had a glass of red wine with some leftover rib roast, slipping Angus a few choice morsels, and was in bed by ten, as if it were any other day.

Kitzi and Martin dutifully watched the ball drop, stuck a rubber cork in their champagne to save the bubbles and turned in.

Arlene stood out on her balcony and banged on her new saucepan, celebrating with her neighbors.

Susie had been away for only four days, so it wasn't even a week since she'd seen Peter.

"It seems longer," he said in bed.

"It does," she said, and kissed him.

Sober and self-conscious, even in the dark, she wore a lace camisole as a nightshirt, covering up her stomach. She'd overdone it at Joan's. As they rearranged themselves, a shooting pain made her flinch, and Peter stopped.

"Sorry, it's my back."

"Are you all right?"

"Just be careful," she said.

And he was.

Evensong

Because New Year's fell on the first Sunday of the month, Calvary moved Evensong to the next weekend. By then they needed it. January was a barren stretch. The holidays were over and the snowbirds had flown, jetting off to Hilton Head and Sarasota, leaving the front pews noticeably thinner. That morning, Communion had taken less than three minutes.

"It might as well have been the early service," Emily said.

"We could have had it in the chapel," Arlene said. "It would have been warmer."

The day had been gray, the Steelers beating the Browns in the last game of the season but still missing the playoffs. Now dusk was coming down, the streetlights flickering. They were sitting in Emily's Subaru in the lot with the heater blasting, waiting for Kitzi. Afterward, they were going to Casbah. At bridge Susie had proposed making it a new tradition, and none of them could think of a reason they shouldn't, though now Arlene worried about driving home. Coming over, she'd used her phone to chaperone her, taking no chances, but it would be dark later, it was supposed to snow, and there was no guarantee she'd remember the way.

Her big resolution was to face what was happening to her. She'd made an appointment with her doctor, hoping he'd refer her to a specialist, but he couldn't get her in till March. In the meantime she was reading about Alzheimer's, borrowing books from the library and researching online. She took the standard dementia test Donald Trump had bragged about acing, drawing a clockface and identifying a horse, a donkey and a camel, and was embarrassed to learn he'd beaten her, a result she shared with no one, though by now it was obvious to all of them that she wasn't right. She was tired of hiding, and there was no point. At bridge she missed an easy trick and apologized. "Sometimes I see things I know I know, and I don't know what they are."

"That must be frustrating," Susie said, and for the first time, instead of merely agreeing, Arlene told the truth.

"Oh," she said, "it's terrifying. You know how people say 'I'm losing my mind'? I am."

Admitting it so openly may have been a mistake. Since then, they'd treated her differently, as if she were slow rather than momentarily scrambled. How could she explain? At the same time the disease was taking her over, it was completely separate from her, another entity. She could stand to the side and watch it happening as if split in two. Even now Emily was regarding her with concern, trying to decide whether she was all there or not.

"Have you talked to Margaret recently?" Emily asked.

"No. Is everything all right?"

Meaning, Emily inferred, is she drinking again? It had been the problem for so long that it was hard to believe it was over, like any war. Henry had been in the Battle of the Bulge and used to tell a story about the Germans tying white flags to their rifles right before they attacked. After the first time Margaret lied to him, he never let his guard down again, and Emily couldn't say he was wrong. Maybe, as Arlene said, Margaret would always be a work in progress, but she wished he could have seen her at Christmas.

Now more good news. Since she'd hung up with Margaret, she'd been waiting to tell Arlene in person.

"Sarah and Tim are getting married."

"No!"

"Yes."

"That's why she wanted you to come for Thanksgiving."

"To see if he passed the test."

"Congratulations. That's wonderful. She's been through so much."

"She has."

"When? Where?"

They were still discussing the arrangements when Kitzi's Honda swung into the lot, taking the space beside them.

The cold made Arlene catch her breath. She hugged Kitzi and had to dab a smudge of lipstick off her cheek.

"Are you ready for some Monteverdi?" Kitzi asked.

"I'm ready for some baba ghanoush," Arlene said.

"New coat?" Emily asked.

"Old," Kitzi said.

"I like it."

"Thank you. Shearling's supposed to be back in style again. Sorry I'm late."

"You're not," Arlene said.

Except they were, letting the cold into the vestibule as the choir was gathering to process. Viv glared as if they were trespassers.

They waved to Susie, grabbed their programs and tried to sneak down the far aisle, their footsteps giving them away.

If this morning's congregation had been thin, the evening's was anemic. At a glance, Kitzi could see they were regulars—not a soul under seventy—and badly outnumbered by the choir. Any hope she had of them providing cover as they slipped into their pew dissolved. They had to brazen it out, and then when they'd sat down and were shedding their coats, the organ called them to their feet again.

Like a teacher taking roll, she noticed the Cunninghams were missing. They couldn't still have Covid. She'd look in on them tomorrow. She'd been so busy conspiring with Francoise to find Jean a suitable place that she'd let everything else slip. Again she heard Joan telling her to delegate, though Joan herself was threatening to start a new branch at Longwood, hyping it like a realtor—location, location, location. She'd almost died, she was still in a wheelchair, yet it made sense to Kitzi. The new year was a time for new beginnings.

It was true for the whole country. After months of suspense, both Democrats had won their runoffs, tipping the Senate—a miracle, on the heels of the Dobbs ruling—and each time she recalled the news, it buoyed her. That one was a Baptist minister from Atlanta only made the victory sweeter. Who would have thought Georgia would restore their faith in America?

They'd arrived too late for Viv's announcement, so Emily leaned across Kitzi and reminded Arlene to silence her phone.

Thank you, Arlene mouthed. Emily could be a pill, but, honestly, what would she do without her? (Sarah was getting married!)

The hornpipe blared a fanfare and the crucifer and candle bearers started down the aisle. Behind them, Viv sent the sopranos off in pairs. The rear of the church was deserted, tempting the procession to speed by the empty rows. Susie measured her steps, keeping pace with Phyllis. While she loved early music, she had no background in Latin, only scattered words picked up from the liturgy. *Deus in adjutorium meum intende.* God something for us intends? Like Monteverdi's ancient harmonies, Latin was mysterious. Its rhythm had a majesty English was missing, and she wished she'd been forced to take it as a child. It wasn't too late. New studies said the brain was capable of absorbing language at any age, she was just lazy. When she and Richard went to Florence, she'd tried to learn Italian by herself using Duolingo—*il ragazzo*, the boy (ding!)—but then when they were there she was too scared and let him order everything.

As she passed Emily and Kitzi and Arlene, she dipped her head. Cleaning out Joan's had brought them closer, and she was looking forward to dinner. There'd been a funeral that afternoon, an older man named Greene she didn't know. Except for running home for a bite of lunch and some Advil, she'd been there all day. Filing into the stall for the third time, she felt like a juror assigned to an endless trial.

She was punchy but totally sober. After their night together New Year's Eve, she and Peter were doing Dry January, including her Vicodin. He'd introduced her to a shiatsu masseuse their drummer used, which helped. Now, instead of falling into bed drunk, they stayed up and talked about what they wanted. He'd missed her over Christmas, he confessed, and she could admit she'd missed him too. They were through pretending they were free. She would keep her own place, he would keep his, for now, but it seemed that naturally, without any premeditation, their arrangement had changed. Though he wasn't coming to dinner tonight—it was too soon, he had work—he'd agreed to go with her next month, and she was brimming with the news.

After the Magnificat, Father John read from the Gospel. He had to stop and cough, hacking, dredging up phlegm, a remnant of the cold that had sidelined Viv at Lessons and Carols.

He started over. "These are my words that I spoke to you when I was still with you."

They listened, intent, though he was hard to hear, parsing the Parable of the Good Shepherd for a moral they might live by. They weren't too old to learn. They knew they weren't perfect.

Domine ad adjuvandum me festina, they sang.

O Lord, make haste to save me.

It was true, they felt that urgency now, the need to finally make things right, or as right as they could be. They had only so much time.

Together they knelt and bowed their heads. Outside, night had fallen. A fine snow was sifting down, silting their windshields, coating the roads.

They prayed for Pittsburgh.

They prayed for Calvary and Tree of Life, murmuring along with Father John and then by themselves, inwardly.

They prayed for Henry and Martin and Peter and Walter.

They prayed for Alyssa and Dwayne, for Margaret and Sarah and Tim and Justin, for Kenny and Lisa and Ella and Quinn and Sam.

They prayed for Joan and Darcy and Oscar.

They prayed for the Cunninghams.

They prayed for Gene and Jean.

They prayed for Luanne Beers and Lillian Cochran and Marion Gill.

They prayed for Mr. Greene.

They prayed for Angus and Rufus and Duchess.

They prayed for everyone they'd loved and everyone they'd lost.

They prayed for patience and wisdom and courage.

They prayed for justice.

They prayed for peace.

They prayed for mercy.

They prayed for grace.

And then waited.

"Amen."

Out of the silence, the organ leapt and soared, jubilant, heralding the good news. Forgiven, born again, they rose as one and joined their voices to the Lord.

Acknowledgments

Grateful thanks to my early readers:

Paul Cody & Liz Holmes

Lamar Herrin

Michael Koryta

Trudy O'Nan

Alice Pentz

Mason Radkoff

Susan Straight

Elizabeth Strout

Luis Urrea

Kate Walbert

Sung J. Woo

Special thanks to Cathy Raphael, who first told me about the Pittsburgh Humpty Dumpty Club over dinner at Churchview Farm, and to Judy Grumet for sharing her experiences as a club member. Deepest gratitude to David Gernert, Rebecca Gardner, Ellen Goodson Coughtrey, Will Roberts, Anna Worrall and Nora Gonzalez for taking care of business at the Gernert Company, and to Sylvie Rabineau, Carolina Beltran, Nikki McGovern, and Dovid Rafailovich-Sokolov for holding down the Hollywood end at WME. To Morgan Entrekin, Zoe Harris, Deb Seager, Rachael Richardson, Natalie Church, and David Chesanow, thank you all for welcoming Emily and Arlene back to Grove Atlantic, where their story began.